More of Me

Prologue

"WE NEED YOUR HELP."

Looking up from the report he was reading, William Montgomery could not conceal his surprise. His ever-independent son Mackenzie was actually admitting he needed his help? Quickly masking his glee, William simply said, "Anything."

Mac shifted uncomfortably. "Here's the thing," he began and then growled slightly. "Gina got a call from her mother this morning. Apparently she fell and broke her hip. She's going to need surgery and someone to take care of her, so as soon as we can arrange it, Gina's heading to San Francisco to spend a couple of weeks there."

William shrugged and smiled. "Okay. I don't see what that has to do with me, but…okay."

Mac shot his father a look of annoyance. "I have a trip scheduled that will have me in London for at least a week."

Again, William simply shrugged and nodded. "I'm aware."

"The wedding is only three months away, Dad. A lot needs to be done. We had scheduled a meeting with the wedding planner to go over venues and whatever else it is that you're supposed to do with wedding planners." William was unsure exactly why Mac was involved at all. From what he had heard, Gina knew exactly what she wanted, and Mac would do anything to make her happy.

"So you need me to meet with the planner and help while you're gone? Is that it?" Mac nodded. "Consider it done. When do you need me to do that?"

"Now."

"Now?" Mac nodded grimly, and William straightened in his seat and did a quick mental checklist of what he had planned for the afternoon. "It's a little short notice, Mac," he admitted. "I'll get Rose to cancel my afternoon appointments, and we'll make this happen. Will you have time to sit with us for at least a little while?"

"Absolutely. As a matter of fact, Casey is here now, with Gina in my office. We can call them in here or go down the hall…"

William stood. "We'll go to them." William stopped to let his assistant know what was going on; then he and his son walked together down the wide hallway. At the door to Mac's office, the sound of female laughter greeted them.

"Ladies," Mac said as he crossed the room to kiss Gina on the cheek. "My father has graciously agreed to help us out during our absence. Casey Peterson, may I introduce my father, William Montgomery?"

"It's a pleasure to meet you, sir," she said with a smile and a twinkle in her blue eyes, standing to shake his hand. "I hear that you had a hand in getting Mac and Gina together."

William gestured for her to sit back down and took his own seat. "While I'd like to take the credit for it, they were meant to be together." He smiled at the couple who were sitting close together on the sofa before turning his attention back to Casey. "So, what can I do to help?"

"Well," Casey began, looking for confirmation from

Gina, "one of the first things we had planned for next week was to make a final decision on the venue. Mac and Gina have it narrowed down to two places, and it's probably a good thing that you can offer a third opinion, because they are having a tough time." She smiled at them both before continuing. "Once that's settled, we will be making final decisions on menus, flowers, programs"—she rifled through her folder to make sure she covered everything—"and of course the invitation will go to the printer immediately after all locations and times are confirmed. The sooner we get the information to the printer, the sooner we get our proofs back and can get them out in the mail." She looked up at the three of them. "How does that sound so far?"

William's head was spinning a little. "So far? How much more is there?"

Casey went through the file again. "A lot of this can be done via email and over the phone with Gina, but I know she is going to be busy with her mother. We're making arrangements for her gown to be sent to a bridal shop in San Francisco, so she can get started on her fittings, and her bridal party will be taken care of here in Charlotte. From what I understand, Maggie Montgomery will be overseeing that, correct?"

Gina nodded. "She's Jason's wife and the epitome of organization."

"Maybe Maggie would be a better fit for this," William interrupted. "Or maybe your mother?" he suggested to Mac.

The couple both shook their heads. "Mom is taking care of coordinating all of the travel arrangements for family and friends, as well as all the pre-wedding activities that she wants to host. We don't want to add another thing to her plate, Dad," Mac said. "Besides, with all the hard work you put into getting us together, we thought you'd enjoy being involved with the wedding."

William gave a knowing smile. "You make it sound like it's a good thing, but I think you're trying to get some sort of revenge on me. This is not my thing," he said apologetically. "Not that I can't do it… It's just that I don't know if I can give it all of the attention it deserves."

"If I can just interrupt for a second," Casey said, leaning forward and placing a hand on William's arm. "There may be times that you're needed out in Wilmington, but I will be sure that it works for your schedule before I make any appointments. I promise to keep any disruptions to a minimum."

"Wilmington?" William said, turning toward Mac and Gina with a bit of surprise. "When did the two of you decide to have the wedding in Wilmington?"

Mac and Gina looked at one another and smiled. "We always knew we wanted the wedding to be on the coast, so we spent a week scouting locations. We spent a weekend in Wilmington," Gina said, "and we knew that was the place. We had a great time there," she added with a blush.

William grinned from ear to ear. He knew that Mac and Gina were perfect for one another, and watching the two of them together gave him endless pleasure. He only wished Gina's father had lived to see this day. "Okay, Wilmington it is!" Just as he was about to address Casey about getting things scheduled, William had a brilliant idea. "You know," he began, "your uncle Robert has a couple of houses at Wrightsville Beach and he mentioned to me that Ryder was spending the summer there. Maybe he can help with some of this whenever I'm not available."

"Dad, that's a lot to ask of a cousin. I mean, we've always been close, but from what I understood from the last time he and I talked, Ryder was on sabbatical because he's exhausted. I can't ask him to give up his much-needed vacation time to help plan our wedding."

"Ryder Montgomery is your cousin?" Casey asked in a weak voice.

William's head snapped around. "You know Ryder?"

With a slight blush, Casey nodded. "We…um…his family rented a home on the beach some years ago just down the road from mine. We dated…briefly…when he was there. It was a long time ago. I thought he lived in California now?"

"He does," William said, suddenly pleased with the direction of the conversation. "He moved there right after graduation." He turned and smiled at Mac and Gina. "Isn't this a small world? With Casey and Ryder knowing one another, it will make their working together that much easier! I'm sure Ryder won't mind helping out when he knows that it's Casey he'll be working with."

"Dad—" Mac began as a warning.

"Nonsense," William cut him off. "It's great how things work out sometimes. Don't get me wrong," he said, addressing Casey again. "I'm still here to help where you need me, but my nephew will be able to take care of things that require immediate attention." Clapping his hands together, he stood. "I love when a plan comes together. Now if you'll all excuse me, I'm going to call my brother and then get Ryder on the phone. It was a pleasure to meet you, Casey, and I'm looking forward to working with you." He kissed Gina good-bye and hugged Mac on his way out the door.

For a long moment, no one said a word. Finally Casey broke the silence. "Wow, he certainly is a force of nature isn't he?"

Both Mac and Gina nodded. "You have no idea."

Chapter 1

"WHAT HAVE I GOTTEN MYSELF INTO?" CASEY mumbled to herself later that day as she climbed into her car. She had been thrilled at the opportunity to coordinate this wedding; Mac and Gina had been dream clients. They were well organized and had a clear vision of what they wanted their wedding to be, and Casey had seen nothing but blue skies ahead.

Until now.

While she knew it wasn't fair to blame anyone—especially not Gina's mother for falling and breaking her hip, or Mac for needing to be out of the country—being faced with the prospect of seeing Ryder Montgomery again, the need to blame someone was strong.

Blame yourself for still allowing even the thought of Ryder to make you crazy.

Casey hated when her inner voice was right. Twelve years later, and just the mere mention of his name had her body tingling. When the heck was that going to stop? The drive back to the coast was long, and with no one for company other than her inner voice, she knew there was no avoiding it.

Normally Casey had all of her clients come to her; the three-and-a-half-hour drive to meet with Mac and Gina had been an exception. When Gina had called her and told her their lives were in a state of chaos, Casey had taken pity on them and offered to drive the nearly two hundred miles to get to them. Her clients' happiness always came first, but this was the first time that, in making that happen, Casey would be making herself miserable.

Destination weddings were all the rage, and although coastal North Carolina wasn't exactly what most people envisioned as a destination, Casey still liked to make sure that every wedding felt like a dream come true.

Mac and Gina were textbook in theory, and there was no doubt how in love they were; however, the distance that they were willing to travel was certainly an issue. As much as Casey hated to admit it, having someone local available to help with the major decisions would have been a big bonus. But why did that local someone have to be Ryder Montgomery? Why now, after all these years, did he suddenly have to return to the North Carolina coast? Why couldn't he just have stayed thousands of miles away and left her alone?

Even if he had, he's related to the groom, and you would have run in to him eventually.

"Oh, shut up," she cursed herself. "No one likes a know-it-all." Flipping on the radio to block out any more words of wisdom from her subconscious, Casey let herself settle into the long drive and did her best to focus on singing loudly to every song rather than on what was going to happen when she came face-to-face with Ryder again.

Being on the beach before sunrise was nothing new to Ryder Montgomery. He'd been living on the beaches of San Diego for more than ten years and taking an early-morning run along the coast was part of his routine. As he stood and inhaled the scents of the Atlantic Ocean, Ryder knew that for some reason, Wrightsville Beach would always be home.

He hadn't made a whole lot of time to come home since he'd left, but that didn't mean that everything wasn't still familiar, comforting. Stretching, Ryder tried to decide which direction to head in, and then, as if it had been yesterday and not years ago, he took off in the one direction that had always called to him.

The sun was just starting to make its debut as he made his way down the beach all by himself. No one else was privy to the start of this day, and that was the way he liked it. Soon the sand would be covered with residents and tourists alike, and Ryder knew that by that time, he'd be safely ensconced back in his home. Not that he was antisocial—far from it. It was just that right now, at this point in his life, he needed a little quality alone time. Work had been brutal for the last several years, and as the one heading up the West Coast branch of Montgomerys, a lot of heavy responsibility had been placed on his shoulders.

Right now, the only responsibility he wanted was deciding what to eat for breakfast and nothing more.

Up ahead, a flash of bright green caught his eye. Not breaking stride, Ryder did his best to focus on it. One more person out on the large expanse of coastline shouldn't have been an issue; it was the placement of that person that had his nerves more than a little on edge.

There was no way that it was possible.

It was both too much to hope for and everything that he dreaded all at once.

The closer he got to the house at the end of this particular section of the beach, Ryder knew that all of his
hopes and fears were about to collide.

Casey Peterson.

Ryder slowed his pace as his mind raced to what he
was supposed to do. She was standing out on the deck
on the back of her house, looking out at the waves and
the sunrise. The wind was blowing her wavy brown hair
out behind her, and his fingers actually twitched as he
remembered how silky it was. Soon, his other senses
jumped on board the memory train, and he could no
longer smell the surf, only the scent of vanilla. Casey
always smelled like warm vanilla, and he had enjoyed
nothing more all those summers ago than tasting every
inch of her.

This was so not the relaxing morning run that he
was used to. Now, every inch of him was on alert, and
Ryder considered doing a quick about-face back toward
his home before she saw him. Who was he kidding?
Chances were that Casey wouldn't even remember him,
and if she did, she'd either ignore him or find something
heavy to throw at his head.

He was hoping for option one but had a feeling that
she'd definitely go for option two.

He'd been a royal jackass back then. Cocky to the
point of being obnoxious. Even though he knew that she
was too good for him, Ryder had no choice but to get
involved with her.

And then to let her go.

Twelve years was a long time to hold a grudge
though, he thought to himself. What would happen if he
continued on his run, stopped at the base of the stairs that

led up to her house, and said a quick hello? In business, Ryder was the poster boy for confidence, but suddenly, when faced with having to confront an ex-girlfriend from way too long ago, he felt as if every ounce of that confidence had been left back in San Diego.

How bad could it be? Wasn't it better just to rip the damn Band-Aid off all at once? Casey lived less than a mile from his family home, they were bound to run into one another eventually. Why not just get it over with so they could move on with their lives?

Because she may be pint-sized compared to you, but she has the ability to knock you on your butt.

Truer words had never been spoken—or thought.

When Ryder had told Casey that he was leaving right after graduation, the look on her face had nearly destroyed him. While the Montgomerys had money and a secure social status, Ryder had been determined to make a name for himself on his own, far away from where anyone knew who they were.

Even if it meant leaving Casey behind.

Hell, her blue eyes, so full of hurt and disappointment, still haunted him. Looking back, Ryder knew he had done the right thing. But now, as he got closer to the base of those steps, he found that he was more than a little afraid to face the woman who had been everything to him.

Never one to walk away from a challenge, Ryder jogged the last few yards to the foot of the stairs and looked up just as Casey was looking down. He knew the instant she recognized him because her face went from serene to wary to disgust in a matter of seconds.

"Hey, Casey," he said, hating the uncertainty in his

voice. Where the hell was the cool confidence that was always with him?

"Wow," she said with barely concealed disapproval. "You certainly didn't waste any time."

Ryder looked at her with confusion. "Waste any time? What are you talking about?"

"Mac and Gina's wedding? Your uncle said he'd be calling you, but I figured you'd at least wait until I actually needed to involve you before showing up here. And even then I figured you'd just come to the office."

That did nothing to alleviate his confusion. "I'm afraid you've lost me, Case," he said and saw her stiffen, Everyone used that nickname, but when he called her that, it had always made her melt.

"Didn't William call you?"

"No."

"How about Mac?"

Ryder shook his head.

"What are you doing here, Ryder?" Wariness laced her voice.

"I'm on sabbatical…"

Casey shook her head. "No, what are you doing *here*?"

Ryder took a deep breath and then just shook his head again. "I don't know. I came out to do my usual morning run and this is where I ended up."

She looked at him with disbelief. "So this is all just a weird coincidence?"

"I don't know," he admitted honestly, and before he knew what he was doing, Ryder found himself walking up the stairs toward her. When finally they were face-to-face, Ryder knew he was in deep trouble. The years simply faded away; Casey was just as beautiful as he remembered. Maybe even more so. Her big blue eyes stared up at him. "Hey," he said softly, his own dark gaze captivating hers.

She was in trouble. Deep, deep trouble. One look at the man that Ryder had become and Casey was almost ready to melt into a puddle at his feet. He was taller than she remembered and much more muscular. Standing before her in a pair of black athletic shorts and a gray T-shirt, she knew without a doubt that he was in prime physical shape. But once her gaze settled on his face? His whiskey-colored eyes, his disheveled sandy brown hair…and that dimple barely making an appearance in his right cheek made one thing abundantly clear.

Her perfectly organized world was about to be turned upside down.

Chapter 2

THERE WERE A MILLION THINGS RYDER WANTED TO say, but no matter how right they sounded in his head, he knew that he had his work cut out for him where Casey was concerned. Now wasn't the time to start talking about the past or if she was interested in them getting reacquainted. He knew it was best to stick to safer subjects—no matter how much it killed him.

"So what's this about Mac and Gina's wedding?" he finally asked.

Casey sagged with relief. With Ryder so up close and personal, it was hard for her to remember why she didn't want to be, well, up close and personal with him. "They've had some unexpected emergencies and are going to be away for a while."

Ryder nodded. "And this has to do with me…how?"

"Well, we need to finalize a bunch of their wedding details, and with neither of them accessible to make decisions, they asked your uncle to step in." When Ryder still looked at her with confusion, she explained, "His schedule is pretty full, and he mentioned that you were here for the summer and might be able to help out when he was unavailable."

His eyes went wide. "Me? What do I know about wedding planning? And what does this have to do with you?"

She chuckled. "It's what I do for a living, Ryder. I'm a wedding planner."

It was all starting to come together now and Ryder nodded. "And the wedding is here on Wrightsville?"

"No, it's actually in Wilmington, but either way, it's a lot of driving back and forth for your uncle—or anyone in Charlotte for that matter—and I guess they were all just looking for the best options."

"When did all this get decided?"

"Just yesterday." Casey explained the situations that Mac and Gina were suddenly faced with, relieved that Ryder was taking it all so well. "I can text and email and call to my heart's content, but there are things that I will need someone to physically be there for." When Ryder continued to stare at her, she quickly added, "It probably won't be more than a couple of times, so it won't be too big of an issue. I told William that I would work around his schedule."

Ryder considered her words and came up with his own conclusion—Casey didn't want to work with him. If he had to read her nervous chatter, he'd say that she would go out of her way to work around his uncle's busy schedule just so Ryder wasn't involved. It was all the opening he needed to get himself reacquainted with her. Ryder Montgomery never walked away from a challenge. And Casey had clearly just presented him with one.

"You can count on me, Mac," Ryder said an hour later as he lounged on a chaise on his back deck overlooking the ocean. "Fax me everything I'll need, and I'll get with Casey and take care of it."

"Are you sure? Dad said he'd be willing to help. I

know that you were looking forward to this downtime. I hate infringing on that."

"Nonsense, what is family for?"

Mac laughed. "I don't think you realize what you're getting yourself into. Hell, most of the time I find myself zoning out. There's only so much I can take of flower arrangements and place cards and linens. It's a damn nightmare."

"Well, just as long as you trust me to make the right decisions," Ryder said lightly, thinking that this day was starting out perfectly.

"There won't be any that you'll have to make single-handedly. Well, with the exception of the venue. You might end up being the tiebreaker on that one. Gina and I just couldn't choose. They're both great and I'm sure that Casey can arrange for you to take the grand tour of each one."

"I'll be sure to call her today and set that up." Ryder wasn't about to mention to his cousin that he had already searched out the beautiful wedding planner, or that he was thinking of more than wedding plans where she was concerned. "Don't worry, Mac. If I have any questions or concerns, I'll reach out to Gina first, then you, and then your father."

Mac sighed with relief. "I don't know how I can ever repay you, Ry. Everything hit the fan at once, and Gina was torn as to what she was supposed to do. I know she'll be able to go and take care of her mother and relax knowing that we have someone right there overseeing things. Thank you."

"Like I said, what's family for?"

———~~~———

"So he's going to do it?" Gina asked when Mac hung up the phone.

He nodded. "He's not doing anything but being a beach bum for the next three months, so I think this will be a good project for him—work, but not too much. I can't imagine Ryder being able to sit and do nothing for three whole months. He's a Montgomery—we go crazy if we don't have something to do."

Walking over to where Mac stood, Gina got on tip-toes and wrapped her arms around his neck. After all this time, it still amazed her that Mac was hers and that she could touch him and kiss him whenever she wanted. She took advantage of that and gave him a kiss that told him exactly how pleased she was with the situation. "What am I going to do without you for two whole weeks?"

Mac's mouth was already working its way down the slender column of her neck. "I could cancel my trip," he said between kisses. "Just go to San Francisco with you."

Gina's head fell back as she purred. "That would be selfish of me." She didn't sound the least bit sorry for it as she moved her body even closer to his.

Tearing his mouth from her sweet-smelling skin, Mac swung Gina up into his arms and strode toward their bedroom. "That's okay," he said with a low growl. "Because I'm about to be a little selfish myself." Kicking the bedroom door closed behind him, Mac lowered his fiancée to the bed and followed her down. "And I'm not sorry about it either."

—⁓—

Casey arrived at her office at ten and looked at her calendar while she waited for her computer to boot up. She had planned on taking her usual morning walk on the beach to get her head clear and ready for the day, but seeing Ryder and talking to him had made clear thinking impossible. If anything, her head was crowded with memories of their past and thoughts of having to work with him now.

And why couldn't he have gotten fat or lost all of his hair? Why did he have to be even more devastatingly handsome than he had been all those years ago? Casey knew without a doubt that if Ryder showed even the slightest interest in her again, she'd quickly lose the battle to stay detached.

And then she'd be brokenhearted when he left again. *Dammit.*

She looked up at a knock on her door and smiled as her partner, Julie, walked in carrying her baby daughter. "Knock, knock," Julie said, dropping a diaper bag and purse on the nearest surface. "Sorry to intrude, but I have a huge favor to ask."

"Sure. What's up?"

Julie sat down opposite Casey and used her best pleading expression. "My sitter is down with the flu and Thomas has meetings all day, and I'm scheduled to go and do a walk-through and a cake tasting with the Millses. I hate to ask because I'm sure you're busy, but… could you watch Savannah for me for a couple of hours?"

Casey never turned down an opportunity to babysit for Julie's daughter; she was precious and it gave Casey her baby fix. Lately her own biological clock was ticking louder and louder, and just a couple of hours alone with Savannah seemed to keep her in check. "No problem. I don't actually have anything on my calendar today other than drawing up some contracts, but Erica can help with that."

"You are a lifesaver," Julie said as she sagged in her seat. "She's had her breakfast and I just changed her, and she'll probably go down for a nap soon. I can bring in all of her paraphernalia so that your work won't be disturbed too much."

"That would be great," Casey said with a smile. She knew that things could change in an instant with a baby, but having all of the things that Savannah was familiar with here in her office would make things a little bit easier should the baby get distressed over anything.

Julie handed her daughter over and quickly turned to start moving things into Casey's office. "Loving you!" she called over her shoulder.

Looking down at the baby in her arms, Casey said, "We're going to have fun today...yes we are!" Savannah smiled and cooed at her, and Casey's heart simply melted. She held the little girl close and breathed in the scent of baby shampoo and talcum powder. There was no sweeter smell than a baby.

"You look good with her, Case," Julie said as she set up the portable crib in the corner of Casey's office. "You are going to be a fabulous mother one day."

"Any idea when that will be?" Casey said wryly.

"Don't rush it," Julie said with a chuckle. "They are sweet to hold and snuggle with, but they come with a ton of responsibility—and equipment." Looking around the office, she motioned to the crib, stroller, toys, diaper bag, and car seat. "She practically needs her own wing in the house."

"I think we need all of this stuff more than she does. Something that makes noise and is colorful to look at, and a pair of arms to cuddle her with, and she's happy as a clam."

Julie snorted with laughter and then covered her mouth. "You keep telling yourself that. And while you're riding your magical unicorn home, let me know how it goes when those arms that are busy cuddling need to actually answer the phone or cook dinner or get dressed or—"

"Okay, okay, I get it. Sheesh! Don't worry about us. Go and get your bride and groom set with their food and venue; Savannah and I will be fine." She looked down and felt her heart skip a beat as Savannah smiled so sweetly at her. "Just remember to keep your phone on," she added for good measure.

"Uh-huh." Coming around the desk, Julie kissed her baby girl on the head and promised Casey she'd get back as soon as possible. Once the door was closed behind her, Savannah's lip began to quiver.

"Oh no, sweetheart," Casey said softly. "It's okay. We're going to have fun together. I promise." She wasn't sure if the baby actually understood her—or believed her—but she was thankful that the lip quiver didn't turn into a full cry.

An hour later, Savannah was down for a nap and Casey was going through her messages. There were several inquiries from potential clients, and once she had responded to them all, she began going through her roster of current clients and confirming what she needed to be doing for them.

Mac and Gina's wedding was at the top of her list, and not only because of her meeting with Ryder earlier. There was still so much to do, and it was going to be the first time that she was having to make all of the crucial decisions without the bride being right there beside her. Picking up her phone, she dialed William Montgomery's work number and waited patiently while his assistant put him on the line.

"Casey," he said, and she heard the smile in his voice. "How are you today?"

"Fine, thanks. I just wanted to see what your schedule was like for the end of the week. Would you be available to take the drive down and tour the two venues?"

His silence seemed to drag on before he finally spoke. "Actually, I have a pretty full schedule this week. Can it wait until the middle of next week?"

"Unfortunately, no. If we don't reserve now, we risk losing one or both. I would hate for that to happen."

"I haven't had the opportunity to speak to Ryder, but—"

"How about I see what I can do? Maybe if I sweet-talk both of the managers, they'll hold the date for me until you are able to come and see them for yourself?"

"That won't be necessary. I'm sure Ryder can do this one thing for me. After this, I promise to be more accessible. This all just came out of the blue, and so I wasn't prepared for it. But now that I know that you're going to need me to come down there, I'll block off some days and we can go through everything. How does that sound?"

She supposed that it could work. If it meant only having to work with Ryder one afternoon rather than

multiple ones, Casey would be able to mentally prepare herself.

Maybe.

Hopefully.

"Casey?"

Oh, right. William was waiting for her response.
"That should be fine. You can have him call my office,
and we'll set up an appointment. Tell him that it will be
quick and painless."

"I'm glad we found a solution. I'm sure Ryder will
be in touch," he assured her and then promised to do the
same the following week.

When Casey hung up the phone, she noticed that
Savannah was starting to stir and was surprised to see
that it was lunchtime. Standing, she walked over to the
portable crib and smiled down at the baby's sleepy grin.
"Well hey, sweet girl. Did you have a good nap?" She
continued to chat and coo as she went about getting
Savannah changed and situated so that they could see
about lunch.

"Who's my sweet girl? Huh? You are; you're my
sweet girl." Savannah kicked her tiny legs and flailed
her arms about as she laughed at Casey's silly tone.

That's how Ryder found them.

———∿∿∿———

Casey had a baby? What the…?

Ryder wasn't sure why he was surprised or why
he felt like he had been kicked in the chest. Twelve
years was a long time, and Ryder was certain that
Casey hadn't been pining for him all that time. But
still, the thought of Casey married and having babies

with some random man and the reality of having to see it for himself were two completely different things. He kept telling himself that he didn't want to know, that maybe ignorance was bliss, but the sight of Casey smiling down and cooing at her baby girl hurt more than anything Ryder had ever experienced.

Forcing himself to put on his business face, he knocked on the office door. The startled look on Casey's face clearly mirrored his own, but Ryder was sure that the shock of seeing him standing in her office was nothing compared to the shock of seeing her with a baby.

We should have had babies. Casey should be here right now taking care of our baby.

The voice in his head was so loud, so clear, that Ryder had to look around to make sure that there wasn't someone else there actually speaking the words out loud. Doing his best to shake himself out of his stupor, Ryder cleared his throat and stepped further into Casey's office. "Sorry to interrupt," he began uncomfortably. "I talked to Mac earlier and figured there was no time like the present to try and get the venue tours scheduled. I hope you don't mind me showing up without an appointment."

Situating the baby more comfortably on her hip, Casey forced a smile. "No, no…this is fine. My schedule was pretty clear this morning. I was just about to get lunch for Savannah."

Nodding, Ryder forced his own smile. "If this is a bad time…"

Casey stepped around the desk and motioned for Ryder to follow her. "I just have to heat up a bottle." She led him down the hall to the small kitchenette. She chatted to the baby rather than Ryder until she had the bottle heated. "I spoke to your uncle earlier, and the soonest he could come out here is the middle of next week. I really wanted him to look at the venues, but at this late date, we risk losing them both if we don't act now."

"Late date? The wedding is what? Three months out?"

She laughed out loud and startled the baby in her arms. Doing her best to soothe Savannah, she got her settled before facing Ryder again. "Believe it or not, most places are booked sometimes two years in advance. Normally I don't like to take on an event on such short notice, but your cousin and his fiancée were very persuasive."

Now it was Ryder's turn to laugh. "That sounds like Mac."

They walked back to Casey's office, and she sat behind her desk to finish feeding the baby, motioning for Ryder to take a seat. "Anyway, it's not an ideal situation, but we lucked out and found not one but two venues that actually have the date they want available. But we have to act fast. I can get us in to look at them both this afternoon, I'm sure. I'll just have to make a couple of calls." That was when Julie's earlier words about having her arms full came back to her. She looked up at Ryder and smiled sheepishly. "Or I will once she's done with her bottle."

"I can hold her if that will help."

Casey looked at him as if he'd suddenly grown a second head. "You…you want to hold her?"

Standing, Ryder came around the desk and held out her arms. "Sure. I'll admit that I haven't held a lot of babies, but I have held a couple in my time. Plus, you'll be right here if she absolutely hates me."

Warily, Casey stood and placed Savannah in Ryder's waiting arms. The baby cooed up at him, and while she was still occupied in sizing up the newcomer, Casey made quick work of her calls. The manager of each venue had no problem with them stopping by for a tour, and when she hung up the phone, Casey couldn't help but smile at Ryder making goofy faces to keep Savannah smiling. Her first instinct was to say that he was a natural, but it seemed far too intimate a comment, and if she was going to survive the afternoon with him, she knew she was going to have to keep herself in total professional mode.

"Okay, I have arrangements made with each of the locations, and we have our first appointment at three today."

Ryder nodded but didn't look up; the baby's big blue eyes held him mesmerized, but no matter how hard he studied her face, he didn't see a trace of Casey there. "She must favor her father," he said as casually as he could.

Glad that Ryder wasn't looking at her, Casey wondered at his odd comment before she realized that he must think that she was Savannah's mother. She did some quick thinking. It might be just the thing to make sure that Ryder kept his distance and didn't tempt her. "She does, actually," she said and then rose to take the baby from him. "It's barely one; why don't you meet me back here at two thirty and then we can head over to the first venue?"

Ryder didn't want to leave; suddenly he wanted—no, needed—to know what had been going on in Casey's life since he had moved away. "Have you had lunch yet?" he asked, grasping at straws.

"Um, no. Savannah had only just woken up when you

arrived, and I needed to get her changed and fed first. I was going to call in something to the deli and go pick it up."

Ryder waved a hand at her. "Tell you what, tell me what it is that you'd like, I'll go and pick up lunch for the both of us, and then you can fill me in on my cousin's wedding. I've never done anything like this before, and I don't want to look like a complete idiot when we tour these places today."

"There's not that much to know—" she began, but Ryder cut her off.

"When I'm at a wedding, all I pay attention to is whether there's an open bar or not. I have no idea about seating arrangements or acoustics or if there's someplace nice for pictures. Please, Case, I don't want to let Mac or Gina down."

How could she possibly argue with that?

"All right," she sighed as she placed Savannah down in the portable crib and found her notepad to write down her lunch order. Handing it to him, she smiled weakly. "I appreciate you doing the run for me. It's not always easy getting in and out of the deli quickly with a baby in tow."

Not trusting himself to comment on that, Ryder simply smiled and said, "I'll be back as soon as I can."

Chapter 3

"I CANNOT BELIEVE THERE IS THIS MUCH TO KNOW."

"And believe me, I'm just giving you the *Reader's Digest* version."

Shaking his head, Ryder took a minute to let the information sink in. For ninety minutes, he had listened to Casey talk about all the features that are important to a bride and groom for their wedding venue. He was going to get even with Mac at some point, of that he was certain. Between the number of tables versus the number of guests, table placement, band placement, acoustics, flowers, and bridal party accommodations…his head was spinning. Who knew that so many ridiculous considerations went into planning a wedding?

"Okay, so this first place," he began as he rubbed his temples, "this is the one that has better beach access for the actual ceremony—"

"But—" Casey interrupted.

"But," he cut her off, "has the smaller deck area for the cocktail hour, right?"

Casey nodded her head with approval. "Impressive. You were paying attention."

"It's my job to pay attention to details—no matter how monotonous," he mumbled. "So the issue with the deck could lead to them either having to shave the guest list a little or risk having people feel like sardines."

"Exactly. However, the main banquet room is exquisite, and both Mac and Gina loved the menu."

"So they've already toured both of these places and tasted the food, but couldn't decide on which one they liked better?"

"Exactly."

"Crafty bastards," he muttered under his breath.

"Excuse me?" Casey asked with a giggle.

"Well, it occurs to me that for all we know, there are no emergencies to deal with, but they just don't know how to break the damn tie."

"Ryder, trust me when I tell you this—no bride would willingly walk away from her wedding plans three months before the wedding if it weren't an emergency. I've been doing this for eight years; I know what I'm talking about."

He supposed she was right. Women took weddings very seriously, and although he had never met his cousin's future wife, Ryder was sure Gina would be no exception. "I'll take your word for it."

"Good." They pulled up to the large oceanfront estate. It was once a private home but had been transformed into a catering venue. "The event coordinator's name is Martin, and he's been doing this for twenty years. Don't hesitate to ask questions, and he has already agreed to hold the date for us so that you'll have a little time to decide. Just don't take too long; he's really only giving you until Sunday."

"But it's already Thursday," Ryder said, his voice laced with panic.

They were walking up the large front steps when Casey, against her better judgment, reached out and touched Ryder's arm to stop him. "We're seeing both places today. That will give you a couple of days to mull it over. Trust me, it's not going to be that bad."

"Easy for you to say. If it wasn't so bad, then Mac and Gina wouldn't have me here doing this because the decision would have been made already."

"Touché."

They were greeted at the entrance by a well-dressed man in his fifties wearing a perfectly tailored suit and a big smile. "Casey," he said, shaking her hand warmly with both of his. "It is always a pleasure to see you."

"Same here, Martin," she said with a smile. Introductions were made, and then Martin took them on an extensive tour of the estate. The final room was Martin's office, where he offered them each something to drink while they made themselves comfortable. When he left the room to fetch their beverages, Casey turned to Ryder.

"So? What did you think?"

"It's amazing," he said with just a hint of uncertainty.

"But?"

He shot her a sideways glance at her perceptiveness. "But…I'm not one hundred percent convinced that this is the place. I mean, it all looks great when the place is empty and everything is neat and set up like a display. What does it look like when there's an event in progress? How is the service? How do they organize the transition from wedding on the beach to cocktail hour to reception?"

"Wow, you really have been paying attention. Again, I'm impressed."

"I told you," he said, holding out his hands, "I'm a detail-oriented guy."

Just then, Martin returned with their drinks and sat down behind his desk. "Well, Mr. Montgomery, any questions?"

"Do you have any events this weekend that we can maybe…observe?"

"Ryder!" Casey hissed at him and then turned and smiled apologetically at Martin.

"It's all right, Casey," Martin assured. "I can understand that this is a big decision and he wants to make the best-informed one he can. We have an event here tomorrow. The ceremony will take place at six p.m. on the beach, cocktails begin at seven, and dinner will be served at nine. You are both more than welcome to come and observe."

"Thank you," Ryder said, relieved that he hadn't committed any kind of faux pas. "I appreciate your willingness to let us crash."

"Well, I prefer to not think of it as crashing. You'll be able to observe the ceremony on the beach and walk around during cocktails, but after that, you'll have to watch from afar for dinner. We respect our bride and groom's privacy and the fact that they paid for the event, and we don't wish to take advantage. We can arrange for a tasting for you both with each course—set up in a separate room, of course—this way you can see for yourself how the food is presented." He looked expectantly at both Ryder and Casey. "How does that sound?"

"It sounds like you've done this before," Ryder said with a big grin. "And it is exactly what I'm going to need in order to make sure that I do the right thing by my cousin. Thank you."

—∿∿—

The drive to the second venue was made in silence. Casey knew that Ryder didn't need any more coaching, and honestly, she was more than a little on edge at the thought that they were going to have to go and observe an event the next night.

Who knew his attention to detail would be so annoying and yet so arousing? How was she supposed to keep her professional shell in place when they had to spend so much time together?

"Ready?" Ryder asked, effectively snapping Casey out of her own reverie. She nodded, and together they headed for the entrance. This facility was an exclusive hotel resort; everything was all-inclusive. "So guests can stay right here on site and not have to drive, right?" Casey simply nodded again. "That's a definite plus in my book; no need to have an open bar all night and then send everyone on their way to drive under the influence."

"Casey! So glad to see you!" They were greeted by a wiry, handsome man who was close to their own age, and Casey was wrapped in a friendly hug.

"How are you, Tyler?" Casey said with a big smile. She introduced Ryder and noticed that he wasn't as friendly as he had been earlier with Martin. She looked at him quizzically, but quickly returned her attention to Tyler. "So, are you ready to give us the grand tour?"

An hour later, they found themselves in Tyler's office, and Casey was a bit unnerved by how quiet Ryder had been on the tour. At the sound of Tyler's phone ringing, he excused himself and left Casey and Ryder alone.

"I'm guessing that you hate this place," she said bluntly.

"What? No, why?"

Casey gave him a look of disbelief. "You've been

quiet and reserved the entire time we've been here, while you were a chatterbox at the last place. So what gives? What don't you like about this place?"

Ryder raked a hand through his hair in agitation. "Honestly? I think the place is great. I like that the ceremony isn't out on the sand, and yet the deck is large enough to seat everyone and still give a spectacular view of the water. The rooms for both the cocktail hour and the reception are the perfect size and the hotel rooms for the guests are top quality."

"But...?"

"But...I don't know. I have to wonder, again, how it all actually looks while an event is going on. Is it going to be like pretty-boy Tyler and just all be a facade?"

Casey couldn't help the laugh that escaped. "What in the world are you talking about?"

Ryder leaned in close and kept his voice down just in case Tyler reappeared. "Guys like Tyler are all the same: impeccably dressed and with all the right things to say. But at the end of the day, they're all just a pack of smarmy jackasses who probably hit on the guests or...I don't know. He just rubs me the wrong way."

"So this has nothing to do with the actual facility," she stated just to be clear, "and simply about your dislike of Tyler. Do I have that right?"

"Well, when you say it like that, it sounds ridiculous."

"That's because it *is* ridiculous, Ryder. I've worked with Tyler dozens of times, and he is a quality guy. He does an impeccable job on each and every event and pays attention to detail, and I've never seen or heard of him hitting on anyone. Actually, I believe that he's been involved with someone for years."

"That doesn't mean anything," Ryder said begrudgingly. "Plenty of people are involved and yet screw around. How do you know he's not going to go hitting on the bridesmaids?"

"Because he's more likely to hit on the groom or the groomsmen," she said as her lips began to twitch. The look of shock on Ryder's face was priceless.

"You mean he's…um…so Tyler's…"

"Gay? Yes. Do you feel better now?"

He relaxed visibly in his seat. "As a matter of fact, I do," he said. Just then Tyler walked back in and apologized for leaving them alone. "No worries, Tyler," Ryder said with more enthusiasm than he had shown on their entire tour. "Do you happen to have an event this weekend that we can come and scope out? I'm more of a visual guy, and I want to see it all in action before making my decision."

Tyler was thrilled that they wanted to come back and gave them information on a wedding they were hosting on Saturday. "This one's going to be a little different than what your cousin is wanting to do," he began. "The ceremony is going to be at four in the afternoon, cocktails at five, and dinner will be served at seven." He looked up and addressed Ryder. "They're an older couple and a lot of the relatives are seniors, so they wanted the event to be over by ten."

Ryder nodded in understanding. "Sounds perfect to me. As long as I can get a general feel of how the rooms will look and how the spot for the ceremony will be laid out, I'll feel better informed to make my decision. I appreciate you letting us come back and do that."

"No problem," he replied. "I would much rather you

be comfortable with your decision so that you'll be confident when you tell your cousin why you chose us."

Casey smiled at the confidence in Tyler's words and
saw that Ryder did not take any offense to them. They
each thanked him for his time, and soon they were back
in Casey's car and heading to her office. Once again
they drove in silence, and when they arrived, she was
surprised that Ryder didn't immediately leave. He followed her inside.

Realizing that she wasn't getting rid of him anytime
soon, she simply headed into her office and got herself
situated behind her desk. "So? Are you leaning toward
one or the other?" she finally asked, her tone neutral.

Ryder took a seat across from her and made himself
comfortable. "I can see why Mac and Gina weren't able
to decide. They're both great places. I think it's going
to come down to the presentation of everything this
weekend." He looked around her office as if searching
for something.

"What are you looking for?"

"I was just looking for all of the baby stuff that was
here earlier." When Ryder had left earlier to pick up their
lunches, Julie had come back and retrieved her daughter
and all of her equipment. Casey had simply said that
her business partner had Savannah, and Ryder hadn't
questioned it. "I'm sorry I kept you out so long. Will
you have a problem going to these events this weekend?
I didn't even take your schedule into consideration when
we were making arrangements with either of those guys.
I'm sorry."

She was touched by his concern. "If I couldn't make
it, I would have spoken up earlier. You happened to

catch me on a weekend where I personally do not have any events to cover." Glancing at the calendar on her desk, Casey picked up a pen and marked their appointments on the appropriate dates.

"I wasn't just referring to other events," he said quietly. "I don't mean to take time away from…your family." Casey could tell he was fishing for information. Well, she wasn't going to make things easy on him.

"No worries. Like I said, if I wasn't able to do it, I would have spoken up earlier. If you don't mind," she said as she rose again from her seat, "it's been a long day, and I do have some calls to make before I can leave. I'll meet you tomorrow afternoon at our first wedding. How about we arrange to get there at five, so you can observe some of the preparations?"

"Why don't I just pick you up? You only live up the road from me or, if you prefer, I can meet you here."

A realistic excuse refused to come to her mind, and before she could overthink it and make herself crazy, she said, "We can meet here."

There was no denying the pleasure on Ryder's face. "You won't need to go home and get ready first? Do we need to dress like the other guests so that we blend in?"

She nodded. "I'll make sure to bring a change of clothes with me. Believe me, this isn't my first time being an innocent wedding crasher." She chuckled at the thought and soon Ryder joined her. "I appreciate you making the time to do this for Mac and Gina. I promise that after Saturday night, you'll be off wedding planner duties. Your uncle said that he was going to clear a couple of days from his calendar so that he can drive down here and take care of the rest."

The thought of only having until Saturday night to spend with Casey had Ryder feeling panicked. He'd have to do his best to convince his uncle that his time was far too important to Montgomerys to take off and deal with this, and that he, Ryder, was more than capable of taking care of all of the details.

He just hoped that Casey would warm up to the idea as he had.

And that maybe, just maybe, she'd finally feel comfortable enough to start sharing a little bit of her personal life with him so that Ryder could get his head on straight and know where he stood with her.

Chapter 4

FRIDAY AT FIVE O'CLOCK ARRIVED MUCH SOONER THAN Casey was prepared for. She was standing in front of the full-length mirror in her office, checking her appearance. The simple hot-pink sleeveless dress was the perfect choice for what they were doing tonight, and yet as she stared at her reflection, Casey couldn't help but frown.

"I was going to say you looked great, but that face you're making tells me you don't think so. What's going on?" Julie was leaning in the doorway to Casey's office watching her friend get ready. "This is a routine thing for you. Why the frown?"

Casey had already shared her history with Ryder, so it didn't take long for Julie to figure out why Casey looked so ill at ease. "I'm being crazy, right?"

Julie shook her head. "No, you're not being crazy. There isn't a woman alive who doesn't want to make an ex eat his heart out."

"I suppose." Fidgeting with her earrings and then with her hair, Casey finally gave up and turned away from the mirror. "I've done this what seems like a thousand times with clients, and yet the thought of doing it tonight with Ryder has me feeling like a nervous wreck."

"Look, if you're that uncomfortable, I'll go in your place. Tom is home with Savannah, and he would more than understand if I told him what was going on. Just say the word and I'm there for you."

As tempting as it sounded, Casey felt guilty at the thought of taking Julie away from her husband and baby just so that she wouldn't have to deal with a situation of her own making. "You are a great friend and I love you, but I can't avoid Ryder forever. We still have tomorrow night's event, and who knows if I'll have to work with him more before Gina Micelli is back in town. And then, naturally, I'll have to see him at his cousin's wedding. I better get used to being around him now."

"If it's any consolation, at least you won't really be alone with him. Granted, I would have made sure that I drove myself to and from the wedding tonight, but other than that, Martin is going to keep the two of you in the thick of things, so you won't have a whole lot of time to think about the fact that you're out with him."

"I guess so." Casey wasn't a hundred percent convinced, but she had run out of time to think about it because at that moment Ryder appeared behind Julie.

"Ready to go?" he said casually, and she nodded, smiling brightly.

"Sure, all set."

"Good luck tonight," Julie said to them both. "And tell Martin I said hello and that I'll see him next weekend." And then she was gone.

—◆◇◆—

Ryder could only stare. Casey had blossomed into a beautiful woman since they had dated, and the sight of her dressed up took his breath away. His first instinct was to compliment her and then kiss her, but then a flash of color on her desk caught his eye.

A baby rattle.

Dammit.

Jealousy raged within him. Casey hadn't shared one bit of personal information with him, and yet after he'd seen her with Savannah the previous day, he thought for sure that she'd talk about her life. Her husband. But nothing. What did her husband think of her going out tonight and again tomorrow night with a former boyfriend? Had she told him about Ryder?

Were they even still together? Casey wasn't wearing a wedding band, so maybe the guy wasn't in the picture anymore. But maybe he was, and there was some other reason she didn't wear a ring. The baby was pretty little—maybe her fingers had swelled? He'd heard about that happening to the wife of one of his colleagues. She'd had to take off her rings for almost a year.

"Ryder?" Casey asked when he continued to just stand and stare. "Are you okay?"

He shook his head to clear it. "Sure, fine. Sorry, my mind wandered for a second." He looked nervously around the office and couldn't bring himself to meet her eyes. "Shall we?"

Grabbing her purse, she motioned for him to lead the way as she locked her office door.

They walked in silence out to his luxury sedan, and Ryder played the part of the perfect gentleman as he held the door open for her. Once they were both inside and on their way, Casey asked "So, how is your family?"

Ryder felt himself relax. His family was a safe subject, and he was relieved that Casey had found something for them to talk about. For the life of him he didn't know why this was so difficult. Over the years he had run into former girlfriends all the time without giving it a second thought. Why was it that seeing Casey was wreaking such havoc on him? Forcing all thoughts of their romantic past aside, he smiled and did his best to answer her question.

"Well, let's see…my brother Zach is up in Oregon now. He's a total outdoorsman, and although he's a big part of Montgomerys' West Coast operations, you're more likely to find him climbing a mountain than sitting at a desk."

Casey laughed softly. "I remember he was always involved in every kind of outdoor activity going on here in the summer. I used to feel exhausted just talking to him about the things he was doing."

"Zach's great, but sometimes I wish he would just…I don't know…cut back on the thrill chasing. It's not necessary for him to always be on the hunt for the next dangerous experience."

"Is he married?"

The question bothered Ryder. Why would she want to know? Was she interested in Zach? Had she had a crush on him years ago and she just happened to get stuck with his brother?

"Ry?" she asked gently.

"What? Oh, sorry. Um, no; Zach's not married. That would mean that he was willing to sit still for longer than a minute."

Casey merely nodded. "Okay, so Zach's still a risk taker. What about James?"

Ryder couldn't help the smirk that spread across his features at the mention of his youngest sibling. "Well, since he's always had issues with not wanting to blend in with the rest of us, he never did join the family business.

Remember how he dropped out of high school and went to work for a landscaper?"

Casey arched a dark brow at him and nodded in approval. "There is nothing wrong with going against the grain. I'll bet he's very happy."

"Well, I don't know about happy. Did I mention that he then went to the police academy and became a detective?"

She spun in her seat and faced Ryder. "Wait a minute, I thought he was going to be a landscape architect." Ryder nodded. "Then how can he be a detective?"

"Funny story," Ryder began as he turned the car down the long and winding lane to tonight's venue. "He decided he was bored, started out at the police academy, and moved up the ranks fairly quickly. He's still interested in horticulture, and so he does the landscaping gig in his spare time."

"Sounds exhausting. I'm guessing that he certainly isn't married."

Ryder shook his head. "Nope. I think that something happened a long time ago that made James wary about getting involved with anyone. He doesn't talk about it and we don't ask, but it's pretty much a given that he's single and that's exactly what he wants to be."

"Wow," she said with a sigh. "I wonder what could have happened to make him just give up on love?"

"Maybe someone broke his heart," Ryder said quietly, forcing himself to keep his eyes steady on the road ahead and not turn to look at Casey. They were quiet for a long time when he finally mentioned his sister. "Summer is doing great."

"Oh my goodness," Casey said, and Ryder could hear

the smile in her voice. "She was so young when I last saw her; she was barely a teenager."

"Well, she's all grown up now, and if my brothers and I had our way, we'd have her locked up in an ivory tower."

"Like a princess?"

"Exactly. She's scary smart and beautiful, and yet she seems to always go out with the wrong kind of guy."

"Maybe you just think they're wrong because no one is good enough for your baby sister."

Ryder merely shrugged. "Could be. Either way, Summer thinks she can take on the world, and she wants to do everything."

"What does she do for a living?"

"This week?" Ryder asked with a chuckle. "Let's see, I think she's a preschool teacher."

"This week?" Casey asked with real curiosity.

"Summer is an amazing woman, and like I said, she's scary smart, but she's also got a short attention span. She didn't want to come to work at Montgomerys, but then sometimes she complains that we won't find her a position. She's taken photography and even had a couple of successful shows out in California for her work. Then there was the summer that she toured with the Broadway musical *Rock of Ages*." At Casey's look of complete shock, he added, "She has an amazing singing voice."

"That's quite a résumé," Casey said and relaxed back in her seat. "I don't have that kind of talent. I always loved weddings and party planning, and when Julie and I met in college, we joined forces and came up with the idea of starting our own business. It hasn't been easy, but we're good at what we do, and we're pretty successful."

"Good for you, Case," he said and sincerely meant it.

"If anything were to happen to the business, I don't know what I'd do. Unlike Summer, I have no other talents to fall back on."

"Then you'll have to make sure that nothing happens to the business," he said with a wink.

That one simple gesture had butterflies taking flight in Casey's belly, and she knew that her resolve was weakening where he was concerned. She had to keep him talking, had to keep the conversation on somewhat safe and neutral topics, so that they weren't sharing anything personal. "How about your parents? How are they?"

"Dad puts all of us to shame," he said. "The man works full-time, goes to the gym several times a week, and still manages to spoil my mom and make time just for the two of them. They're getting ready to head to Italy for a couple of weeks, and to prepare for it, he arranged for both of them to take Italian lessons." He snorted in disbelief. "I mean, I work a sixty-hour week and barely manage to microwave my dinner before falling asleep on the couch, and the man is out there like someone half his age and having it all."

"It must run in the family, because after meeting your uncle William, I was damn-near ashamed of myself. The man had boundless energy and didn't seem fazed by any of the chaos going on around him."

"That sounds exactly right." They pulled up to the luxury home and Ryder parked a fair distance away so as not to interfere with the guests and the valet service. Stepping around to the passenger side, he held out a hand to help Casey out of the car, not letting go as they made their way to the party.

~~~

The weather was perfect.

The ceremony was beautiful.

The food was fit for royalty.

And Ryder was miserable.

Martin had arranged for them to have a tasting of everything that was being served at both the cocktail hour and the reception, and had set them up in a private dining room to sample it all. Unfortunately, he was sitting alone with twenty plates filled with every kind of food known to man while Casey was out in the hall talking to potential clients. He knew he shouldn't be annoyed, and yet he was. Honestly, Casey didn't need to sample the food, and really, neither did he. Mac and Gina had done all of that, and he should just flip a damn coin and be done with it.

Only Ryder knew that he never walked away from a job.

Or a challenge.

And if he had the chance to do it all over again, he would never have walked away from Casey.

Her laughter rang out in the hallway, and he was half-tempted to get up and ask the couple she was speaking with to call her on Monday and go and enjoy the wedding for themselves. But that would be a little high-handed, and while he couldn't be one hundred percent certain, he had a pretty good idea that Casey would not appreciate his interfering with her job.

He hated her job right now.

They were supposed to be quietly ensconced in this private dining area, with its soft lighting and wonderful food, having intimate conversation.

At least that's the way Ryder had pictured it in his mind all day.

Too much free time and now he was having romantic daydreams.

He really needed to work.

He was just about to serve himself from a plate of assorted hors d'oeuvres when Casey came back into the room and carefully shut the door.

"Have you eaten yet?" she asked as she pulled up a chair opposite him at the table. Ryder shook his head and simply made her a plate and handed it to her before he made one for himself. "I am so sorry about that. I didn't think they'd ask so many questions. I was almost praying that you'd come out there and interrupt."

So much for that pretty good feeling…

"I didn't want to overstep my bounds," he said honestly as he placed a crisp linen napkin in his lap. "Your business is very important to you, and I figured that you've already tasted this stuff and you'd come in when you were done."

"I really am sorry, Ryder," she said as she reached across the table and placed her hand over his. "Tonight you're the client. I should have simply given them my business card and asked them to call and make an appointment. It was unprofessional of me to walk away from you. I'm sorry."

Her eyes implored him to accept her apology, and Ryder knew that he would. There was never a doubt about it. He gave her a smile and relaxed a bit in his seat. "Apology accepted. Now, tell me what's good here."

—∿∿—

After tasting all of the offerings, they went and stood in the back of the grand ballroom and watched as people danced and ate and laughed. "The room is beautiful," Ryder said as he stood behind her. Because of the music and not wanting to intrude on the festivities, he said the words carefully in her ear, resisting the urge to wrap his arms around her and pull her close. "I think this would make a great venue for Mac and Gina."

Casey had to crane her neck and turn around to answer him. She was on sensory overload at their proximity and the smell of his cologne. She wanted to simply wrap herself around him and forget all about wedding planning for just a little while. Her conservative nature won out, and she sighed and said, "Don't get swept up in it. You still need to see the second place, or you will forever wonder if you made the right choice."

She pulled back to resume her original position watching the crowd, when Ryder's hand gently cupped her shoulders and held her in front of him. He knew her words were targeted for what they were doing, but he couldn't help but feel that they also had everything to do with their past. Back then he had gotten swept up in the idea of making it big in the business world and had walked away with a single-minded purpose; he had never taken the time to consider how much more he could have had if he had simply slowed down and explored a future with Casey.

"I'm sorry," he said quietly, and it took Casey a moment to realize that he had said anything. He had opened this particular can of worms, and he was tired of avoiding the elephant in the room. Reaching down,

Ryder took her by the hand and led her out of the noisy room, down the hall, and out onto the beach, where he repeated his apology.

Casey wasn't sure what was going on and decided that her best course of action was to play dumb. "Sorry? For what? Do you want to go? We have no time limit on how long we have to stay."

Unable to help himself, Ryder cupped her face, forcing her to look up and him and stop rambling. "This has nothing to do with the wedding, Casey, and you know it. I'm apologizing to you. I should have apologized more than ten years ago. Hell, I never should have left the way that I did."

"Ryder…" she began, not wanting to have this particular conversation.

"No, let me finish this," he said firmly. "I was wrong back then. I had been groomed my whole life to work for my father's company, and even though I knew I was going to end up there, I wanted to do it on my own terms. I was so focused on that goal that I didn't realize all I was giving up. You meant everything to me back then, and I treated you poorly. I was so determined to be a success in the business world that I lost focus on what I could have had in my personal life."

"Ryder—"

"I know it's been a long time, probably too long, but I just want you to know that I am truly sorry. I hate knowing that I hurt you. Seeing you again and facing you after all these years has been harder for me than any business negotiations I've ever done."

"What is it that you want from me, Ryder?" she asked quietly.

He wanted everything that he had no right to ask for. "I want a chance to get to know you again, Case. I want to talk to you about your life. I don't want to be just a client to you and a stand-in for my wayward cousin. I know I'm asking a lot, and I have no right to ask for you to be even remotely nice to me, but…well…I've missed you."

His honest admission was her undoing. Keeping a professional distance with Ryder seemed like the right thing to do, especially when she thought that she was simply dealing with the selfish Ryder Montgomery she had known all those years ago. But the man standing before her, with the wind blowing his hair and his eyes imploring her to have a little faith in him, made it impossible to say no.

In light of his own honesty, Casey felt that she owed him the truth too. "I don't know if I can trust you again, Ryder. You broke my heart back then, and it took me a very long time to get over you."

"I know and I'm sorry…"

"We have no choice but to work together for the time being, but I promise to try and not be so focused on my job that I don't stop to have a conversation with a friend. Is that okay?"

He wanted to say that he didn't want to just be her friend, that he wanted the opportunity to prove to her that he was trustworthy, someone who knew now how to appreciate what he had right in front of him. Ryder wasn't sure if now was the time for him to push. Looking down into her face, he saw hope and purity and honesty.

For now, he'd take what he could get.

Chapter 5

WHEN RYDER HAD DROPPED CASEY OFF BACK AT HER office, he had secretly hoped that she wouldn't be anxious for the night to end. Not that he had been thinking of anything inappropriate, but maybe she would have wanted to go and sit someplace a little more quiet than a wedding reception and talk.

He had been wrong.

Now he was staring at his reflection in his bedroom mirror, adjusting his tie for tonight's wedding. Since Casey wasn't working today, he had convinced her to let him pick her up at her home. Ryder had no idea what to expect; she hadn't mentioned her husband or, for that matter, her baby. Didn't women usually go on and on about their children? If Ryder hadn't known any better, he'd have sworn that Savannah wasn't hers. But how was that possible? He'd seen her with his own eyes.

A quick glance at the clock showed that it was just about three o'clock, and he had told Casey that he'd be there to pick her up at three fifteen. Ryder was known for his punctuality, and so with one final glance at his reflection, he walked down the stairs and out to his car. The entire time, he gave himself a mental pep talk about how he needed to be pleasant and cordial to Casey's husband when he arrived to pick her up. No ogling her, no comments on the way she looked— which he was certain would be beautiful—and he needed to use his professional veneer, simply shake the man's hand, and leave.

It all sounded good until he was actually in the driveway of their home and having to get out of the car.

Ryder sat gripping the steering wheel until his knuckles turned white. "You can do this," he muttered. "You've run into many ex-girlfriends and their now-significant others and always managed to be polite."

That's because you simply didn't give a damn about them. This is Casey, and you know that she is the one who got away.

The digital clock on the dashboard showed that it was three fourteen, and with a sigh of resignation, Ryder shut off the engine and got out like a man off to his own execution. He climbed the steps to the house that was so familiar to him. How many times had he walked to this door all those years ago? Did her parents still live here too? Wasn't the house a little small for all those people? What did this guy do for a living that he had to glom on to poor Casey and her family rather than providing a home for them himself?

He raised his hand to knock and then mentally chided himself for going on that inner tirade. He was sure that whoever Casey's husband was, he was a decent guy.

A decent guy who clearly can't provide for his family, but...whatever.

"Shut up," he mumbled and knocked on the door. When it opened, Ryder had been prepared to meet the man he already hated, but instead he was greeted with a warm smile by Casey herself.

"Right on time," she said, opening the door for him and stepping aside to let him in. "I just need to grab my purse and we'll be on our way."

Before Ryder could say a single word, she had walked away and down the hall toward the bedrooms. He remembered the layout perfectly, and smiled at the memory of how many times he had snuck in here after Casey's parents had gone to bed and spent the better part of the night with her in her bedroom. The thought alone was enough to arouse him, and he did his best to count backward from one thousand just in case he had to meet anyone.

A quick look around, along with checking to make sure he wasn't hearing things, and Ryder realized that no one was home. Maybe they all had gone out someplace since Casey wasn't going to be home, but if it were *his* wife going out with another man—who she happened to have dated, even if it was a long time ago—Ryder would be here to make damn sure that said man knew he was not cool with the whole thing. Didn't this guy even care?

He was just about to step further into the house when Casey came back into the foyer and smiled. "Ready when you are!"

In another lifetime, he would have said to skip the damn wedding and dragged her to the tiny bedroom at the back of the house and found another way to spend the night.

—∿∿—

The sun was a little bright at this time of day, and being outside with no tent was a little hard on the eyes. Ryder looked around at the small gathering—maybe seventy-five people—and saw that most of them were wearing sunglasses or shading their eyes. If Mac and Gina wanted their wedding here, he would ask about some sort of tent or inquire about what time of day their ceremony was going to take place.

He and Casey stood at the back of the group, and once the bride and groom had kissed, they walked away before anyone really noticed them. As they made their way back toward the resort building, Casey asked his opinion so far, and he mentioned the sun.

"Well," she said as they walked toward a common area, "your cousin wants a ceremony at sunset, or close to it. That will make the glare of the sun a little less daunting. But we can certainly ask about some sort of covering. I don't think we want to go with a whole tent, because that will defeat the purpose of a wedding near the beach." The room where the ceremony had been held jutted out from the back of the resort and onto a pier so you had the spectacular view without the hassle of the sand. "We'll have to look into that."

They strolled around and made small talk about the venue in general, and then Casey received a text that the cocktail hour was starting. They walked back inside and observed the layout of the room and the appetizers being passed, and made comments on the basic flow of it all.

"I like the fact that it's not a sit-down type of thing," Ryder said. "The menu is pretty phenomenal, and you want people to enjoy themselves and the food. I think I like the menu here more than yesterday's."

Casey nodded. "It's a lighter fare here and the presentation is wonderful." A waiter came by and offered them each a crab puff, which they readily accepted. "I always feel bad about this part."

"What part?"

"I feel like I need to be hiding behind a potted plant

or something. I don't think I would like anyone lurking around at my wedding."

That struck Ryder as odd, but he didn't comment. "Well, we could always decline the food and wait for the tasting during the reception."

With a shrug, Casey nibbled at the crab puff and sighed with delight. "They really do have great food here." She put a hand up over her mouth and giggled.

"What? What's so funny?"

"I'm not supposed to say stuff like that."

"Like what?"

"I'm not supposed to offer my opinion like that, especially when you have to make this decision. It needs to be your choice and not influenced by me."

She looked so adorable, Ryder thought to himself, that the urge to kiss her was nearly overwhelming. Knowing this wasn't the time or the place, he took her by the hand and pulled her behind a large potted plant. They were both laughing by the time they settled in to watch the crowd. "Do we need binoculars or anything?" he asked teasingly.

Casey swatted at his arm. "You're making fun of me."

"Just a little."

"This is serious stuff, Ryder. Mac and Gina have entrusted you with picking their venue, and you know them better than I do. The decision has to be yours and yours alone. I can't do anything to sway it."

Placing his hands on her shoulders, Ryder forced Casey to look at him. "First of all, I don't know Gina. I've never met her, and all I know about her is what Mac and the rest of the family have said about her. She seems like a great woman and Mac loves her, and believe me when I say that I want to do right by them. I don't think commenting on whether or not you're enjoying the food is going to sway my decision. Food is food. I'm trying to get a feel for the place overall. I think it's fun to stand back here and watch all of the activity going on. I feel a little like James Bond."

Now she really laughed. "Really? How many 007 movies have you seen where he hides behind a large fern and eats crab puffs?"

"Well, maybe not exactly like James Bond, but you get my point. We're here on a secret mission, and I'm enjoying myself."

They stood behind the plant for several minutes, just watching people milling about. They seemed to be having a good time. Before they knew it, the guests were being led to the main banquet room. "I guess that's our cue to head to the private dining room for our tasting," Casey said, stepping out of the shadows. She was turning to make sure Ryder was behind her when she bumped into someone. "Oh!"

"Were the two of you hiding back there?"

Casey turned back and faced an elderly woman who had to be in her eighties. She was standing there in a bright yellow sequined dress, hands on her hips, frowning at Casey and Ryder. "It's not polite to partake in hanky-panky at somebody's wedding, you know," she said.

"What?" Casey managed to squeak out. "Oh, no… ma'am. There was no hanky-panky going on back there."

"Did you find out what they were doing back there?" Another elderly woman stepped up in an equally loud dress. She was looking at Casey and Ryder with suspicion. "We're in a hotel for crying out loud. Seriously, get a room."

Ryder stepped around Casey and faced the two women. "Ladies, as we said, there was no...hanky-panky going on and there was no need to get a room."

"You see that, Minnie," the one in the yellow said as she elbowed her friend. "Young people. Here they are in a perfectly romantic setting, and they're more interested in the food than in fooling around. What's the world coming to?"

"I hear you, Izzy." Lady number two, Minnie, made a tsking sound. "So basically you're crashing the wedding."

Ryder turned and looked to Casey for help. She stepped to his side and faced to the women again. "We're here looking at the resort for an upcoming event. I'm afraid we were just sort of...people watching. You know, making sure that the flow of the room was good and that the servers were able to handle the crowd and keep everyone happy."

"Then why were you hiding out in a dark corner?"

"What?" Casey cried in despair, her eyes immediately going to Ryder's before she could find her voice again. "No...no, it's not like that. Really. You see, I'm a wedding planner. I've done many events here, and we're trying to decide whether or not to book this particular resort for a wedding."

"Well, that's a damn shame," Izzy said. "You two are just adorable, and now you're telling me this is all about business?" She turned to Minnie. "Back in my day, when an attractive man pulled a woman behind a potted plant, he had the good sense to kiss her." Minnie nodded, and then Izzy poked Ryder in the chest. "Don't you have any sense, son?"

"Me?" he wheezed. "I'm just here to make sure this place will be perfect for my cousin and his fiancée. Casey's just here to do a job, and besides that, she's married!"

"What?" Casey said, her complexion paling. "Why would you say that?"

Both women took a step back and grinned, seemingly pleased with this turn of events.

"What do you mean?" Ryder asked. "I came to your office. I saw your daughter. You told me that she favors her father."

"And so you put all of that together and that was your conclusion?" Casey said, a little guiltily. She crossed her arms over her chest and thought furiously about what to say next.

"What conclusion was I supposed to come to, Case? You haven't shared a damn thing with me since I came back to town! Last night we said we'd spend some time getting to know one another again, and yet you haven't shared one damn bit of information with me about your life! What was I supposed to think?"

"I don't know," she snapped and made to turn away, but Ryder's hand latched on to her arm to stop her. She spun and faced him again. "Savannah is my partner Julie's daughter. That day you came into the office, I was just babysitting. Didn't you think it was odd that I would have all of that baby stuff in the office one minute and then it was all gone when you came back from getting us lunch?"

"He bought you lunch?" Minnie asked. "Such a gentleman."

Casey ignored the woman and continued her defense. "And did you think it was normal for me not to have one picture of Savannah or my supposed husband anywhere in my office? I mean, you were in there several times. Didn't you take notice of that?"

"No, I—"

"And then, when you came to pick me up today," she said, picking up momentum, "did you see even a hint of another person living in my house?" Ryder didn't know what to do or say, so he simply stood there and stuttered until Casey cut him off. "Well? Did you?"

"Did you, son?" Izzy asked.

Both Ryder and Casey turned and glared at their audience before facing one another again. "All right. I'll admit that I jumped the gun and came to the wrong conclusion, but you know, you've been a bit secretive with me."

"Ya think?" she snapped. "Did you honestly think you were going to walk back into my life twelve years later and I was going to be happy to see you?"

"I wouldn't be happy," Minnie said.

"Me either," Izzy agreed.

"You walked away from me back then, Ryder. You promised you'd find a way to make it work. You swore we'd have everything we wanted, but it didn't take long before the phone stopped ringing. You were chasing the life you wanted, and it obviously didn't include me."

"That's not fair, Casey. You know why I left—"

"No," she cut him off. "All I know is that we clearly wanted different things. You talked a good game while we dated, but it was all a bunch of lies."

"I hate a liar," Minnie whispered, and Izzy nodded, entranced by Ryder and Casey's argument.

"They weren't lies, Case. Things were just… I didn't know how to give you what you wanted!" he pleaded.

"Then you're a fool, Ryder. All I wanted was you." Silence hung between them, and though she had waited a dozen years to say those words to him, it didn't give her the satisfaction she had hoped for. When he continued to just stare down at her, she threw up her hands in exasperation. "Look, it's all in the past. I'm not married, I don't have children, and right now I have a job to do. You need to make a decision by tomorrow about which venue you are going to pick for my clients." Taking a step back, she faced the two elderly women who were just as speechless as Ryder. "Ladies, I hope you enjoy the reception."

Once again, Ryder reached out and stopped her departure. "This isn't over, Casey," he said tightly.

"Yes it is, Ryder," she said with finality and pulled her arm from his. She hadn't gone more than three steps when Minnie came up beside her.

"You know," she began, "there were a few last-minute cancellations, so there are going to be some empty seats and uneaten meals. Why don't you two come inside and enjoy the reception? You'll be better informed."

Casey shook her head. "While I appreciate the offer, it's not our place to interfere with a wedding; that would be completely inappropriate, and I wouldn't want to do that to the bride."

"Nonsense," Izzy said coming to stand with them. "This is my niece's wedding. Well, she's not technically my niece anymore. She used to be married to my nephew, Barry, and he was a complete moron. We always told him that if he let Mary go, we'd be on her side, didn't we, Minnie?"

Casey looked at them both in confusion.

"We're both related to the bride's ex-husband. Actually, there are five of us here sharing a table who are related to that moron." Minnie rolled her eyes. "We were thrilled when Mary found her Mr. Right. Fred may not be as good looking as Barry, but he's a decent man with a secure job and he loves Mary. They're going to have a very happy life together."

"Well, that all sounds very lovely and I hope that they do have a wonderful life, but it's still not appropriate for us to just make ourselves at home at this wedding. We have an arrangement with the management—"

"Nonsense," Izzy said and reached over to grab Casey's hand. "Come and sit with us and be in the middle of the action. If anyone gives you a hard time, Minnie and I will set them straight."

"Aunt Izzy? Aunt Minnie? What are you two doing out here? Why aren't you inside sitting down and enjoying your salads?" They all turned and saw the bride heading their way. Casey groaned.

It took less than a minute for the two women to rattle off Casey and Ryder's situation, and although their version left Casey's head spinning, the bride smiled the serene smile of a woman in love. "My aunts are right; you should come inside and enjoy yourselves. The more the merrier."

"Are you sure?" Casey asked. She looked over her shoulder at Ryder and wondered how he would survive sitting at a table with five ex-aunts of the bride. Suddenly, she was actually looking forward to this. Ryder seemed less pleased.

Mary nodded. "We've already paid for the food. I'd hate for it to go to waste. Please. Join us."

"You are very gracious," Casey said, smiling brilliantly at Ryder, and they found themselves flanked by the three woman and led into the reception hall.

———

An hour later, Ryder cursed his luck. While he was grateful for the opportunity to see the reception service in action—which was superb—the conversation around the table was almost more than he could handle. The women simply gushed over Casey and asked her dozens of questions about the weddings she'd done, and then asked her opinion of the wedding they were currently attending. Once that subject had been exhausted, they had seemed suddenly to remember his presence and started glaring at him, one by one.

"What?" he asked, looking at each of them individually with confusion. "What did I do?"

"How could you break this poor girl's heart?" Minnie was the first to ask. "She is an absolutely delightful young woman, and you just walked away and left her like that? How could you?"

"Well...I..." he stammered.

"And then you come back here," Izzy interrupted, "and you just waltz right back into her life and expect her to trust you? If it were me, I would have told your cousin to find someone else to help out because I certainly wouldn't be willing to work with you." She snorted with disgust.

"Now just a minute," Ryder began in his own defense. "I had no idea that Mac would..."

"Why would you even agree to something like this?" This question came from ex-aunt number three, Marie.

"You knew what you did was wrong, so why put Casey through having to work with you?"

"As I was trying to say—"

"Typical man. Only thinking of himself," Minnie said as she reached for her glass of champagne.

"If you would just let me explain—"

"Oh, we don't want to hear your explanation, young man," ex-aunt number four chimed in. Jean. "We're not the ones who need to hear it. Personally, I don't think Casey wants to hear it either, because what's done is done; you can't change the past. But a decent man would not subject a woman who he hurt to being in his presence like this. You've made her come to this beautifully romantic wedding," she began, gesturing to the room at large.

"It really is romantic, isn't it?" Izzy asked.

"Definitely," Marie said.

"As I was saying," Jean interrupted, "you've made Casey come with you to this beautifully romantic wedding, and you don't think that it hurts her? You don't think that a setting like this has her thinking about what your wedding would have been like?"

"Jean," Casey said gently, doing her best to not crawl under the table and hide, "I'm really not sitting here imagining my own wedding. I do this for a living. I don't sit and compare them to the wedding that I want. And besides, I never imagined myself married to Ryder."

"You didn't?" This came from everyone at the table collectively, including Ryder.

Casey wasn't sure who to answer first. "Honestly, no. We were young, and we both had to finish college, and at the time, I had no idea where I wanted to be when it was all said and done. I just wasn't ready for it to end, that's all. I'm sure everyone can understand feeling like that. No one wants to be dumped, right? Wouldn't you all agree that you'd rather be the one to end a relationship than have someone else do it for you?"

The ex-aunts all nodded in agreement and before they could speak, the DJ called all of the couples to the dance floor for a slow dance. "Oh, you two should go and dance," Minnie said.

"No, that's okay," Casey said politely. "We really shouldn't even be here."

"Nonsense," ex-aunt number five chimed in. Celia. "Dancing doesn't cost anything. Go out there and take a turn on the floor. None of us can do it any longer."

"Speak for yourself," Minnie snapped. "I could handle a slow song if I had a partner."

"Who'd want to be your partner?" Izzy asked, making a face.

"Ladies," Ryder said diplomatically as he stood. "You are all too lovely to be fighting. If I could, I would take each of you out on the dance floor with me right now. But if you don't mind, I think I will take your very sage advice and ask Casey to dance." He held out a hand to her, and his eyes implored her to take pity on him and get him away from the table for at least a few minutes. He thought he saw a hint of mischief there in those beautiful eyes, and he feared that she'd reject him. He was relieved when she placed her hand in his and stood.

"Excuse us," she said to the table at large and let Ryder lead her out to the dance floor.

Once they joined the other couples, Ryder pulled Casey in close as they began to sway to the music. "Thank you."

Casey leaned back a little and looked at him. "I'm surprised you didn't make a run for it sooner."

"They're a tough crowd," he said with a chuckle. "I'm sure they mean well, but they are definitely a handful. It seems unusual that the bride still considers them family. If I were her, I would have run once the ink was dry on the divorce papers and never looked back."

Casey rolled her eyes. "They're not that bad; they're just a little more…vocal than most. They're only stating their opinions."

"Loudly," Ryder said with a hint of asperity. "Look, they seem like they're harmless, but that's only from a distance. Up close and personal, they will eat a guy for breakfast."

"Don't be upset that they pointed out the obvious."

"What obvious?"

"Seriously, Ryder?" Casey said with annoyance. "You don't think it's a little awkward for us to have to be working on your cousin's wedding together? Couldn't you just have said that you weren't available?"

He stopped dancing but didn't let Casey out of his arms. "You can't be serious."

"But I am," she said in the same tone.

"So I should let my cousin's wedding planning suffer due to family emergencies and the fact that I was a jerk twelve years ago, just so that you don't have to feel… awkward? Do I have that right?"

When he said it like that, Casey realized how ridiculous it sounded. "Okay, maybe I'm being a little dramatic…"

"You think?" He gently pulled her back into his arms and began dancing again.

"I'll admit that this hasn't been…terrible. And after

tonight, we're done. We won't have to see each other again until the actual wedding."

He stopped dancing again.

"Wait. What?"

"You'll need to have your answer by tomorrow. You can simply text it to me, and I will go from there with the planning. Your uncle will be coming down next week for a couple of days to go over anything else that needs to be done, and so really, after we leave here tonight, your job is done."

"And so…what? We can't see each other again?"

Casey wasn't prepared for this line of questioning. She had secretly hoped that after his part of the planning was done, he'd be more than happy to walk away. That was what he was good at. Without showing that his question had thrown her a little off course, she simply shrugged. "I don't see why we'd need to."

"How about because I want to see you, dammit?" he snapped. "How about because ever since I jogged over to your house the other day, I haven't been able to stop thinking about you? Or maybe because you said that we could at least be friends, and I'd like to actually have the opportunity to hear about your life? I know that it's Mac's wedding that brought us back together, but that doesn't mean that it's all we have to talk about."

The song had ended and people were starting to stare. Casey felt more than a couple pairs of eyes on them. "Can we discuss this later?" she whispered.

Ryder threw his head back in disgust, then reached for Casey's hand and led her out the nearest door. They were out on the deck overlooking the ocean, and when he stopped, he took her by the shoulders so that she couldn't get away. "I can apologize for the next twelve years, and it still wouldn't be enough," he finally said. "Even if you forgave me, I can't forgive myself. What I did was selfish and screwed up, and I regret it. I can't change it though. If I could, believe me, Casey, I would. All I'm asking is for a chance to get to know you again."

His hands on the bare skin of her arms felt nicer than they should have, and everything that he was saying was making her anger at him simply dissolve. The fact that he was being so sincere and that he truly seemed to be in as much distress over the whole thing as she was spoke volumes.

"What do you want me to say, Ryder? I never thought I'd see you again. This is new territory for me. We were kids back then; we had no idea what we really wanted."

"That's not true, and you know it," he said thickly, pulling her closer. "What we had wasn't some teenage crush; from the first moment I saw you, I knew that you were out of my league, and yet I couldn't stop myself from introducing myself to you and doing everything humanly possible to convince you to go out with me."

Casey smiled at the memory. "You were pretty persuasive."

"Because I knew what I wanted. I knew it then and I know it now." And then he kissed her.

Chapter 6

CASEY KNEW THAT THE KISS WAS COMING AND YET didn't want to do a thing to stop it. She was honest enough to admit—at least to herself—that this was bound to happen. She had dreamed of a time when she and Ryder would spend hours just kissing and holding one another close. But the kisses of an eighteen-year-old boy were nothing compared to that of a thirty-year-old man. And this thirty-year-old man certainly knew how to kiss.

Ryder was slowly going insane from the feel of Casey in his arms. This was not the way he had envisioned their first kiss, but in the moment, it was all he could think of to do. Her lips had gone soft and pliant under his, and when she had let her hands come to rest on his chest before gliding up and going around him, it had nearly brought him to his knees. He touched his tongue to hers and heard her soft whimper.

For all he knew, the wedding was over and people were milling around them, but he didn't care. Casey was in his arms where she belonged, kissing him like he had dreamed, and it would take an act of God to make him let her go.

"Ryder," she sighed when he moved his lips from hers to travel down the silky expanse of her throat. "Wait."

Okay, maybe not an actual act of God, but a soft plea from her.

Reluctantly, Ryder pulled back and looked at Casey. Her skin was flushed and her eyes were slightly glazed, and she was the most beautiful thing he had ever seen. He waited to see what she wanted to say because he didn't want to do anything that would make her uncomfortable or ruin the possibility of his getting a second chance with her.

"What are we doing?" she asked breathlessly.

He couldn't help but smile. "I would have thought it was obvious."

A small chuckled escaped before she could stop it. "That's not what I mean." She looked up into his eyes and saw his every emotion just like she always had. "This is crazy."

Ryder shook his head. "No," he said solemnly, "it's not. It was always like this for us, Case, and it doesn't matter if it's been twelve years, twelve hours, or twelve minutes, it's always going to be like this for us." He watched as her eyes widened, and he hoped he hadn't said too much. Unable to help himself, because it was all or nothing, he said exactly what his heart was telling him to. "I want you, Casey. I've always wanted you. Seeing you again made me realize everything that's been missing from my life."

She took a step back as panic began to build. "No, you don't really mean that, Ryder. It's been too long; you don't even know me anymore."

He took a step toward her, unwilling to let her get away. "I do know you. I know that right now you're starting to feel a little bit panicked, wondering what you've gotten yourself into. But at the same time, you're feeling a little bit excited at what this could be. You hate that we're here right now and you're probably worried that you left your purse at the table and then wondering how you'll be able to go in there and face the five ex-aunts without them knowing that we've kissed out here."

More than anything Casey wanted to deny what Ryder was saying, but unfortunately he was spot on. "How…?"

Ryder reached out and cupped her face in his large hands. "I know because I know you. I can't take back what I did twelve years ago, but I can promise to make it up to you. If you'll let me."

It was on the tip of her tongue to just say yes; Ryder Montgomery was the one. True, she always considered him to be the one that got away, but now he was back and saying everything that she had always longed for him to say. But could she trust him to not break her heart again?

"It's too much, Ryder; it's too soon."

He leaned in and placed a gentle kiss on her cheek. "I'm not going anywhere," he promised. "When you decide what it is that you want, I'm going to be here waiting." And with that, he took her hand and led her back into the grand ballroom, back to their table, where they were met with five pairs of inquisitive eyes.

Luckily, no one made a comment about their absence or about the fact that all of Casey's lipstick was gone, and some of it was on Ryder. Rather than sitting down, Ryder reached for Casey's wrap, placed it around her shoulders, and then handed her the beaded clutch that was on her chair. "Ladies, thank you so much for inviting us to be a part of your niece's wedding. This was definitely helpful to my decision-making process. We hope that you have a lovely evening." With a hand placed low on Casey's back, he waited for her to say her good-byes and then together they left the reception.

"Didn't you want to stay until the end?" Casey inquired as they were walking out into the lobby. "How do you know you'll like the way that they do their dessert presentation?"

Ryder shrugged. "I saw more than enough. I'm not going to lie to you; it's a tough decision, but I think I'll be able to sleep on it and know by tomorrow which one is best."

"You don't know right now?"

He shook his head. "Never make a decision about something this important in the heat of the moment; you'll always second-guess it. I tend to make myself wait at least twenty-four hours before making a major decision."

Casey couldn't agree more. She had a feeling if she had said yes to Ryder out on the deck moments ago that at some point she would have wondered if it was the right decision or if she was simply caught up in the moment. "That's very wise."

They reached his car, and once he saw that Casey was settled in, Ryder walked around and climbed in. They drove in silence, and when he pulled into her driveway, Ryder could feel the tension rolling off her. "There is nothing I want more than to go inside with you, Casey," he said softly. "But I know you're not ready for that. I'm asking a lot from you; I know that, and yet I can't help the way that I feel. I'm not going to sit here and try and persuade you or seduce you into letting me back into your life. The decision needs to be yours." Leaning over, he kissed her cheek and then climbed from the car.

Casey watched as Ryder walked around to open her

door for her, indecision screaming in her brain. She wanted to invite him in, wanted him to take the decision from her because it was just too hard. Ryder reached a hand out toward her and she clasped it and rose from the car, standing toe-to-toe with him. She sighed as she leaned into him.

Wordlessly, Ryder took her by the hand and walked her up to the front door. Taking the keys from her shaking hand, he unlocked the door and gently pushed it open. "I had a great time with you tonight," he said, taking in the beauty of her face in the moonlight. "Thank you for making the time to go with me so that I can do what's right for Mac." Then, he did something that even surprised himself. Ryder took Casey's hand in his and gently placed the keys in the palm before stepping back and wishing her a good night.

Casey watched, dumbfounded, as Ryder walked back to his car. That was it? He seriously wasn't going to do a damn thing to convince her to let him come inside? Didn't he realize that she was teetering on the edge, and it wouldn't take much to win her over? She was certain he was going to turn around and stride back toward her and kiss her senseless.

She hoped that he would.

Then he turned around, and in that moment, Casey was certain that he was coming back.

"Go inside, Case," he said. "It's getting chilly out." And then he climbed into his car and drove away.

With no other choice, Casey walked into her house and shut the door behind her before sliding down the cool surface and wondering what in the world had just happened.

It was barely eleven thirty and Casey still hadn't been able to unwind. It had been a little over two hours since Ryder had dropped her off, and her mind was still in overdrive trying to figure out what had happened. She understood that he was letting her make the decision; he wanted her to be one hundred percent certain of what she was doing.

She both loved and hated that.

In less than a week, Ryder Montgomery had managed to turn her world upside down once again. They were older now and a little more in control of their emotions, and yet that wasn't helping matters right now. The more Casey thought about it, the more she realized that she couldn't hold the actions of an eighteen-year-old boy against a now thirty-year-old man. Everyone made mistakes in their youth, and looking back, it was probably for the best. Long distance relationships rarely worked, and at the time, she had resented his commitment to getting an education thousands of miles away so that he could stand out in a family of well-accomplished businessmen.

But seeing the man Ryder had become? She knew that he had done the right thing. She knew him. Sure, there were some stories of their lives that they would need to share and talk about, but the person at the core of it all would still be familiar.

She sighed.

When Casey had found out she was going to have to work with Ryder, all she could think of was keeping her distance. But now? All she wanted was a chance to be everything that Ryder had mentioned earlier. She wanted—no, she needed to know if it was possible for lightning to strike twice, for two people to find one another again after so many years and realize they were the one thing missing from each other's lives.

It was late.

She had already changed out of her dress and shoes, and was roaming her house in yoga pants and a tank top.

She had no shoes on.

And her hair was a mess.

"Screw it," she murmured, reaching for her keys and walking out onto the back deck and then down the wooden steps that led to the beach. The Montgomerys' home was only a half a mile up the coast, and there was something very soothing about walking in the cool sand, watching the moonlight play on the water.

Each step she took filled her with a sense of anticipation, and yet she kept a fairly leisurely pace. More than anything, Casey needed to prove to herself that she was in control and that she wasn't rushing, although the thought of being back in Ryder's arms had her body humming. The cool air had felt good on her heated skin when she'd first left the house, but now she cursed herself for not at least grabbing a sweater.

Up ahead, she spotted Ryder's family home and stopped. Was she certain? Was she seriously ready to let go of the past in hopes of a future? There was still a chance that things wouldn't work out, and if that was the case, could she handle having Ryder break her heart for a second time? Was she ready to take that risk?

Her feet started moving before her head gave her a definitive answer, and soon she found herself at the base of the steps leading up to the deck. Casey's hands gripped the railing like a lifeline, and she took one last fortifying breath before taking that first step that would finally lead her to Ryder.

When she was finally up on the deck, the first thing that she noticed was that the house was dark inside. No lights were on except for a soft one out on the deck. If she knocked, would Ryder even hear her? With no way of knowing except for simply doing it, Casey raised her hand and knocked on the glass and waited.

And waited.

And waited.

Had he gone out? She was just about to turn and leave, cursing herself for her impulsive behavior when she saw Ryder coming toward her. Her heart rate kicked up at his approach, and when he reached the glass door, he simply stood there and looked at her. Casey couldn't read his expression, and she began to really second-guess her decision to come here.

"Ryder?" she asked with uncertainty. But he said nothing; he simply continued to look at her through the glass. "It's kind of chilly out here. Can I please come in?" She was certain that he'd open the door right up for her, but instead he turned his head and looked as if he was searching for something.

*Oh no…*she suddenly thought with a sickening feeling in her belly. *He's not alone.*

Putting her hand up and taking a step back, she said, "You know what? It can wait. Really. I'm sorry that I disturbed you." Turning and doing her best not to trip over everything in sight in her attempt at a quick and hasty getaway, she didn't hear the door sliding open.

"Casey," he said gruffly and she turned back toward him. "What are you doing here?" His hair was ruffled and he was shirtless, wearing nothing but a pair of cotton pajama pants hung low on his hips.

She nearly swallowed her tongue.

"It…it was nothing," she stammered and continued her less-than-graceful backward walk toward the stairs. "You can just…go back to…whatever you were doing and um…text me tomorrow with the venue that you want me to book for your cousin." She banged her heel on the edge of a lounge chair and cursed.

Ryder came toward her slowly. "Are you okay?"

"What?" she asked nervously. "Oh, I'm fine. Really. Never better." Looking over her shoulder to make sure that the path was clear, she added a final good night before turning her back on him.

And that's when he reached for her and pulled her back against him. Casey's skin was freezing against his hands and Ryder could feel her shivering. He rubbed his hands up and down her arms for several moments while he simply took in the feel of her against him—the smell of the ocean and the vanilla that always drove him wild. "Why are you here?" he whispered against her throat and heard her moan slightly as she did her best to press her body fully against his without being obvious.

"I wanted…"

"Yes?"

"I needed to…"

He kissed her neck and then simply blew on the spot and almost had to catch Casey as her knees buckled. "What do you need, Case?"

"You," she said, her voice shaking "I need you, Ryder."

Without a word, he bent and swung Casey up in his arms and strode back to the house, stopping only to shut the sliding doors and lock them before taking Casey to his bed.

Gently laying her down, Ryder stood and took in the sight before him. Everything about it was right.

"Can I ask you something?" Casey asked quietly. Ryder nodded. "Why didn't you open the door at first? What were you looking for?"

Ryder ducked his head and felt himself blush slightly. "It wasn't quite midnight."

"What?"

"Remember, I told you earlier that it's always best to wait a day before making a decision?" Casey nodded. "Well, I told myself that if it was at least after midnight, it would be all right. I had to wait for it to be at least twelve-o-one."

Casey reached out a hand to Ryder to draw him down beside her.

Neither one bothered to look at the clock again.

Chapter 7

THE FIRST RAYS OF SUNLIGHT WERE BEGINNING TO filter into the room when Casey opened her eyes. There was no confusion—she knew exactly where she was, and it was exactly where she wanted to be. Ryder was curled around her, and she had been held lovingly in his arms all night.

"Hey," he whispered, and Casey smiled at the sound of his voice and the feel of his breath on her skin.

"Hey, yourself," she whispered back and then shifted even closer, so that her bottom was snug against the arousal that was growing behind her. "A girl could get used to waking up like this."

"I hope so," he replied, trailing kisses along her throat and shoulder. "I was very relieved to wake up and realize that I didn't dream this last night; you're really here."

"Yes, I am." A purr of delight escaped her lips as his worked their magic everywhere they touched. She sighed his name and then turned in his arms so she could face him. Reaching up, Casey cupped his face and kissed him on the lips. "Good morning."

Ryder smiled down at her in pure wonder. When he'd heard the knock on the door last night, he had thought he had been dreaming. As he'd made his way to the door and saw Casey standing in the moonlight, he was certain that he was dreaming. After their discussion earlier in the night, he had figured that she would need at least a day, if not several, to decide whether or not she wanted to be with him. Relief had swamped him when he realized that Casey didn't need the time, that she was just as anxious for him as he was for her. There was so much about her life that he wanted to know, and as much as his body was screaming for him to make love to her again, he didn't want her to think that what he was looking for was only physical.

Putting a little distance between them, Ryder lay on his back and tucked Casey in at his side. "So tell me," he began, "how is it that you're still here in Wilmington, in your parents' house? Are they still here?"

She shook her head. "They retired to Arizona several years ago. I was just getting the business going and wanted to stay local, and so I offered to buy the house from them. They immediately declined and said that they wanted me to put my money into the business. I thought that the plan was for me to just live in the house and pay the utilities, since the mortgage was completely paid off. It wasn't until after they moved that I received the papers saying they had deeded the house over to me."

"That was very generous of them."

Casey nodded. "I was a little angry at first; I didn't want them to give up on their dreams for their retirement because of me. My parents are pretty private people, but after weeks of me arguing with them, they showed me their financial statements and assured me that deeding me the house wasn't hindering their lives at all. Apparently they had saved more than they spent throughout their marriage, so they are living quite comfortably in the desert right now."

"Good for them."

"They're the only people I know who willingly moved away from the beach," she said with a laugh. "Most people work their whole lives so that they can live on the beach and mine wanted nothing more than to move far away from it."

"Well, in their defense, they lived with it their whole lives; it was time for something different."

"I suppose." She was silent for a moment, simply enjoying listening to Ryder's heartbeat while her fingers skimmed their way across his chest. "Tell me about California."

Ryder shrugged. "Not much to tell. I have a house similar to this one, and it's right on the beach. My office is less than five miles away, and I moved there, went to school, got that branch of the company up and moving, and now…" His voice trailed off.

Casey pulled herself up and looked at him. "Now…what?"

He studied her face. Even without makeup, she was the most beautiful woman in the world to him. "Now…I want more."

There were at least a dozen ways that Casey could read into that statement, but decided to not jump to any conclusions and let Ryder explain himself. When he didn't expand right away, she began to fish a bit. "You want to grow the company some more?"

Ryder shook his head. "No. I'm a little burned out with the business. I've worked seventy to eighty hours a week since it started, and now I'm confident that some-one else can take over and I'll be okay with it."

"One of your brothers?"

Again he shook his head. "I don't think that either

of them are all that interested in putting in that kind of time. Actually, I know that James doesn't want anything to do with it and Zach has his own agenda. He does a lot of our international stuff. I don't think he'd want to be tied down to one place."

"So you'd let an outsider take over?"

"I don't think of it like that. Besides, it's not just my brothers who would be up for the position, I have at least another half-dozen cousins—besides Mac and his brothers—that would be good candidates to slip right into the position."

"And what would you do with yourself?"

I'd spend the next forty or fifty years making things up to you. Ryder reached out and stroked a hand down Casey's cheek. "I'll still be involved in one way or another, but just not as the CEO of that particular branch of the company. My dad and my uncles have offices all over the country, and I think if I put it out there, one of them would find a place for me."

Casey was growing frustrated with Ryder's some-what elusive answers. "Where would you want to go?" She couldn't help but ask.

"Well, that would depend," he said softly, his eyes never leaving hers.

Now they were getting somewhere. Casey sighed and rested her cheek into the palm of Ryder's hand. "On what?"

It was now or never. Ryder usually took his time working things out in his head; he always had a plan. For some reason, however, where Casey was concerned, he couldn't wait. He had already lost so many years with her, and he wanted their future to start now.

"I want to be wherever you are, Case," he said solemnly, watching her expression.

She sighed his name. "I think I would like that very much."

"Really?" he asked, unable to believe that he had heard her correctly.

"Really." Casey leaned forward and touched her lips to his, loving the fact that this was reality and not something that she was dreaming. Ryder was here; she was in his bed, in his life, and as he rolled her beneath him, she knew that he was her future.

By the time they surfaced from the bedroom, the sun was starting to set in the late afternoon sky. Ryder had grilled a couple of steaks while Casey had prepared a salad, and they were eating out on his deck watching as the tide crashed on the shore.

"I never get tired of that sound," she said as she took a sip of wine. "I can sit outside for hours, no matter what time of day it is, and just listen to the waves."

"It is a great sound. So tell me what your schedule is usually like. What does a typical week in the life of a wedding planner look like?"

She laughed at his question. "There is no typical week," she said with a smile. "My weekends are usually pretty full during the season, but just like with you, things come up unexpectedly, and while most of my days are nine to five, there is the occasional time where I have to go out at night to tour a venue with a couple."

"That's understandable. How do the next couple of weeks look for you?"

Casey had to take a moment to get her head back in business mode. "Let's see, I have a consultation on Monday afternoon, a tasting to go to on Tuesday, I think your uncle is coming out either Wednesday or Thursday and—"

"Why?"

"Why what?"

"Why is my uncle coming down? I thought that we had everything covered?"

"For the most part we do, but when I last spoke to him I was trying—"

"You were trying to get rid of me," he said with a hint of disbelief. "Why?"

Casey looked at him with exasperation. "Seriously? Haven't we covered this already? I didn't want to work with you, Ryder. I was sort of annoyed that you had come back to town and were involved in this wedding at all. I didn't think too highly of you after the way things had ended between us, but now…well, it just took a little time for me to stop being childish and to see that it was time to stop living in the past."

He nodded. "So do you still need my uncle to come down here, or can I simply finish helping out?"

Casey reached across the table and took his hand in hers. "You have gone above and beyond the call of duty. But maybe…hey, wait a minute. Have you decided on the venue? Do we need to call Mac and Gina and let them know?"

Ryder burst out laughing. "You'd think I would have remembered that, right? I have decided on the second venue. In the end, I like the fact that it was an all-inclusive resort and that the guests can stay there after the reception. I hate to think of anyone having to drive. The food was great, the service was top-notch, and the rooms were luxurious."

"Call your cousin and let him know while I call and book it. They were only holding the date for me until today, and it's already later than I had planned on calling." It was only then that Casey realized she had left home last night with nothing but her keys and the clothes on her back. When she looked back at Ryder, he was smirking. "What's so funny?"

"You just suddenly looked a little lost and it was adorable. Let me call Mac and then you can use my phone to make your call."

"Fine," she muttered, but wondered if maybe she should run home for some of her things. Maybe it would be better for her to go home anyway; she didn't want to make Ryder feel like she was ready to move in with him or anything. She did have work to do in preparation for her week. Once he got off the phone with Mac, she'd make her excuses and head home.

"Wow, that was impressive," Ryder said, snapping Casey out of her inner dialogue.

"What was?"

"That whole conversation you were having with yourself. It was fascinating to watch."

"I wasn't having a conversation with myself. Much."

Ryder stood and took Casey in his arms and kissed her. "Yes, you were. Much." They laughed and Ryder stepped away, grabbing his phone and pulling up Mac's number. He was surprised that he actually caught him. Truth be known, he had no idea what the time was over in England and wasn't sure if he was waking Mac up or catching him in a meeting.

"Hey, Mac. It's Ryder. Did I catch you at a bad time?"

"No, I am actually done for the day here. Thank God," he sighed. "What's up?"

"I made a decision on the venue and wasn't sure if I needed to call you first or your dad. I don't have Gina's number, and although Casey does, I thought maybe you'd want to hear it from me first."

Mac chuckled. "Did you want to claw your own eyes out by the time you were done?"

Ryder laughed along with his cousin. "It wasn't as bad as it could have been. I had the opportunity to observe two different weddings—one at each venue—so that I could see how well organized they were during an event."

"Gina had wanted to do that, but our schedules never quite meshed. So? Which one did you choose?"

"I chose the all-inclusive one."

"Yes!" Mac said. "Honestly, that one made the most sense to me. Gina really liked the other place because they do the ceremony on the beach, but personally, I'm not a huge fan of sand."

Ryder rolled his eyes. "While that is the lamest excuse I have ever heard, I can understand it."

"So the place was good in action?"

Ryder relayed the details of the wedding the previous evening, including the five ex-aunts he and Casey had sat with. They were both laughing and Ryder made a mental note to send a bouquet of flowers to each of them. They may have been major pains in the rear, but if it hadn't been for their egging him and Casey on, they might not be where they were right now. He looked over and saw her clearing away their dishes, wearing nothing more than one of his shirts. It looked good on her.

It was going to look even better when he peeled it off of her.

"Ry? You there?"

"What? Sorry. My mind wandered for a minute. What did you say?"

Mac chuckled again. "I asked how things were going with Casey. When she mentioned that the two of you used to date, I almost cringed. My dad is on a matchmaking kick after having a hand in mine and Lucas's and Jason's love lives. I thought for sure he was going to get up and do a jig at the thought of doing it again."

"Well, remind me to thank him," Ryder said, unable to hide the smile in his voice. "I looked Casey up even before I got the call about you needing help with the wedding, and thanks to the time we had to spend together, I think that things are damn-near perfect."

"I'd ask exactly what that means but I don't think it's necessary," Mac said. "She's a great girl, Ry. I have no idea what your history is with her, and really, it's none of my business, but from what I know of the both of you now, I think you're perfect for each other."

"I agree," Ryder said and smiled warmly when Casey turned and smiled at him, her eyes full of promise. He needed to get off the phone. Now. "So listen, are we good? Are you okay with Casey going ahead and booking the date?"

"Gina said you were the tiebreaker so I'll call her now and let her know you've made your decision, and tell Casey to take care of the rest."

"Will do, Mac. Good luck with the rest of your trip. When are you heading back home?"

"I've got another couple of days here in London and then I'm meeting up with Christian on Wednesday."

"Really? For business?"

"Nah, we haven't seen one another in years, and you know how this family is," Mac said with a hint of humor. "We have more cousins than we can count, and it's rare that we're in the same place at the same time. I looked him up before I got here and Wednesday worked for the both of us. We're going to hang out for a bit, and then I'm catching a flight to San Francisco to meet up with Gina."

"Well, tell our wayward cousin that I said hello," Ryder said. "Will he be coming for the wedding?"

"We have two hundred people coming, and I think a hundred of them are Montgomerys!"

"So Gina doesn't have a big family, I'm gathering."

"Luckily, no; otherwise we'd have had even more trouble finding a location."

"Well, my work is done, Cousin," Ryder said, even more anxious to get off the phone when he saw Casey bend over to pick something up. "Gotta go."

"I know that tone," Mac said. "Tell Casey I said hello and thank her for all she's doing."

"Consider it done," Ryder said as he hung up. He knew there were calls that Casey needed to make, but his need for her was too great. Walking up behind her, Ryder wrapped his arms around her and gently nipped at her neck. "You look really good in my shirt, Case."

She purred and arched into him. "Thank you. Wanna see what I look like out of it?"

It was as if they were of one mind. "Sweetheart, you have no idea how much," he growled as he let his hands roam up and down her torso. "But I don't want to feel rushed, so make that call and book the place, and then I'm turning the phone off."

Casey looked over her shoulder at him and smiled a wicked smile. "One mind."

———

By Wednesday, Ryder was more than a little frustrated with the direction of his life. After finding Casey again after all this time, he didn't want to be apart from her. They spent every night together, but her days were full. If he was working, he was sure that it wouldn't seem so bad, but with nothing to do but sit around and wait for her to come home, he was slowly losing his mind.

The one thing he had managed to do was call his uncle William and tell him that it wasn't necessary for him to come to the coast, that he had it all under control. Even now Ryder chuckled at how pleased his uncle had sounded.

"Are you sure, Ryder?" William had asked. "I managed to clear a couple of days in my calendar so Monica and I could drive down and help Casey out."

"It's really not necessary," Ryder had assured him. "The venue is booked, and Gina and Casey have already talked and emailed and Skyped to go over the invitations and programs. They are supposed to have another Skype meeting with the florist today, so really, it all seems under control."

"You seem to know an awful lot about how it's all going," William said with a hint of amusement in his voice. "I thought you were simply taking care of the venue. Have you been talking to Gina?"

Ryder knew his uncle was fishing, and although the stories making their way through the family told Ryder everything he needed to know about his uncle's matchmaking abilities, Ryder wanted to tease him a little more. "I actually talked to Mac. I hear he's meeting with Christian today before coming back to the States. It's going to be great to have all of the cousins together for the wedding, don't you think?"

"Yes, yes," he said absently. "It's going to be wonderful. I haven't been with my brothers in far too long. And the thought of all of you kids in one room is enough to make my head spin. Maybe you should tell Casey that we'll need to put the resort on high alert. You all can be a handful!"

"Uncle Will," Ryder began lightly, "we're not kids anymore, and we all know how to behave ourselves. Maybe you should tell Gina to handle that."

"Oh, I'm sure that Gina has enough to deal with. Her mother's surgery went very well and she seems to be recovering nicely. I'm hoping that she and Mac won't have to stay out in California for too long. But surely you and Casey will have everything under control for them. Heck, you'll probably be an old pro at it by the time the big day comes! Maybe even pro enough to plan your own wedding!"

It was hard to simply not bust out in laughter. "Wedding? Oh, you've got the wrong guy, Uncle. Once this wedding is done, I'm heading back to San Diego."

"What? But…but…you said that you were going to take a step back from the company. We've all been discussing which of your cousins was going to take your place! You can't tell me that you've changed your mind. What on earth is going on down there, Ryder? What about Casey?"

"Casey? What about her? She's the wedding planner and she's doing one heck of a job, but…well…that's it. We took care of the venue, and she didn't need my help on anything else. She's pretty efficient at what she does." Ryder smiled at the images in his mind of how efficient Casey was at nearly bringing him to his knees on a daily basis by simply being in the room.

"To hell with being efficient," William said. "You mean to tell me that the two of you worked together and then that was it? No sparks? No lingering chemistry?"

"Not really." Ryder wasn't sure how he was keeping it all together.

"Well, then you're clearly doing something wrong, Ryder!" his uncle yelled. "I hope you didn't treat Casey as some sort of colleague or—"

"But she is a colleague of sorts. She's handling Mac and Gina's wedding, and as such, it would be inappropriate for me to make some kind of move on her."

"Nonsense. She's a beautiful woman and clearly at one time you thought so too. What's wrong with you?"

"Nothing," Ryder said as if he didn't have a care in the world. "People change; they grow up. I did meet a very cute cocktail waitress at the first venue we looked at."

"Maybe I do need to take a ride down there," William muttered. "Honestly, it's like not one of you boys can see what's right in front of your face." He continued to mutter to himself before announcing to Ryder that he was definitely coming to the coast.

"Okay, okay…I confess," Ryder finally said. "I

looked up Casey before you and Mac even called me. I went out for a run and found myself at the foot of the stairs leading to Casey's parents' house. It's her house now and so I was lucky there."

"And…?" William prompted.

"And…" Ryder began, "there were still the sparks and the chemistry."

"I knew it! Ha-ha! Four for four!"

"Uh-uh," Ryder said, tsking at his uncle. "I searched out Casey before you called, so you cannot take credit for this match. Sorry."

"Well, that's just ridiculous," William snorted. "If it wasn't for me, you two wouldn't have worked together."

"I'll be honest with you, I didn't need a reason to seek Casey out. Even if there wasn't a wedding to be dealt with, I would have done whatever it took to make her see that we belong together."

"You just can't let me have this one thing, can you?" William teased.

"Absolutely not. Mac has filled me in on all of your antics with him and Lucas and Jason, and while the intention was there, it wasn't needed. The girl is mine, and I'm not letting her go."

"Atta boy! I am so happy for you! Does this mean that you're moving back East?"

Ryder nodded even though his uncle couldn't see it. "Yes."

"Does Casey know?"

"I told her that I want to be wherever she is. I've been feeling a little lost for a while now, but once I stood on the deck that morning and saw Casey again, I knew exactly where I wanted to be."

"Well then, I guess it's all right that I don't get to add you to my list of successful matches, because the end result is still the same."

"Don't worry; if it means that much to you, it will be our secret. When everyone's together for Mac and Gina's wedding, you can brag about your streak as a successful matchmaker."

"You were always my favorite, Ryder," William said.

"Remember that when you're faced with another dozen Montgomerys in a couple of months."

"Oh, don't you worry. I'm sure I'll have my hands full with all of them."

And Ryder had no doubt that he would. "You don't plan on playing matchmaker to all of them, do you?"

"Me? Would I do something like that?" His voice was laced with mischief, and if Ryder knew one thing about his uncle, just like all the Montgomerys, he never stepped away from a challenge.

Chapter 8

RYDER FINALLY SETTLED INTO A ROUTINE OF SORTS over the following weeks. Without much discussion, he had essentially moved into Casey's home. He liked being there. The house was smaller than his, but it felt more like a home. Plus, his parents had come down for a weekend, along with Uncle William and Aunt Monica, so it was better for everyone for him to simply stay at Casey's for privacy's sake.

Luckily, William hadn't gloated too much. It was beyond obvious how pleased he was to see his nephew and Casey together, but he had managed to rein in his giddiness at the turn of events when they had all gone out to dinner together.

Casey's work schedule was never the same twice, and Ryder had to learn to go with the flow a little more than he was comfortable with. At the same time, it allowed him to have some time alone to figure out his own future. Casey was his future, of that he was certain, but he needed to figure out what he was going to do with himself career-wise.

There was no appeal to having to go into an office on a daily basis, and if he was being honest with himself, Ryder didn't need to work. Financially, he was more than secure, and he would always draw an income from Montgomerys. The problem was that he needed some-thing to do. Sitting around the house all day was fast losing its appeal. When he had set out on his little sabbatical, he had been looking forward to doing nothing all day, but the reality wasn't nearly as fun.

"You're frowning again," Casey said as she walked in the door and found Ryder sitting on the sofa. "You are going to have to find some sort of job or project to keep you busy, because all of this sitting around is clearly starting to get to you."

He rose and walked over to kiss her hello. "I can't help it; being without you all day makes me cranky."

"Aw," she cooed, wrapping her arms around him. "Poor baby. Whatever are we going to do with you?" Before she could even blink, Ryder had reached down, lifted her up and over his shoulder, and began to head toward the bedroom. "Ryder!" she shrieked with laughter. "What in the world are you doing?"

He threw her down onto the bed and gave her a wicked grin. "It's been a long day. I had way too much time to think of all of the things that I want to do with you."

"Ooo," she purred. "I like the sound of that."

Ryder placed a knee on the bed and reached out to take her shoes off first. His hands traveled up her calves and lingered on the sensitive spot behind her knees. Casey was wearing a black pencil skirt and white blouse, and where she had looked all crisp and neat a few minutes ago, she was quickly looking thoroughly mussed.

And very sexy.

"Ryder," she said breathlessly as his hand continued to travel up her thighs until he found her panties. He lingered only a moment before hooking a finger on them and quickly pulling them off.

"I missed you," he said huskily, coming to lean over

her. "I don't know how I made it through my days all the time I was away from you, but now that we're here together, I can't seem to stop wanting you."

"I don't want you to stop," she said.

"Good."

And that was the last thing he was able to say before claiming her lips with his.

———⁓———

"So I was thinking," Ryder began later that night, as they sat and watched the sun setting from the deck, "the wedding is only a couple of weeks away and everything seems to be in place. Why don't we invite Mac and Gina down for the weekend so I can actually meet my cousin's fiancée, and you can take care of any last-minute business with them?"

Casey turned to him and smiled with surprise. "That sounds like a wonderful idea." There wasn't really much else to go over with Gina that couldn't be done over the phone, but since she was now back in North Carolina, Casey was sure a last-minute get-together couldn't hurt. "I'll call her in the morning and see if they can do it."

"I was thinking that they can either stay here with us or down the road at my parents' place. Which do you think?"

"It could be fun to have them stay here with us, but they may want a little more privacy. We'll give them both options and let them decide. I hate the thought of your place up the road sitting there empty even though it's like that most of the time."

Ryder shrugged. "It's a great house, but it was always meant as a vacation home. When we were younger, I couldn't understand why my parents kept it, but now I'm glad they did." He reached out and took Casey's hand.

There had been quite a few things on Casey's mind lately that she wanted both to talk about and to avoid. Things had been going so perfectly—almost too perfectly—and she was afraid of rocking the boat. But sitting in the cool night air, watching the sun set, she couldn't help but voice her thoughts.

"What about your house back in San Diego? Have you thought about what you're going to do with it?"

Once again he shrugged. "Not really."

"I mean, I know you said that you want to be here with me, but you have to be realistic, Ryder; you can't simply walk away from your life in California. You have a home, a car, an office…you're going to have to deal with them at some point."

"And I will," he said agreeably.

"I'm just saying that it seems to me like you're not dealing with it." Casey wasn't sure why the topic was nagging at her, but it simply was.

Ryder turned his head and looked at her. "What's this all about, Case? I had planned on being here for three months. I made sure everything was being taken care of back home. Why is this such a big deal all of a sudden?"

Casey sighed. "I don't know. I guess there's a part of me that's still a little insecure. I think right now everything is fine and good and right, but what happens when the wedding is over and you have to go back to California? What if the transition doesn't go the way you want it to? What if you suddenly decide that you need to stay there a little bit longer? Or not come back at all?" God, she hated how needy and clingy she was sounding, but it was hard to let go of old insecurities.

"Hey," Ryder said softly when Casey looked away from him. "Where is this coming from? You know I want to be here with you. I don't want to go back to my life in California. It was empty and meaningless. This is where I want to be, Casey."

"You said that once before," she whispered.

"I know," he said. "I was a kid back then. I thought I was invincible and could control every aspect of my life. I really thought I'd be able to have the career and come back here to you. I made a mistake; I've apologized. I don't know what else I can do to make you believe me."

Her eyes were filled with tears when she faced him again. "I know you think I'm being silly," she sniffled. "It's just that I can't help but make comparisons to how things were before. Everything seemed to be going so perfectly, and then you left and didn't come home. Now I know that you have to go back to San Diego after Mac's wedding, and I can't help but fear that the same thing is going to happen."

"Baby," he said softly, coming to sit beside her on her chaise, "nothing is going to keep me from coming back to you. This is where I want to be. I want us to finally have a life together. I want to marry you, have babies with you." It certainly wasn't the way Ryder had planned on proposing to Casey, but right now felt exactly like the perfect time.

"You do?" she asked with quiet surprise.

"I do," he said, leaning his forehead against hers. "You're everything to me, Case." He wiped the tears from her cheeks. "I don't ever want to be the reason for you to cry. I'm sorry that I ever was. I love you."

A smile grew across her face at his words. In all of their time together in the last weeks, neither had spoken the words out loud. Casey knew for sure that she had never stopped loving Ryder, but fear of what the future held kept her from saying those three little words to him. "I love you too."

Slowly, Ryder leaned in and kissed her with all the pent-up passion he had inside. "I never want to leave you again."

Casey sighed as she relaxed into Ryder's arms. "I don't want you to leave me again," she said quietly. "I know you'll have to travel for business and go back to San Diego to take care of things, but I like knowing that you'll always come back."

"Always, Case. It just took me a little longer this time."

Chapter 9

"ARE YOU SURE YOU'RE READY FOR THIS?"

"Absolutely."

"You know it's not too late to change your mind."

"Why would I want to?"

"Anything could go wrong out there. Are you sure you thought of everything?"

Mac looked at his two brothers, who were doing their best to try and get him riled up. "The only thing that matters is watching Gina walk up that aisle toward me. I don't care if it's raining. I don't care if nobody else shows up. None of that matters. All I want is Gina."

Lucas rolled his eyes. "You didn't need to go through all of this nonsense to get Gina. Hell, what she sees in you, I'll never know. She would have married you at the drive-through at Taco Bell if you asked her."

"Please. I have a little more class than that."

His brother Jason snorted. "Class? That's what you're going with? Although I have to admit, this place is exceptionally classy. Good choice."

"You can thank Ryder for that. He made the final decision."

"Yes," Lucas said, "and remind me to thank him. I'm glad you didn't expect me to run around playing wedding planner for you."

"As if I would," Mac said with mock disgust. "But seriously, I don't know how we could have pulled this off without him. I don't know how to even begin to thank him."

"I saw him earlier and met Casey; I think you've thanked him enough," Jason said with a laugh as he straightened his tie. "I guarantee you we'll be back here in no time for their wedding."

"I'm sure Dad would just love that," Lucas said, coming to stand next to Jason to make sure his own tie was in place.

"What? What would I love?" William Montgomery asked as he entered the groom's room.

"The fact that Ryder and Casey are going to get married," Mac said, tying his shoe.

"Ah, yes. Ryder and Casey. Another happy match, might I add. I am just too good at this!"

Lucas rolled his eyes. "Why don't you quit while you're ahead? You got lucky, old man," he teased. "Leave the rest of the family alone."

"Now, how can I do that? Have you seen all of your cousins? There's about a dozen of them out there, and none of them are married. What is it with your generation that you have to be pushed into getting married? Back in my day, we got married young because that's what we wanted."

"Back in your day, there weren't so many distractions," Jason said as he walked over to his father and played at adjusting his tie. "You know, you talk about wanting us all to be married, but you and your brothers have managed to keep all of us busy with the company. It's not always easy to find the balance between work and a personal life, especially when we were younger. Personally, I don't think I could have settled down quite so easily if I had met Maggie ten years ago."

"Probably not," William agreed. "But now that you are settled down, you see how wonderful marriage can be." He stepped back and looked at his three sons. Each one of them had him beaming with pride. "You all look so handsome. Your mother is going to burst into tears at the sight of you."

"Not again," Mac said under his breath, and Lucas elbowed him in the ribs. They both laughed and then Mac faced his father. "You sure you're okay with your role today?"

William instantly sobered. "Nothing would have pleased Art more than to know that I was the one walking his daughter down the aisle. In a perfect world, he'd be here today to do it himself, but I'm honored to do that in his place."

"Gina was nervous about asking you."

"I'm sure it wasn't an easy decision for her, but I'm glad I can do this for her. And for Art."

A knock at the door had them all turning. Casey walked in and smiled at them all. "You Montgomerys certainly know how to make an impression," she said with a laugh.

"Oh no," William said, craning his neck to see out the door. "Is everyone behaving?"

"Behaving? Yes. But the male members of the family are causing a near riot among the female staff."

"Aren't there only male members of the family?" Jason teased.

"Oh, knock it off," William scolded. "Sure, they're outnumbered, but you know darn well that Summer and Megan are out there too."

"I don't think of them as women," Lucas said

with a smirk. "Last I saw them, they were just kids—
tomboys, actually."

Casey walked up to him and poked him in the chest.
"Well, let me tell you, the two women I just met are certainly not tomboys, and I think they would be offended
to know you still think of them like that."

"Old habits die hard," Lucas said in his own defense.

"Well, I just wanted to come in here and get you,
William," Casey said as she turned to him and smiled.
"Gina is ready for you." Then she turned to the brothers.
"And it's time for the three of you to take your places
outside." It was almost comical how these confident
men suddenly looked a little nervous. "Oh, come on.
This is the third wedding in three years from what I
understand. This should be a cakewalk for you."

With that, Casey opened the door, instructed her
assistant to take William to Gina's room, and then led
Mac and his brothers out onto the pier. As she was
making her way back inside, an arm snaked out and
pulled her off her path.

"Ryder," she hissed with a laugh. "I'm working."

He kissed her soundly until she melted in his arms. "I
know, I know, and you're very good at it. I just wanted
to take a minute and make you relax. You were looking
a little too intense. That can't be good for you."

Ryder's hands were on her hips and she swatted him
away. "You're the one who needs to relax. I've done
this more times than I can count. Today is all about the
bride, and it is my job to make sure everything goes off
without a hitch. I need to stay focused."

"Fine," he said with a pout. "Go and focus."

She smiled and leaned in for one last kiss. "I'll

be honest with you, this is not an easy bunch to stay focused with."

Ryder's brows furrowed in confusion. "What does that mean?"

"I mean look around this place! It is wall-to-wall testosterone. I've never seen so many good-looking people at one event. Your grandparents must have been gorgeous!"

"Hey, hey, hey," he said, not liking the fact that Casey was even noticing his cousins. "There is no reason for you to be focusing on anyone other than the bride. And me."

Casey smiled. "Believe me, you are more than enough."

That seemed to satisfy him. "Good. Now go and take care of Gina. I'm sure Mac is anxious to get this show on the road."

"Such a romantic," she teased and walked away.

Ryder watched the sassy sway of her hips as Casey walked away in the mile-high stilettos that he loved so much and said a silent prayer of thanks that she was his.

———

An hour later, there wasn't a dry eye in the house. After the beautiful ceremony in which the bride and groom spoke the vows they had written, doves were released, along with dozens of white balloons in memory of Arthur Micelli, who had lost his battle with cancer less than a year ago and was not there to see his only daughter married.

Casey had to wipe her own eyes several times, thankful that her job required her to be on the go, so she couldn't stand still and think too long about the emotional ceremony. Soon she was directing people to the cocktail hour and then hurrying off to help the bridal party get their pictures taken.

It was a hectic pace, and she adored it. For some reason, weddings had always drawn her in. She loved the romance, the planning, the promise…and being a part of people's big day was something she never tired of. Standing off to the side, Casey watched as Mac and Gina Montgomery posed for their first official portrait as man and wife. The way Mac looked at his bride said more than any words could. Casey was familiar with that look because it was the same one Ryder gave her.

Ryder.

Sigh.

If anyone had told her that he would come back into her life and they would pick up where they left off, she would have laughed at them. But now? Now Casey was beyond grateful for the second chance. She had learned never to take anything for granted, and the next few weeks promised to challenge them.

The entire Montgomery family was going to be in town for the next four days. They had all kinds of events and get-togethers planned, and lucky for Casey, she was good at remembering names and faces. There were a lot to remember with this bunch! Once everyone was gone, she and Ryder would have only two days to themselves before he left for San Diego. He had asked Casey repeatedly to go with him, but this was her season. She had several weddings on her calendar, and even though Julie had offered to take on the extra work, Casey was committed to her clients and didn't want to disappoint them.

Ryder was disappointed, but Casey knew this was all

part of how their lives were going to be, and if they couldn't handle it early on in their relationship, then they were never going to be able to deal with it. The timing was bad. Things had come up that she hadn't had time to talk to Ryder about. It couldn't be helped; she wanted everything to be perfect, and right now it was all too chaotic to be perfect.

She hated chaos.

"We're going to head down to the beach for a few shots," the photographer said to her and she snapped out of her reverie.

"That's fine," Casey said with a smile. "I'll have my assistant go with you just in case anyone needs anything, and I'm going to check on the guests and make sure that the cocktail hour is going well." Confident that the bridal party was in good hands, Casey walked over to where the guests were all eating and drinking and laughing and smiling. It didn't take long to spot Ryder in the crowd. Doing her best to focus on her job, she circled the room and checked with Tyler to make sure everything was on schedule. Once she was assured that all was well, she made a beeline for Ryder.

He greeted her with a kiss and a plate full of assorted hors d'oeuvres. "I'm working, Ryder," she said even as she accepted the plate.

"You have to eat. I know you didn't eat more than a cup of yogurt for breakfast, and I haven't seen you stop since we got here. Trust me, eat a little something now, and you'll feel rejuvenated."

She quirked a brow at him. "What makes you think I need to be rejuvenated?"

One arm snaked around her waist to pull her close,

and then his mouth brushed up against her ear. "Because I know that you exhausted me this morning, and I had the luxury of staying in bed far longer than you."

Casey blushed. "I exhausted you? I kind of like that."

He kissed her, then took a tiny quiche and held it to her lips. "Are you doing okay? It was a little warm out there. You look a little flushed."

She swatted his hands away for the second time today. "Stop fussing. I feel fine."

Ryder wasn't so sure. He knew Casey's job was demanding, especially on the day of the event, but lately she seemed a little paler, more tired. Maybe he needed to talk to Julie about hiring more people to help them out so that neither of them would have to work so hard.

"Whatever it is that you're thinking, stop it," she said between bites. The food was delicious and she hadn't realized just how hungry she was until she started eating.

"What are you talking about?" he asked innocently.

"I can hear the wheels in your head turning. So whatever it is going on in there, stop it. I'm fine. You've never been to one of my events before. This is nothing out of the ordinary, so please stop worrying."

"I'm just thinking that if you had another assistant…"

"Ryder," she warned.

"Okay, okay, I get it. You know what you're doing, and I'm interfering. Sorry."

"I appreciate your concern, but during the busy season, this is how it is. This season is a little more demanding than usual because we've had so much going on. With your family in town and all the arrangements for you to go back home for a week…I guess I'm just a little more mentally stressed."

"I still wish you'd come with me. I think you could use the time away."

She smiled at him, reaching up to cup his face in one hand. "It would definitely be nice, but now isn't the right time. I can't leave my clients like that. I know Julie would take them and most of them would be fine, but they signed on with me, and I've worked with them all for so long that I would hate to miss out on the big day."

"I understand. I hate it, but again, I understand. Besides, since I'm not selling the house, we can go back whenever we want and have someplace to stay."

"That would be nice. What about one of your cousins subletting the place? Have you all decided which one is taking over?"

Ryder shook his head. "I think it was a monumental task to get us all here for the wedding. We're getting together Tuesday afternoon and sitting down to discuss it all; my dad, his brothers, and all my cousins who are working for Montgomerys. It should be wild."

"I can only imagine." Popping a crab puff in her mouth, Casey sighed with pleasure and handed her plate back to Ryder. "This has been a lovely break, but it's time to go and search out the bridal party. I'll see you at the reception."

"You're going to play guest at that point, right?"

She nodded. "By that time, all of the hard work is done, and my assistant and Tyler can handle anything that comes up. And if they can't, I'll be right there."

Ryder kissed her cheek. "Good. I want you by my side in there, and I want to dance with you."

Casey blushed and thought about the last wedding at which they had danced. "Hopefully we'll be sitting with people who aren't going to be yelling at us the way the ex-aunts did."

A hearty laugh escaped before Ryder could help it. "They may not be elderly women, but my brothers and sister will surely find something to fight about."

Over the course of the day, Casey had the opportunity to get reacquainted with Ryder's siblings, and she was looking forward to spending quality time with them over dinner and during the next four days. She had spent some time with them years ago, when she and Ryder had dated, but as kids, they were more interested in being alone together than with their families.

"I'm sure they're not that bad."

Ryder smiled and winked. "Wait and see." Before he could say any more, Casey was off and running to finish her final duties for the day. Looking around, Ryder was impressed. He was pleased that the venue was everything that Mac and Gina had wanted and that he had the opportunity to help with that decision.

"You did a good job," his brother James said as he walked up beside Ryder. "I hear you helped pick the place."

Ryder shrugged. "I was just the tiebreaker."

"I have to admit, it's kind of crazy how it all worked out."

"How so?"

"Well, what are the odds of Mac using Casey as the wedding planner? You have to admit, Ry, that's one hell of a coincidence."

"I can't deny that, but I had gone and looked up Casey before I even knew about the wedding. That was simply fate lending a hand to make sure I didn't let her get away again." Ryder searched the room just in case he could catch another glimpse of her, but Casey was nowhere to be seen. Actually, the main reason he had chosen to take a sabbatical in Wrightsville Beach was because he was hoping to look for Casey.

"Still, it's kind of cool how it all worked out. You're lucky." There was a sadness in James's voice that he found hard to hide at the moment.

"What's going on, James?" Ryder asked as he pulled his brother to a quiet corner of the room. "You've been in a funk for way too long. Is it work?"

James shook his head. "It's nothing. I'm fine."

"Bull. Something is definitely going on with you, and I have to tell you, we've all noticed it, and it's been going on for far too long."

His brother looked up at him first with anger and then with resignation. "I envy you," he said quietly.

"Me? Why?"

"You went out on a limb, and now you have Casey back."

"Who do you want back?" Ryder wracked his brain for the women he knew of who James had dated. Having lived on opposite coasts for a dozen years wasn't helping.

"It doesn't matter," James said, taking a long drink from his champagne glass. "It was a long time ago, and she's better off without me."

Ryder reached out and forced his brother to look at him. "That's a load of crap and you know it. I walked away from Casey and basically blew her off because I selfishly wanted to prove a point to our family, and you know what? I may have achieved that success and earned my place in the company, but it's a hollow victory when you reach it alone. Maybe it's not too late for you. Who is she? Do you know anything about her life now?"

James shrugged. "She's got a business here on the Outer Banks. I thought about looking her up while I'm here, but I don't even know where to begin. Her family wasn't overly fond of me back when we dated. They thought I was some sort of degenerate."

Ryder laughed out loud. "You? Why would they think that?"

"It was all during my rebellious period."

"Ah." Ryder nodded. "Leave it to you to meet someone while being a high-school dropout and mowing lawns for a living. Thank God you outgrew that phase."

"The thing is, it's because of the way her family treated me that I went so crazy trying to overachieve in everything else. I wanted to prove them wrong."

"James, you don't need to prove anything to anybody. You were a kid; you were going through a phase. Don't let these people make you feel bad about yourself."

"Too late."

"Are you sure you would even want to be involved with someone who has a family like that?"

"It's not her family I'm interested in," he said and turned to look around the room. "I don't know. You were fortunate things worked out the way they did. You and Casey were always meant to be; we all knew it, even back then. It's not like that for everyone."

"I hate that I had no idea you were dealing with something like this for so long," Ryder said. "I'm sorry."

James turned and forced a smile. "Hey, this is supposed to be a happy day. I didn't mean to drag you down. It was a long time ago and I guess I'm just feeling a little nostalgic right now. Between the wedding, you and Casey, and being so close to…" He cut himself off before revealing too much. "Anyway, no more talk of the past. Weddings are about the future, and there's a room full of family here that we haven't seen in a long time. Let's go mingle."

Ryder watched his brother get absorbed into the crowd, but he wasn't fooled. James was definitely struggling with this situation and he had no idea how to help him. If only he knew the name of the mystery woman, maybe he could help out. Out of the corner of his eye, Ryder saw his uncle walk into the room, and he smiled. Maybe Uncle William wouldn't mind if someone actually asked for his help in making a match this time.

Chapter 10

RYDER HAD BEEN GONE FOR TEN DAYS—THREE DAYS longer than he had planned. His frustration was mounting, and yet there wasn't a damn thing he could do to change it. His cousin Christian had volunteered to take a one-year position as the CEO of Montgomerys' West Coast office, but he was stranded in London on a business deal that he was trying to finish up. Ryder knew that he could leave and come back and that everything would be fine, but there was more to handing over the reins than he had originally thought.

He talked to Casey every day, several times a day, and yet as time went on, he was beginning to hear the disappointment and uncertainty in her voice. Business was keeping her busy and for that Ryder was thankful, but knowing he was causing her stress was killing him.

"Christian tells me he should be here by the end of the week," he said to Casey that night during their call. "All the papers he was waiting for are being signed today; then he has to wrap things up at his office and will be here by Friday. If all goes well, I'll be home on Sunday."

"Okay," Casey said.

"Case," Ryder began, "I know this isn't going the way we thought it would, and I'm sorry. Do you have any weddings this weekend? Maybe you can fly out on Thursday and be here when Christian gets here and we'll fly home together."

She made a noncommittal sound. "I have appointments on Friday and Saturday with clients who I don't want to reschedule and a wedding on Sunday. It's fine, Ryder. You'll get here when you get here."

He knew that tone.

He hated that tone.

"If this is going to work, you are going to have to get over what I did, Case. If you doubt me every time I go away, then we're doomed."

She sighed with frustration. "It's not that I doubt you, Ryder; it's not. I'm disappointed because, well…I had plans for us, and I hate not knowing when you'll get here so I can actually put them into play."

"Plans? What kind of plans? Sexy plans?"

Casey laughed. "You're an idiot, and so I'm not going to tell you what kind of plans. You'll just have to get your butt back here and find out."

"You're killing me. You know that, right?"

"Good." They were silent for a moment. "I miss you."

"I know, baby. I miss you too. I hate this. I hate that it's taking so long to wrap everything up, but I owe it to everyone to make sure that Christian gets here and is ready to take over. He's going to live here in my house, and we can video conference whenever he needs anything since I'm not doing anything substantial with my time for the next month or so. I could just leave and let him settle in on his own, but I don't think that would be fair."

"I know you're right," she said reluctantly. "It's just that we've waited so long to be together, and I want us to start planning our lives. There was so much to do, between Mac and Gina's wedding, and then all of your relatives being here, and then you having to go back and settle everything in California, that we haven't talked about…us."

"I don't have to be there for us to have that conversation," he said softly, wishing more than anything that he were there with her right now.

"It's silly, I know, but I want us to be together when we talk. I love our conversations on the phone, but it's not the same."

"We can Skype," he suggested.

"Still not the same, Ryder," she said and then yawned.

"You're going to get tired of seeing me so much when I get back, you know," he reminded her. "I took an extra month off so we'd have some time together, and I guarantee you're going to get to a point where you want to kick me out the door."

"Maybe," she said with a laugh.

"Definitely." Ryder settled in more securely on the sofa and felt himself relax after another long day. "Soon, sweetheart. Soon I'll be home, and we'll talk to your heart's content. I promise."

Casey couldn't wait for that to be so.

A late-afternoon wedding had Casey returning home Sunday night exhausted. Per her last conversation with Ryder, he was boarding a plane to come home, and with a little luck, she'd have some time to shower and change and freshen up before he arrived. This particular wedding had been a handful because the parents of the bride were divorced, so most of the day had been spent making sure no fights broke out.

It had come close no less than half a dozen times.

In all the chaos, Casey hadn't even had time to stop and eat. "Maybe I'll grab some soup before I shower," she sighed as she opened the door to the house.

And froze.

There were candles lit everywhere.

Soft music was playing.

And there, no more than five feet in front of her, stood Ryder.

"What…? How…? When did you get here?" she asked, dropping her purse to the floor, not sure where to look first.

"I was already on the ground here when we talked earlier," Ryder said, walking slowly toward her. Wordlessly, he took Casey by the hand and led her down the hall to the master bathroom, where he had a hot bath ready and waiting for her.

"How did you know when I'd be home?" she asked, still dazed that he was here.

"I asked Julie to call and give me a head's up so I could have everything ready for you." Finally, Ryder leaned in and kissed her, a gentle kiss meant to soothe, not arouse. He took the clip out of her hair and ran his fingers through it while massaging Casey's scalp. "I heard that this wedding was a bit more challenging than most, so I want you to relax."

Slowly Ryder unbuttoned her blouse while Casey kicked off her shoes. "A girl could get used to this sort of thing," she said with a small smile.

"I'm hoping that this particular girl does, because I plan on pampering you tonight."

Casey liked the sound of that. Before she could comment on it, Ryder had unzipped her skirt and it pooled around her ankles. She kicked it aside and stood before him in nothing more than two bits of white lace. "I had planned on freshening up before you got home. I'm a mess."

"You're beautiful," he said firmly, gazing intently into her eyes. "I missed you so damn much." And then he kissed her with all the pent-up passion of the last few weeks. Casey wrapped her arms around him to pull him close, and Ryder picked her up and carefully placed her on the vanity counter. It was cool against her skin, but she didn't seem to mind.

"I missed you too," she said breathlessly as Ryder's mouth traveled down the column of her throat, nipping at her shoulder before working his way back up. His hands were seemingly everywhere, and suddenly all thoughts of relaxing and pampering were gone; all Casey wanted was Ryder. Right here, right now.

She shifted slightly and pressed up against the part of him that was the hardest, drawing Ryder's mouth back to hers. His hand roamed up her spine and deftly unhooked her bra before pulling it away. His mouth never left hers as those skillful hands moved around and cupped her breasts, making her gasp with pleasure.

"Please," she whispered.

Ryder finally tore his mouth away. "I promised myself I'd let you soak in a nice hot tub and relax before we did this, but I can't wait either. I need you."

One mind.

───⁓⁓⁓───

Later, they sat together in the big tub, Casey's back to Ryder's chest. They talked about the wedding from hell, and he told her about Christian's arrival in California and how he expected things to run at Montgomerys without him.

"I think Christian is going to fit right in," Ryder was saying as he leisurely played with the bubbles that were covering Casey. He loved hearing her purr with every handful of water.

"I'm glad it all worked out. I'm sure it's going to be a little bit of an adjustment for him after living in Europe for so many years."

Ryder shrugged. "Maybe. I think he's been wanting to come back to the States but wasn't sure where to go or where there'd be a place for him."

"Then it's a win-win for everyone." She sighed and relaxed more against him, her head resting on his shoulder.

"What about you?" he asked softly. "What is your schedule looking like?"

"You're in luck. I managed to clear my schedule for the next two weeks."

Reaching up, Ryder tipped Casey's head back so she could see the pleased look on his face. "Really?"

She nodded. "I wanted us to have some time to ourselves. There were a couple of consultations on the calendar, but they weren't major and my assistant and Julie can easily take care of them. I just needed to get through this one wedding before I could relax."

"I'm sorry your day was so rough." He wrapped his arms around her and held Casey tight. "So what should we do with all this free time we suddenly have?" he asked lightly.

Casey chuckled. "For starters, we should get out of

this tub before we get all pruney." She felt his chest rumble behind her with his own soft laughter.

"Agreed." Ryder shifted a bit so they could both sit up more. "How about this? You dry off and relax, and I'm going to go and grill us some steaks, and we'll have a quiet dinner out on the deck."

"Sounds like heaven," she sighed and watched Ryder rise from the tub and reach for a towel. *No man should look so good,* she thought to herself, and then smiled because he belonged to her. Reclining into the tub, she murmured, "Five more minutes," and closed her eyes.

Ryder retrieved his clothes and got dressed before heading down the hall to the kitchen to get their dinner started. His brain was spinning. It didn't seem to matter how much time they were together or apart; it didn't matter how many times he made love to her, he wanted her more.

Taking the ingredients for their meal out, he smiled. His goal had been to surprise Casey tonight and so far he had. He had a couple more tricks up his sleeve, and he couldn't wait to see the look on her face when he pulled them out.

The steaks were on the grill and he was pulling out a salad he had made earlier when he heard Casey padding into the kitchen. She was dressed in silky lounging pants and a cami. Her hair was in disarray and she still managed to take his breath away. He handed her a glass of wine and smiled. "Feel better?"

"Mmm…much," she said, declining the wine. "I

don't think I realized how tense I was until I got in that tub and felt it all just melt away. If I drink any of that I'm afraid I'll fall asleep at the table." Walking over to the refrigerator, she poured herself a tall glass of ice water and added a slice of lemon.

Ryder took Casey by the hand and led her out onto the deck. The air was a little cool, so he lit the heat lamp and pulled out a chair for her. "Ryder, I can help…"

He held up a hand to silence her. "You worked all day. Let me cater to you."

Before she knew it, Ryder was placing a plate in front of her loaded with a steak grilled to perfection, a Caesar salad, and freshly baked bread. "Thank you."

"My pleasure."

They ate in silence, simply enjoying the fact that they were together as they listened to the waves crashing on the shore. When Casey was finished, she sat back in her chair and sighed. "I had planned on having a bowl of soup, but this was way better."

Ryder chuckled. "I should hope so." They sipped their drinks and held hands for a little while until Ryder stood.

"What are you doing?" she asked.

"I have dessert too."

"I thought we had that earlier," she said with a wicked grin.

"Sweetheart, that was just the beginning." Collecting the plates, Ryder went into the house and returned a few minutes later with a bowl of fresh strawberries and another of whipped cream. He placed them on the table and then walked back into the house. He returned with a bottle of champagne and two glasses.

"Champagne?" Casey said, looking at him with confusion. "What's the occasion?"

Ryder sat down and turned his chair so he was facing her. "When I first came back to North Carolina, I always knew I was going to look for you. Never in my wildest dreams did I let myself believe we would end up where we are now." The look of love on Casey's face told him she felt the same way. "I know I don't deserve you and that I have a lot to make up to you."

"Ryder," she began, but he stopped her words with one finger to her lips.

"We met up again at a pretty chaotic time, and I feel like we missed some key things." Casey's brows furrowed as she listened to him. "Part of me wanted to go slow with you, to prove that I was sincere and that I was taking our relationship seriously. But you blew my world away when you showed up at my house that night."

She blushed. "We had already lost so much time. I didn't want to go slow."

He leaned in and kissed her. "I love your impatience." Taking one of her hands in his, he continued. "I told you that I love you and talked about marriage and babies and I forgot one very important thing."

"What was that?" she asked softly and then gasped when Ryder dropped to one knee in front of her.

"I fell in love with you twelve years ago, Casey," he began solemnly, "and I was foolish enough to walk away. I don't ever want to do that again. You're everything to me and I want you to be my wife." He pulled a small velvet ring box from his pocket and opened it to reveal a brilliant emerald-cut diamond ring.

"Oh, Ryder," she sighed as he placed the ring on her

finger. "It's beautiful." A single tear rolled down her cheek as she reached out and cupped his face. "Yes."

Ryder leaned in and cupped a hand around her nape, greedily claiming her lips with his. Waves continued to crash, the moon continued to rise in the sky, and Ryder felt like he could go on kissing Casey forever. Her hands raked up into his hair, and he knew that if he didn't pull back soon, he would end up taking her right here on the deck.

Not the most romantic way to end a proposal.

When he did finally pull back, he wiped away that lone tear and sat back in his seat. "I hate that it took me so long to give this to you," he said, motioning toward the ring. "I wanted to be back here days ago. I'm sorry I didn't do something more romantic or take you out someplace. It's just that…I knew from the first moment I saw you again that I wanted you back in my life forever. And once you said you loved me too, I was anxious to start working on our own forever."

"Mmm…" she purred, alternating between looking at the man she loved and the sparkling diamond on her finger. "I like the sound of that."

"How is it going to be planning your own wedding?" he teased. "I'm sure you have a lot of great ideas."

Casey reached over and grabbed a strawberry and seemed to contemplate his words. "Actually," she said with a smile, "I was thinking Vegas."

"What? You mean like a Vegas theme?"

She shook her head. "No, I'm talking let's get on a plane and fly to Vegas and get married in a little chapel and book the gaudiest penthouse suite and have our honeymoon there."

The look on Ryder's face was priceless. "Case, you can't be serious. Weddings are your business. I thought for sure that you'd want something big and beautiful like you did for Mac and Gina."

Sighing, she leaned back further in her chair. "Too much work, and besides, we don't have that kind of time."

Now his expression was one of pure confusion. "Time? Why don't we have time? I figured we'd do something here on the beach, and my schedule is extremely flexible. Don't you have any weeks free? Are you booked up this far in advance?"

She giggled and reached for another succulent strawberry, covered it with cream, and held it up for Ryder to taste. He moved her hand away and she rolled her eyes. "I have plenty of weekends free, and though our calendar is looking very promising for the upcoming year, that's not what I'm talking about."

"I'm at a loss here; you're going to have to spell it out for me because I don't understand why you would seriously opt for a cheesy Vegas wedding with an Elvis impersonator rather than something more elegant like what you create for a living."

"I never said Elvis impersonator."

Now he rolled his eyes. "It's kind of implied, Casey. So come on. What gives?"

With a huff, she sat up straight in her chair and put the strawberry down and took both of Ryder's hands in hers while staring him in the eyes. "We don't have a lot of time because I have no intention of wearing a maternity wedding gown. I'd like to have wedding pictures while I'm still rocking a slim figure, if it's all right with you."

"Maternity gown…slim…wait. What?" He stood up

so fast that his chair fell backward. "Are you telling me that you're…that we're…"

"Having a baby?" she finished for him. Ryder nodded mutely, his eyes wide and a little dazed. "Yes, that is exactly what I'm telling you."

―⁓―

There were dozens of reactions Casey had prepared herself for. As Ryder righted his chair and walked into the house, she realized that this reaction wasn't one of them. Standing, she followed him into the house and found him in the bedroom packing a suitcase. Suddenly her dinner began to rise in her throat at the same rate panic was rising within her. Was he leaving her? Was it all too much? Had he not been serious about wanting to spend forever with her?

"Ryder?" she asked, her voice laced with uncertainty. "What are you doing?"

He stopped suddenly, seemingly shocked that Casey was in the room with him. "We're going to Vegas. Now." Then he was back in action as he whipped out one drawer after another and tossed piles of clothes into the large open case on the bed. He only stopped when he heard Casey's hysterical laughter. "What? What's so funny?"

"You!" she said before doubling over with more laughter.

"Why? You said you wanted to get married in Vegas, so we're getting married in Vegas."

"I didn't mean tonight, Ryder!" she cried, straightening herself up and walking over to sit on the bed beside the suitcase. "I love that you are ready to jump on a plane at a moment's notice, but don't you think we should talk about this?"

Pinching the bridge of his nose, Ryder took a deep breath and then focused on Casey. "What is there to talk about? We're having a baby; we need to get married. Now."

"Whoa, whoa, whoa," she said, holding out a hand to stop him. "We don't *need* to get married. I thought we already *wanted* to get married."

Ryder sat down beside her and stared at her in wonder. "We're really having a baby?"

"Honestly and truly," she said, unable to suppress a grin at his awed tone.

"Why didn't you tell me sooner?"

"You were supposed to be home days ago. I had it all planned out that I was going to make you a romantic dinner and tell you. But you got delayed and then you showed up here tonight and stole my thunder."

He leaned in and rested his forehead against hers. "Forgive me?"

"Absolutely," she sighed and kissed him gently on the lips. "I love you, Ryder."

"I love you too, Case. I can't believe this is all happening."

"My head is spinning a little," she admitted and then regretted her words when Ryder jumped to his feet.

"Are you okay? Do I need to call a doctor? I can't believe I almost gave you wine with dinner!" He began pacing the bedroom in search of some unknown object.

"Ryder, I'm fine. I just meant that my head is spinning because everything is happening so fast."

"Oh," he said, relief washing over him. "Okay." Sitting back down beside her on the bed, he reached out tentatively and placed his large hand over her flat belly. "I still can't believe it."

"Me either."

"So what do you want to do now?"

Casey rested her hand over his. "Right now, I want you to put all of these clothes back in their drawers and I want to crawl into bed with you. I did not enjoy sleeping alone all the time you were away."

He chuckled, then put the clothes away and placed the suitcase back in the closet. Casey stripped down to her panties and was reaching for a nightie when he came up behind her and wrapped his arms around her. He placed a gentle kiss on her neck.

"And after that?"

Turning her head, Casey looked at Ryder with confusion. "After what?"

"After we crawl into bed, then what?"

She gave him a sexy smile and said, "I think I'd like a little more of what we started earlier."

"Such a dirty mind," he said and playfully swatted her bottom. "What about Vegas?"

"Seriously, Ryder," she said with a huff as she stepped out of his arms. "Do we have to decide this right now?"

"The idea of a long engagement was not appealing to me at all, if you want to know the truth. It doesn't have to be Vegas; we can go anywhere you want and we can be married by next weekend. I don't want to wait to make you my wife, Casey."

She wanted to be annoyed because he was rushing her, but at the same time, she loved him too much. "How about this? It's Sunday night. You just got home from California. We can call our families tomorrow and tell them we're getting married and make arrangements for them to meet us in Vegas on Friday. What do you say?"

"I say that you are the perfect woman for me, and I am thankful every day that you came back into my life."

She smiled serenely at him. "Thanks for jogging over that morning."

"Thanks for not throwing something heavy at me."

She giggled and took Ryder by the hand and led him over to their bed. "Thank you for coming back for me."

Ryder kissed her then and with that, there were no more words, only sighs and caresses. As he lowered Casey to the bed, he said one final prayer of thanks for all he had been blessed with.

Read on for a peek at an all-new Montgomery
Brothers romance from Samantha Chase

Return
to You

Prologue

THERE'S NOTHING LIKE A GOOD CHALLENGE TO PUT A little pep in your step and to get the heart pumping. In the last several years, William Montgomery had put a lot of pep in his step, and his heart had never felt better. Who knew matchmaking could be so rewarding? Getting his three sons married to their perfect matches had certainly been a challenge, but it was nothing compared to the one before him right now.

"Are we sure about this?" he asked cautiously as he scanned the file he held in his hands. William absolutely adored his role as the family matchmaker, but this particular situation was a little more sensitive. One look at his nephew, and he saw that it wasn't being taken lightly on his end either.

Ryder Montgomery nodded. "Believe me, it wasn't easy to get even that much information out of him. Luckily, James gets chatty after a couple shots of tequila."

William chuckled and flipped through more pages. "It seems to me like you're onto something here, but I want to be sure before we move forward. Have you talked to any of your other siblings? Anyone willing to give us a hand with this?"

"Actually, there's someone here I think can help." Ryder stood and walked to his uncle's office door and opened it. "Her name came up in the conversation at the

wedding, and it didn't take much to track her down."
He motioned to someone in the reception area and then
stepped aside. "Uncle William, this is Jen Lawson."

William stood and welcomed their visitor with a
smile. "Thank you for being willing to meet with us.
Please, have a seat."

"I have to admit that I feel a little overwhelmed by all
of this," Jen said as she sat down. "When your nephew
contacted me, I thought he was crazy."

Another small chuckle escaped before William could
help it. He looked over at Ryder and smiled. "Well, we
Montgomerys tend to be a little unorthodox at times."
His expression turned serious as he leaned forward on
his desk. "My family means the world to me. In a million years, I never would have imagined Ryder coming
to me with such a request. As of late, most of my nieces
and nephews seem to run in the opposite direction
when they see me coming. I'm sure he's mentioned my
recent hobby…"

"You mean the whole matchmaking thing?" she said
with a saucy grin.

William looked at the woman and smiled broadly
before turning to his nephew. "I like her," he said. "I
think she's going to be an asset to this whole thing."

"What exactly are you planning?" she asked.

"It's been a little over ten years," William began,
"and this conversation Ryder had at my son Mac's wedding was the first time James even mentioned what happened back then. He's distanced himself from his family
and is leading a very solitary life. I can't bear to see it,
and I think it's gone on long enough."

Ryder pulled up a chair and finally sat back down.

"He's my brother, but to be honest, I had no idea exactly what had happened. We were close growing up, but once we hit our teens…well, things changed. Back then, he was rebellious. He and my dad fought all the time and were always at each other's throats. Then he finally left and went to live with some distant relatives of my mother's. I'm ashamed to admit this, but I was too self-absorbed to pay much attention to what was going on. Apparently my parents had some kind of inkling of what had happened at the time, but they kept his secret for him. None of us had a clue."

Jen looked between the two of them and leaned back in her seat. "I still can't believe that James is from such an affluent family." She shook her head in disbelief. "I mean, back then, when we all knew him, he was working as a landscaper, had no car, and seemed to be dirt poor. I think that speaks highly of his character—especially knowing what I know now—but why would someone purposely make their life more difficult when they didn't have to?"

"I think he found having the Montgomery name to be more of a burden than a blessing," Ryder said. "It's opened a lot of doors for us, but my brother wanted to get by on his own merits and not because of his name. On top of that, my father was grooming all of us for corporate careers. That was never James's style. I think he felt that he had to take drastic measures to be who he wanted to be."

"That's one of the drawbacks of being from a big family," William said with a sigh. "There's a lot of pressure on the Montgomery men to continue the family traditions in the business. James wanted to make his own way. As long as he lived at home, that wasn't possible. My brother Robert was not pleased that James moved so far away—in spite of their differences. Unfortunately, he had no choice but to let him make his own mistakes."

"I still can't believe all he went through," Ryder said. "I don't know if there was anything I could've done at the time, but I hate the thought of him going through it all alone."

"It was worse to be there living it with them, with Selena and James," she said sadly. "I never felt so helpless in my life."

All three grew silent for a long moment before William straightened in his chair. "And that's why we're doing what we're doing. Enough time has passed. This situation should never have gotten to this point, and I think between the three of us, we can rectify it." He stared intently at the woman before him. "I need to know that you are fully committed to this. You are going to be the most directly involved, and you're going to need to keep your story straight in order for it all to work out."

She gave a small smile. "Actually, your timing couldn't be better. When I get back home, it seems I will have a legit reason to get in touch with James. Selena is going to be the problem."

William wanted to probe into the woman's predicament, but right now his nephew's future and happiness were on the line. "Do you keep in touch with her? With Selena?"

She nodded. "We talk at least once a week, but she hasn't come home in…well…" She shrugged her shoulders and looked at the two Montgomery men. "A long time."

Clapping his hands together, William said, with a wicked grin, "Well, then, it's about time Miss Selena Ainsley received an offer to come home that's too good to refuse." Standing, he reached over his desk to shake her delicate hand. "Ryder will fill you in on all the details, and if there's anything else you need from me, please feel free to contact me. Anytime. Day or night." Reaching down, he found a business card and then wrote on the back of it. "That's my personal phone number on the back. I expect to hear from you periodically to keep me up to date."

"I wish I had your confidence, sir," Jen said hesitantly as she took the card from him. "I'm afraid too much time has gone by, that maybe it won't all work out."

"I have an excellent track record, my dear. My sons were all stubborn and convinced they didn't need any help with their lives, and now? They're all married with children on the way. Which reminds me." He turned to Ryder and grinned. "How is Casey doing?"

Ryder smiled at the mention of his wife. "She's finally done with the morning sickness and is getting her energy back. I have to remind her to take it easy most days. All in all, we are both beyond excited for this baby's arrival." He turned to the woman. "And don't let my uncle fool you; he'll try to take credit for my marriage too, but I was already on a mission to win Casey back."

"You can tell yourself that all you want, Ryder, but you and I both know that if it hadn't been for me, there wouldn't have been a wedding for you to work with Casey on."

Ryder rolled his eyes and couldn't help but smile at

his uncle. "I was already in the area and had no idea about the wedding when I walked over to Casey's beach house. Sorry, old man, but this match is firmly on me."

William winked at his female guest. "I'm four for four, no matter what my nephew says."

She chuckled. "With a track record like that, I don't think James and Selena stand a chance."

"Atta girl!" William bellowed with characteristic gusto. "I knew we'd win you over. I look forward to hearing from you in the very near future." And with that, he excused himself and fairly skipped out of his office.

William smiled and nodded to his assistant Rose on his way out. "If you need me, you can reach me on my cell. I think I'm going to take my lovely wife out for a celebratory lunch."

Rose was used to her boss's cheery moods and his multiple excuses for celebrating. "What are we celebrating today, sir?"

"Another successful match."

Yes, there was nothing like a challenge to put a little pep in your step, and if this challenge turned out the way he thought it would, William Montgomery's feet weren't going to touch the ground for a long time.

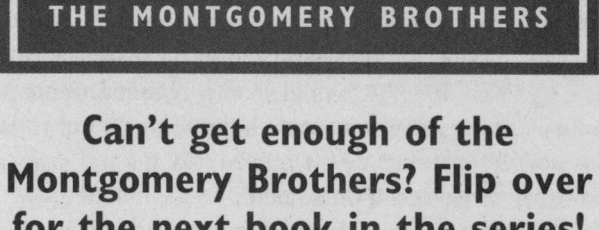

Stay *with* **Me**

More *of* **Me**

THE MONTGOMERY BROTHERS

Can't get enough of the Montgomery Brothers? Flip over for the next book in the series!

Prologue

STANDING OUTSIDE ON A CRISP SEPTEMBER MORNING, William Montgomery swore that the sun was shining directly on him. The morning dew sparkled on the lush acres of green grass before him as he awaited the arrival of his dearest friend to join him for a round of golf.

The last two years had left him feeling blessed; two of his three sons were married, he had a grandchild on the way, and he was about to spend some quality time outside with a friend on a beautiful day. Yes, William was most definitely a blessed man. Inhaling deeply, he lifted his face to the sun, smiled, and thanked the good Lord above.

"Now that is the face of a man at peace," a voice said from behind.

Turning, William greeted his lifelong friend Arthur Micelli and shook his hand. "That I am, Art, that I am. How could I not be?"

A sad smile crossed his friend's face. "As long as you appreciate it, Will. Embrace it."

Something in Arthur's tone caused a trickle of alarm. William wanted to come right out and ask if everything was all right but knew better than to charge into what could quite possibly be a delicate situation. So instead of asking what was on the tip of his tongue, he segued into the next order of business. "You ready for eighteen holes?"

Arthur looked out at the greens ahead of them and sighed. "No time like the present."

Something was definitely up. "I don't know about you, Art, but I don't feel much like walking this one. I'm going to grab a cart, and then we'll get started. What do you say?"

Arthur's shoulders sagged with what William would guess was relief. "Sounds good to me." Within minutes, their bags were loaded and they were on their way. At first, the conversation consisted of the basic pleasantries, but by the third hole, William was ready to get a little more insight into what was going on with his friend.

"You feeling okay, Art?"

His friend chuckled. "You know me too well." Climbing from the cart, he stood and waited for William to join him. They stood side by side for a long, quiet moment before Arthur spoke. "Remember when the kids were little and we'd all get together in the summertime to barbecue and go swimming?"

"Those are some of my fondest memories from when they were all growing up. Just listening to their laughter as they chased each other around always brought a smile to my face." William smiled even now at the thought of it. "Which reminds me, how is Gina doing? Have you talked to her lately?"

The mention of Arthur's daughter seemed to bring on a wave of sadness followed by regret. "We spoke on the phone briefly last week."

"How's she doing?"

"The same. Working for a firm she doesn't seem to like very much and doing her best not to disappoint her mother."

"That's a shame. I really thought Barb would have outgrown that controlling streak."

"I think it got worse after the divorce, and unfortunately, Gina's paying the price for it."

"She's a grown woman, Art; she can move away anytime she wants. California isn't the only place she can live. Hell, she can come back here to North Carolina! Have you approached her about coming to work for you?"

Arthur shook his head. "As much as I would love for Gina to move back here by me, I would never ask."

"Why not?" William asked, stunned. "I would do whatever it took to get my child back in my life."

"Don't you see, Will? She's never had the opportunity to choose to do anything. Barb has made all of her decisions for her. The poor girl has never been allowed to decide what it is *she* wants to do. If I call and ask her to come here and work with me, she'd probably say yes out of guilt and then stress herself out because she'd know that her mother would be angry with her." He sighed wearily. "I don't want to add any more stress to her life. Thanks to me, she's suffered enough."

"That's a bunch of bull and you know it!" William snapped. "Your wife chose to leave and took your daughter with her. If anything, you stepped back in hopes of making Gina's life easier. You're still stepping back!"

"It's hard, William; you don't understand. You and Monica have a great marriage and your sons are all with you. I envy you."

The sadness in Art's voice had William rethinking this line of conversation. "Well, that's kind of you to say, but it's not always smooth sailing. Hell, in the last couple of years, my sons have been more than a little irritated with me a time or two." He chuckled as he thought of how their irritation had faded when they'd realized that dear old dad was doing them the greatest favor of their lives by finding them the perfect wives. So far, Lucas and Jason were enjoying the very lives they had rebelled against, and nothing could please William more. He wished Arthur and his daughter could reconcile their differences.

"Remember when the kids were younger and we always thought it would be great if Gina married one of the boys?"

Art laughed. "We always thought she should marry Lucas because they were the closest in age, but she only had eyes for Mac."

William felt a familiar itch of inspiration. "She sure did, followed him around wherever he went. He may have grumbled about it at the time, but I think that was just to save face."

Arthur couldn't help but smile at the memory as well. "Well, seeing as he's seven years older than Gina, I'm sure it wasn't cool to have her trailing around after him." He turned toward William. "He was always a good sport about it. I was always so grateful that he made sure to be kind. No wonder she had such a crush on him!"

"Lucky for us he's the only one left who isn't married!"

"If only it were that simple," Art said. "They haven't seen each other in, what? Twelve or thirteen years?"

"What difference does that make?" William's voice boomed with excitement. "There's still time! I bet if we got them together, there'd still be a lingering spark. Plus, they're no longer kids. Just think, we could be grandparents together in no time!"

Art turned to his friend with a look of utter devastation. William stopped and looked at Arthur's face, seeing the fatigue etched there and that his color was a little off.

"Art? What's going on?" A cool breeze blew around them and the sun dipped behind a cloud, as if sensing the impending news. His friend's hesitation stopped William cold. "Art?"

"I'm dying."

Chapter 1

MACKENZIE MONTGOMERY WAS TIRED. WEARY TO THE bone exhausted. It wasn't the long hours at the office wearing him out; it was the incessant rounds of well-wishers with their "Congratulations" and "You all must be so happy" that were grating on his every last nerve.

"*Must* I be so happy?" he muttered under his breath. Deep down, Mac knew they all meant well; he shouldn't begrudge their pleasantries. Unfortunately, for the last two years, all he'd seemed to hear was how happy everyone was for his brothers, their wives, their lives... Sure, it was great, but didn't anyone have anything else to think about? To focus on?

"Great news about Lucas and Emma, isn't it, Mac?"

Mac looked up, and there in the doorway stood one of his junior executives with an eager look and a wide smile on his young face. Mac tried to return the smile, but at this point in the day, it made his face hurt. "It sure is."

"Tell them I said congratulations!" the young man said before disappearing.

Mac slumped down into his plush leather chair and turned to face his wall of windows. The sun was starting to set and the view of downtown Charlotte was one of bustling activity. Glancing at his watch, he saw that it was just after five, and he knew he should head to the hospital where the rest of his family had congregated to welcome the newest Montgomery.

A girl. Mac couldn't help but chuckle. His former NFL player brother, who had been so certain he was going to have a son to teach all of his moves to, now had a tiny baby girl. There was a joke in there somewhere, but right now Mac couldn't seem to find it. He'd go, meet the newest member of the family, pat Lucas on the back and hug Emma, and remember to smile at all of the excitement that was sure to be going on around him. But all he really wanted to do was go home, have a beer, and just relax.

The drive to the hospital was short, and he even remembered to stop and pick up a bouquet of flowers for his sister-in-law. As he headed toward Emma's room, the noise level told him his prediction was right on the money. He was greeted by his father first, then his brother Jason, finally making his way to shake the new father's hand before handing the flowers to Emma.

"Oh, Mac," Emma said as tears swam in her eyes. "They're perfect. Lilies for our Lily."

Right, the baby's name was Lily. Happy coincidence? Or maybe he had subconsciously remembered his father telling him that was what they had named her. Neither here nor there, the fact was he had done a good thing and now everyone was staring at him with sappy grins on their faces.

Great.

"Do you want to hold her?" Emma asked, nodding toward the bassinet next to her bed.

Mac was about to break out in a cold sweat. Hold her? *The baby?* Wasn't that against the rules or something? He wasn't the father! He could give her germs or drop her! Lucas must have seen the look of pure terror on his face because he chuckled and said, "I'm not ready to entrust my princess with him yet. He can't even catch a football!" The room erupted with laughter, but Mac took it all in stride since it got him out of infant holding.

"Were you planning on throwing her to me? Because I'm pretty sure the hospital has rules against that," he teased and then smiled when his mother came over and looped her arm though his, pulling him close.

"You'll have to hold her eventually," she whispered with a sassy smile.

"Sure, when she's talking in complete sentences, I'm sure I'll be fine." He heard his father's cell phone ring in the distance and watched as William quickly exited the room. Mac quirked an eyebrow at his mom, but she simply shrugged and then walked over to gaze lovingly at her new granddaughter.

His brother Jason patted him on the back. "Nice side-step with the baby; for a minute there I thought you were going to cry."

Mac took the ribbing, but his mind was on his father. Was something wrong? "Is there a problem at the office I'm not aware of?" he asked his brother, ignoring his comment.

"Not that I know of," Jason said. "Why?"

"Probably nothing, but Dad got a call and sort of bolted from the room." Mac looked toward the doorway to see if his father had returned.

Before Jason could offer any input, Lily let out a small cry and all attention was on the newborn. Mac never understood the attraction of babies, particularly newborns. They were tiny and wrinkly, fragile and ter-rifying, and they cried a lot. He watched in amazement as Lucas walked over and picked up his daughter with such gentleness that Mac almost couldn't look away. He was used to seeing Lucas being rough and physical; after all, years of high school sports and a career in the NFL had toughened him. But watching him now? He seemed at ease handling the tiny pink bundle and handing her to his wife. A collective sigh went out as Emma took the baby and cuddled her. Even Mac got a little misty at the sight of mother and child.

What in the world?

Taking a step back, he saw his father walking back into the room. "Everything okay, Dad?" William's face was drawn and sad. "Dad?"

William reached out and touched Mac's arm and pulled him aside. "Son," he said, his voice cracking slightly, "I need you to do something for me."

There were a million reasons why Gina Micelli should be anywhere else but where she was at the moment. She had a job that needed her, social engagements she had committed to, plants that needed to be watered, bills that needed to be paid…but the fact was that she was walking through the Charlotte Douglas International Airport on her way to see a man who had been vastly absent from her life for more than ten years.

Her father.

Arthur Micelli was a good father on paper; Gina had gone to the best schools and had a wardrobe that was the envy of all her friends. She vacationed all over the world and had a new car every three years. She had been given everything she had ever asked for. Except his time. Her

parents had divorced when she was fifteen, her mother
had taken her clear across the country, and her father
had allowed it.

She glanced down at the Rolex her father had given
her for her last birthday and saw that it was just after two
in the afternoon. She was scheduled to meet William
Montgomery in baggage claim at two fifteen. That made
her smile a little. The Montgomerys had always been
such good friends to her parents, and Gina had nothing but fond memories of the countless times they had
gotten together for barbecues and holidays and even
several vacations.

She often thought about the family and where they
all were now. She knew Lucas had played professional
football, and although Gina was not a sports fan, she
remembered reading about the injury that had ended his
career. She had been devastated for her old friend and
could only hope he was doing well. Jason Montgomery
was a couple years older, and she had seen him a couple
of times in the last few years when he had flown out to
the West Coast for business. It had never been intentional, but they ran in some of the same social circles,
so she usually got the *Reader's Digest* version of what
was new with his family. While hearing how his parents
were doing was always nice, she somehow managed to
listen politely until he got to news about Mac.

Mackenzie Montgomery.

Sigh.

Mac had been her reason for living when she was a
teenager. He was so much older, and they had absolutely
nothing in common, but she had always been drawn
to him. He was serious and studious and much more

reserved than his brothers, but Gina found that even at a young age, she was attracted to that in a man.

He had always been polite to her and had treated her like a kid sister, but by the time she hit puberty, the last thing she wanted was to have Mac think of her like that. Gina had had big plans for turning eighteen and how she would find the courage to engage with Mac on an adult level, but her mother had moved her thousands of miles away before she ever had the chance.

Sighing, Gina picked up her pace and navigated her way through the throngs of people to get to baggage claim. Her father was in serious condition and there was little hope of him living beyond the next three months. The thought caused a tightening in her chest. Even though Arthur Micelli was an absentee father, it didn't mean she wasn't devastated by the thought of losing him.

William had promised to set up an appointment for her to talk with her father's doctors, so they could better explain Arthur's condition. Gina was not particularly looking forward to that. She was here because Arthur was her father; she had no idea how to be with him or how she was supposed to act with his medical team. When she'd made arrangements at work for a leave of absence and her boss had asked how long she'd be gone, Gina had shrugged and said, "I don't know. A couple of weeks, I guess." Surely she wasn't expected to stay until the end? What good would that do? Wouldn't it be better for her and Arthur to settle their differences so that he could die in peace?

A shudder ran down her spine at her own callous thoughts. Gina couldn't think about her father dying, not now. She wasn't ready. In her mind, it was better to act as if he was going to recover and be okay.

Yes, that was what she was going to do. She would thank William for his efforts, but then graciously decline his offer to meet with the doctors. The less she knew, the better. No, her time would be better spent just being with her dad and making peace.

Looking up, she saw the signs for the carousel where her luggage would appear and anxiously looked around for William Montgomery. It had been well over ten years since she'd last seen him, but Gina had no doubt she'd recognize him. Her gaze went over the crowd of people standing around waiting, and that's when she saw him.

Mac.

What was Mac doing here? Where was his father? Why hadn't someone told her there had been a change in plans? She wasn't ready to meet up with the object of her every teenage fantasy. The flight had been over six hours; she stunk like plane and had dressed casually for the flight.

With a quick duck through the crowd, Gina ran for the nearest ladies room and did her best to freshen up. Her long, black hair had been haphazardly pulled back into a ponytail and the curls were begging to be let loose. Pulling the band from her hair, she shook it out and finger combed it to try and tame it. Unfortunately, the hair gods were not on her side and Gina thought she looked like something out of an eighties hair band video.

Sighing with frustration, she gave up the fight against her hair, pulled her small makeup bag from her purse, retouched her lipstick and blush, and used her travel toothbrush to do a quick brush and rinse to freshen her breath. The final touch was a spritz of perfume to her wrists, and then she straightened and turned to look at herself in the full-length mirror.

"Let's hope he doesn't hold too much stock in first impressions," she muttered as she squared her shoulders, took a deep breath, and made her way back out into the crowd and toward one Mackenzie Montgomery.

———

Mac scanned the crowd again in search of Gina Micelli. When his father had asked him if he would pick her up from the airport, Mac had been less than enthused at the idea, but it got him out of being part of the big taking-baby-Lily-home festivities.

It was like trading one form of hell for another.

It had been over ten years since he'd last seen Gina, and he basically had no idea who he should be looking for. He remembered her as a kid: dark hair, glasses, and the typical awkward, gangly teen. He may not know much about these things, but he was sure she wouldn't have stayed that way. Looking at his watch, he huffed with agitation. It was two twenty. He knew for a fact that Gina's plane had arrived on time, so where was she?

With another glance around the baggage claim area, he caught a glimpse of a gypsy. That was the only way to describe the woman who seemingly floated toward the luggage belt. She was petite—maybe five foot four, tops—and she wore some sort of long, gauzy black skirt that flowed with her every step. Peeking out from beneath the filmy fabric were a pair of bejeweled sandals and hot pink–tipped toes. Mac swallowed roughly as his gaze traveled upward.

She was wearing a sheer blouse, belted at the waist,

and underneath it was what promised to be a phenomenal body, covered in some sort of clingy teal-colored
cami that matched the beaded necklace around her slender neck. Dark sunglasses covered her eyes, but Mac
mentally bet himself they were either blue or green, and
knew that either would look amazing against her tanned
skin and jet-black hair.

He shifted his stance and pulled at the collar of his
shirt because it certainly felt like it was getting hot in
the airport. Unable to tear his eyes away, he watched,
fascinated by her every graceful move, as she reached
over and pulled a large black suitcase from the conveyor
belt and then did her own scan of the crowd. When her
gaze landed on him, Mac felt frozen to the spot.

Please don't let this be Gina, he cursed to himself.

"Excuse me." Her soft voice washed over him like
silk. "Mackenzie Montgomery?"

Mac looked down and almost groaned when his
gypsy took off her sunglasses and eyed him warily.
"Indeed I am," he said and hated how gruff his voice
sounded. "It's good to see you again, Gina. I wish it
were under better circumstances."

She looked down at the ground before meeting his gaze
again. "Thank you," she replied softly. "Is your father here
with you? He said he'd be the one meeting me."

Mac explained about Lucas and Emma and the baby,
and he wasn't sure if he saw relief or annoyance on her
face. Either way, her big green eyes were staring up at him,
and he had to force himself to look away. "Here," he said
after a long moment, "let me take your suitcase and we'll
get going." When she didn't make a move right away, he
stopped and looked at her. "Is it just the one bag?"

"What?" she asked, momentarily distracted by the enticing rear view of him. "Oh, yes, I tend to travel light."

"That's a first," he joked and started walking.

Gina had to take two steps for his every one and, when she caught up to him, asked, "What is that supposed to mean?"

He shrugged. "Nothing, it just always seems to me that women pack more than they'll ever need, no matter how long or short the trip. Based on that theory, I'd have to guess you don't plan on staying very long."

"I haven't really decided yet. I'm supposed to meet with some of my father's doctors tomorrow and discuss his prognosis, but honestly, I don't want to think about it. I'd rather focus on spending time with him now, rather than watching a clock that tells me when it's going to end."

Mac wasn't sure what to say to her. From what his father had told him, Arthur's prognosis was not good. He had stage four pancreatic cancer, and his heart was failing. Not a good combination. She looked to be holding up okay, but then again, he didn't really know Gina very well. Mac thought about how he'd feel if the tables were turned and it was his own father who was dying. He wasn't fool enough to believe William was going to be around forever, but the thought of knowing his time was so quickly coming to an end was enough to cause a deep ache around Mac's heart.

Pushing those thoughts aside, he decided to change the subject. "So, Dad tells me you'll be staying in the guesthouse."

Gina nodded. "I know I could stay at my father's house, but I've never been there and I just thought it would be odd. Plus no one else is there, and the thought of being alone in a strange house was a little bit intimidating."

Mac nodded in understanding.

"When your father offered me the use of your family's guesthouse, I was a bit surprised. I figured I'd just stay at a hotel and rent a car."

"My father would never have allowed that. He and Arthur have been friends since they were kids; you're like family. And family takes care of one another."

Just what she wanted to hear, another reference to her being like family. While she didn't mind it coming from William and Monica or even Lucas or Jason, the last thing she wanted was for Mac to think of her like a sister.

"Well, that's sweet of you to say," she said as they stepped out into the sunshine and she placed her sunglasses back on. "I'm very grateful for their hospitality. Plus, I have some very fond memories of the times our families spent together. It will be nice to stay someplace familiar."

Soon they were at Mac's car and Gina settled in as he put her suitcase in the trunk. When he climbed in beside her, it was as if the entire interior had shrunk. He was big—much bigger than the last time she'd seen him. Mac stood easily over six feet tall, and even in his monstrous SUV, he overpowered the space.

He didn't try to make small talk and for that Gina was thankful. As they made their way out of the airport parking lot, she took some time to observe him discreetly. Considering his intimidating frame, he moved with grace. His hands were large and tanned, and Gina secretly wished that he'd reach out with them to offer her some comfort.

But he didn't.

His dark brown hair was cut short and there wasn't a hair out of place. His suit was impeccable as well. She could tell Mac Montgomery was a man who liked order and organization. His car was spotless, his appearance was spotless, and she had a feeling he did not do well with any form of disorganization or chaos.

He'd think she was a hot mess.

She had no real plan for her time here; there was no schedule or itinerary. She had to simply go with the flow and take each day as it came until it was time for her to go. Gina knew it was just a gut feeling, but watching the rigid way Mac held himself reminded her of a person who did everything with a purpose and rarely relaxed.

With a sinking feeling in the pit of her stomach, she thought they'd probably make each other crazy if they spent too much time together.

Although making each other crazy could be fun.

A small smile tugged at her lips. While she had no idea how her days were going to go while she was in North Carolina, Gina knew she and Mac were bound to run into one another, especially if she was going to be staying at his parents' house.

"I don't know if my father mentioned it, but he and my mother are going to be out of town for part of your visit."

Gina nodded. "He did. He said he'd happily cancel their trip so I wouldn't be alone, but I told him that it wasn't the same thing as being alone at my father's. There I have no connection; it's a strange house I've never been to. With the guesthouse, it's part of my child-hood. Plus, I didn't want them canceling their vacation on my account."

"Well, to be honest, he's really worried about Arthur."

She nodded again. "I know he is, but right now there isn't a whole lot any of us can do. Dad wouldn't want your father hovering over him at the hospital; that would make him crazy."

"It would make anyone crazy," Mac said a little too harshly. "I mean, your father has enough to deal with right now with medical staff hovering over him—he doesn't need any more spectators at this point."

"I hope that doesn't include me," she snapped.

"Of course not, Gina; you're his daughter."

"And your father is his best friend."

Mac sighed with frustration. Why were they even discussing this? "There's a difference, and I think you know that. Your father is going to be happy to have you there with him after all this time." He realized immediately how that sounded. "What I mean is…"

Gina held up a hand to silence him. "It's okay, Mac. I know exactly how it is. My parents' marriage was a mess even before it ended, and by the time they decided to call it quits, it was unbearable even to be in the same room with them. I had no choice but to go with my mother to California; Dad didn't protest."

Mac was about to tell her they didn't have to talk about this, but he sensed that maybe Gina needed to.

"At first, my mother used the excuse that we needed time to settle in before letting me come back to North Carolina to visit with my father; then it was my school schedule. Dad came as often as he could, but his business kept him busy here on the East Coast. He made excuses and I pretended to understand, and in the long run, it meant that for the first time in a long time, no one was arguing. It was almost a relief..."

"I'm sorry," Mac said when Gina's voice trailed off. "That couldn't have been easy for you."

She shook her head. "It wasn't. Even when he did come to visit, he never came to the house. I had to meet him other places, because if he and my mother got within ten feet of one another, they'd start fighting." The passing scenery held her attention for a few moments. "He was there for all of the important events, like my graduation from high school and college, but other than that, our time together was spotty. I think he believed that staying away was for the best."

"It was a difficult situation. There was probably never going to be a 'best' for anyone."

Gina turned and looked at Mac. "I think you're right," she said and then paused. "It still would have been nice if he had just asked."

This was all getting a little too deep for Mac. He liked and respected Arthur Micelli. He'd never given much thought to Arthur's estranged relationship with his daughter, and he didn't want to know this much personal information. Truth be known, Mac didn't like to get too deeply into anyone's personal life. It was easier that way. The less he knew, the better. Although he had plenty of friends and business associates, he never invited them to delve too deeply into his personal life, and he was rewarded with the same respect.

Before Gina launched into any more deep family secrets, Mac decided to change the subject. "My mother made sure the house was cleaned and stocked for you; you shouldn't need to do anything."

"That was nice of her," she said, seeming grateful for something lighter to talk about.

"Dad mentioned that you were getting a rental car. Is that really necessary? He has two spares I'm sure you could borrow, plus, with him and my mother going out of town, there'd technically be four cars for you to choose from."

Gina shook her head. "He mentioned that, but I really didn't want to impose any more than I already am. They're giving me a place to stay, and you came and got me from the airport…there comes a point where it feels like I'm taking advantage."

Why did women think this way? "You're not taking advantage, Gina. Trust me, no one will be using the cars and it's ridiculous for you to waste money on a car rental when you don't have to." His tone was firm and authoritative; he was certain that she'd agree with him.

"Well," she snapped, "ridiculous or not, that's how I feel. I didn't ask to be here or for a place to stay. I know how to take care of myself, and I don't need anyone telling me what to do!"

With a ragged sigh and mentally counting to ten, Mac softened his tone. "I'm not trying to tell you what to do. Really. I'm just trying to help you have one less thing to think about. This happened so quickly, I'm sure you're still trying to absorb it all."

He had her there. It had all happened quickly. One minute she was at work, worrying about getting financial statements filed for a difficult client, and the next she was packing a suitcase while making travel arrangements to get across the country to her father.

"Fine," she said begrudgingly. "I'll use one of their cars. I suppose it does make more sense."

Mac wanted to high-five himself but figured Gina wouldn't appreciate that. "Getting from my parents' place to the hospital is really easy. I don't imagine you'd remember your way around here that well."

She shrugged. "It's been so long, I'm sure things have changed."

"They have," Mac confirmed. "But like I said, the route isn't difficult and all of his cars have navigation systems, so you shouldn't have any problems." She didn't respond and Mac was grateful for the silence. Within minutes, they were pulling into the circular driveway of his childhood home. "Here we are."

A wide smile crossed Gina's face and she turned to face Mac. "It looks exactly as I remembered it," she said in a voice laced with excitement. "It's weird. I don't remember much about the home I grew up in, but your house always stayed with me. Probably because to me, it was a refuge." She climbed from the car and almost took off at a run to get to the backyard—much like she had when she was a young girl.

Then she remembered that she wasn't a young girl anymore and there was a very serious-looking man watching her every move. Halting in her tracks, she turned and faced Mac. "It feels like only yesterday we were pulling up here for a barbecue. I used to love being here and running around back to the yard, where we would all swim and play volleyball. It was better than summer camp!"

Mac couldn't help but return her smile. "My folks loved having you around. I think my mom always felt a little gypped that she didn't have a daughter and ended up with three rambunctious boys; while you were here, she got to pretend."

Gina's heart softened at the thought. If only Monica knew how many times she had wished that she was a Montgomery too. "That's sweet. Although it seems like now she has quite a few girls in the picture to level the playing field." Mac looked at her quizzically, so she explained herself. "Well, with your brothers' wives, she has two daughters, and now she has a granddaughter too. All in all, I'll bet after those years of being tortured by her three sons, she's happy to finally have some women in the mix."

"You have no idea," Mac said with a laugh and grabbed Gina's luggage from the trunk. "C'mon, I'll show you to the guesthouse so you can get settled in."

"Thank you," she said and fell into step behind him. Gina smiled as she walked along the stone path leading to the massive backyard and couldn't keep the grin off her face. The property had always been beautiful and all these years later, it still took her breath away. She paused to look at the small koi pond situated just inside the six-foot-tall gate. Yes, it was all still a feast for the eyes.

"Are you coming?" Mac asked, standing and watching her curiously.

Gina realized that she had been standing still for a few minutes. "Oh, sorry, yes," she replied and then watched as Mac walked away. He was all lean grace and solid muscle.

And another feast for her eyes.

Chapter 2

SEVERAL HOURS LATER, GINA WAS WIPING TEARS FROM her eyes—not from sadness but from laughing at some wonderful memories she'd shared with the Montgomerys. Sitting across the dining room table from her in their beautiful home, William Montgomery shared stories of all the adventures he remembered Gina and his sons having so many years ago.

"I'll tell you, your father and I couldn't believe it," he was saying. "There you were, up in that tree, completely terrified and yet refusing to let anyone help you come down."

Gina laughed. "I always hated heights."

"But you didn't want the boys to know that, and I nearly skinned Lucas alive for daring you to climb up so high!"

She took a sip of her wine and waved him off. "Dare or no dare, if they were climbing, I was climbing. I didn't want them to think I was weak. Being so outnumbered around here, I had to make sure I did whatever they did; otherwise I'd be relegated to sitting in the corner with a Barbie doll."

"You never played with dolls," William said. "More of a tomboy, if I recall."

"Much to my mother's dismay," she said with a touch more resentment than she wanted anyone to know. "I preferred running around outside to sitting inside reading or playing quietly. I think she was more upset about my being up in that tree than I was."

"She was nearly hysterical," Monica interjected with a small laugh of her own. "I remember pulling her away and keeping her in the house until you came down."

"It only took three hours," William said, and they all started laughing again.

"The key was never to let them see me sweat," Gina said with a confident smile as she placed her glass back down on the table. She could feel Mac's gaze on her but refused to meet his eyes. Earlier, when he had walked her over to the guest cottage, he had turned beet red when she'd removed the blouse she'd worn over her cami. There was a confidence builder for you: take off your blouse and watch a man nearly dive through a window to escape.

In all honesty, she wasn't doing it to entice him; she'd simply been ready to change out of the clothes she'd traveled in. The clothes she had on under the offensive blouse weren't particularly revealing, but the way Mac had looked at her, you'd have thought she was doing a striptease and swinging from a pole!

Well, it didn't really make a difference, because no matter how attractive he was, it was painfully obvious that Mac did not approve of her. *Sigh*. It was better to accept that now than to torture herself the entire time she was in North Carolina.

"Did Mac show you where everything is in the guesthouse?" Monica asked, interrupting Gina's thoughts. "I tried to think of everything you would need and I had a cleaning crew go in and get everything ready for you."

"It's perfect. I really can't thank you enough for your hospitality."

"Did you talk to your father yet?" Monica asked carefully. Of course, she would know that Gina and Arthur's relationship was strained.

"I called him before I walked over here for dinner. I told him I'd be there around lunchtime tomorrow."

"You'll use one of our cars, of course," William said and caught the glare Gina shot toward Mac.

"I would be perfectly fine renting a car. I don't want to impose any more than I already am."

"Nonsense," both William and Mac said at the same time.

Gina chose to address William. "If you're sure you don't mind and that it won't be an inconvenience, I'll take you up on your offer." At that moment Mac's phone rang and it seemed the perfect time for everyone to get up from the table. "I know it's not very late, but it's been a long day for me, so if you don't mind, I think I'll head over to the guesthouse and crash."

"I'll walk you over," William said, walking around the table toward her. "We'll take a quick detour by the garage so you can choose which car you want to use and I'll give you the keys. This way you can leave whenever you're ready tomorrow."

Gina wished Monica a good night and thanked her for dinner. When Monica embraced her and whispered, "I'm so glad you're home," Gina almost burst into tears. It had been so long since they'd seen each other, and yet she'd felt more warmth and affection than she did back on the West Coast in her own home.

"Thank you, Monica," she said with a final squeeze, and then met William by the back door.

It was a cool September evening with a star-filled

sky. There was an overall feeling of peace as they walked toward the garage, and Gina enjoyed the silence.

"It's okay to be nervous about seeing your father," William said softly.

It was pointless to argue; William Montgomery had a way of seeing into your soul and knowing exactly how you felt and yet never making you feel bad about it. "It's been a long time."

William sighed. "He struggled every day with his decision to let you move across the country. It wasn't easy for him, and unfortunately, there didn't seem to be any way to make everyone happy."

"My mother can be difficult," Gina said, trying to play if off like it wasn't a big deal, but they both knew differently.

"We've missed you—not just your dad, but all of us. You were part of our family."

"I wanted to keep in touch but sometimes it was just easier to let things go than deal with…" she trailed off and saw William nod in understanding.

"That's all in the past, Gina. You're here now, and if you need anything, please don't hesitate to ask."

"You're being far too generous. The house, the car… I'm not used to having things go so smoothly."

"You just say the word and Monica and I will postpone our trip. You shouldn't be alone to deal with all of this."

"Thank you for offering, but I would feel terrible if you missed your trip. Besides, I think it might be good for me and my father to have this time together." She paused and stopped in her tracks. William stopped and turned to face her. "I know you said that you would arrange for me to meet with the doctors in charge of my father but…I don't want to do that."

William quirked an eyebrow at her. "May I ask why?"

She took a fortifying breath. "This trip is not going to be easy for either of us. If I try really hard, I can pretend that this is just a normal visit and enjoy the time he and I have together. Once I talk to the doctors, all I'm going to be able to focus on is how much time we have left together." Unwanted tears filled her eyes and William pulled her into his embrace.

"Whatever it is you want, that's what we'll do." Gina nodded against him, and he rested his head on top of hers.

"I'll tell you what," he began and looked down into her big green eyes, bright with unshed tears. "I'll let the doctors know you're there and to make themselves available should you want to talk to them. Okay?"

She nodded. "Thank you for understanding. I know I should be braver about this, and maybe I'm being naive, but for now, in all honesty, ignorance is bliss."

William took her by the hand and together they walked in silence toward the garage. When they arrived, William opened the door and revealed four vehicles: an SUV, two luxury sedans, and a BMW convertible. Gina couldn't help it—the convertible called to her. She was just about to take a step toward the sleek vehicle but stopped herself.

"Um, which car will you and Monica be taking?" she asked casually.

"We have a car service picking us up tomorrow so really, the choice is yours."

She wanted that convertible; she was a practical person who always made practical choices, but something about that car made her want to be just a little bit wild. Back home, she drove a top-rated sedan. It was luxurious and had every feature a driver could want, with the highest safety rating available.

It was boring as hell.

The BMW seemed to wink at her in the dim light of the garage, and as much as she wanted to ask William for the keys to it, practicality won out. "Either of the sedans will be fine," she said, forcing a smile into her voice.

William put an arm around her and led her away from the sedans and toward the convertible. "Isn't she a beauty?" he asked, not waiting for a response. "I bought her six months ago but I don't drive her much. Monica tells me I look ridiculous in it, like a man having a midlife crisis. So I gave her the keys to it." He sighed dramatically. "Unfortunately, she doesn't appreciate the beauty of a convertible and ends up taking her Lexus over there instead." Without looking away from the car, he reached into his pocket and pulled out the keys.

"I imagine a California girl like you can appreciate a convertible," he said lightly and chuckled at Gina's startled expression.

—◦◦◦—

"Dad, that was Baker on the phone. Apparently they want to meet with us tomorrow," Mac said as he strode into the garage.

William sighed. It was always business with Mac. He appreciated how his firstborn took his position in the company so seriously but sometimes he wished Mac would just relax and enjoy himself! Here was a beautiful woman standing in the room with them and Mac didn't even spare her a glance.

"Did you tell him I was leaving after lunch?"

Mac looked up from his phone and nodded. "He said they can be at the office as early as you'd like." Mac looked over and saw Gina walking around his father's convertible, staring at it wide-eyed. What the hell? He returned his focus to the conversation with his father. "I told him eight a.m. should be fine."

William nodded. "That will work." He turned and watched Gina inspecting the car. "Why don't you get in and get acquainted with it? It's got every feature known to man and the navigation system will get you anywhere you want to go."

"She's using the BMW?" Mac asked with disbelief. "Why? Wouldn't one of the sedans be more appropriate?"

"What's the big deal?" William asked as he tried to hide his amusement. It took a lot to get Mac riled up, and something about Gina Micelli seemed to be doing just that. "Gina needs a car, I told her she could use any that she wanted, and she is."

Mac sighed and pinched the bridge of his nose. "She's not familiar with how to get around here anymore, Dad. Wouldn't it make more sense for her to drive a car that's a little less…complex?"

Gina had heard enough. "Excuse me," she said, fairly stomping over to where the two Montgomery men stood. "For your information, I know how to drive. I've owned cars in my life and I've driven up and down the West Coast without incident. I don't imagine driving around the city of Charlotte, North Carolina, is going to trip me up too much."

"I just don't see why you need such a flashy car!" he replied, his tone rising slightly. "You're driving from here to the hospital and back. What's the point?"

Gina stepped into his personal space and then

immediately regretted it. Not only did the man look good, but he smelled good too. Dammit. "So what you're saying is that only 'practical' cars should be used to drive to and from the hospital?" She snorted with disgust. "Okay, that makes sense."

"All I'm saying is—"

"And who says I'm only driving back and forth to the hospital? Do I have a curfew? Do I need to punch a clock or something? Last I checked, I was here to see my dad, and as an adult not under any kind of house arrest, I'm free to go wherever I want."

Mac's gaze hardened. "So this is what? A pleasure trip for you? Stop in and see your father for a few minutes and then go traipsing around town?"

"Mackenzie!" William snapped. "Why are you badgering Gina? She didn't say she was going traipsing around anywhere, but for crying out loud, if she wants to visit old friends or go out to eat or just go to the store, that's none of your concern."

Gina looked at him with a smug smile and Mac mumbled an apology. She graciously accepted before turning away and going back to the car. She wanted to skip away but she would wait to do that when she didn't have an audience.

———ᴧᴧᴧ———

"What is the matter with you?" William asked as he walked Mac out of the garage.

Mac shook his head. "I don't know, Dad. Sorry. It's been a rough week."

"Really? How? It's been business as usual, as far as I can tell."

Now was really not the time to get into it, but for some reason, Mac felt the need to unburden himself a little. "Between you and me? With Lucas and Emma having Lily, and Jason and Maggie getting married, it's been a bit much. Everyone is looking at me and wondering when it's going to be my turn, and if I have to hear them ask that one more time, I'll lose my mind!"

William observed his son. Mac never admitted to any kind of weakness and this was as close as he'd ever gotten to sharing his personal feelings. "Do you begrudge your brothers their happiness?" he asked cautiously.

"No, no…of course not; I'm thrilled for them both but, well…I just wish that I didn't have to hear about it from everyone all the damn time. I'm beginning to dread going into the office."

Unable to help himself, William pulled his son in for a hug and patted him on the back. "It's the nature of the beast, I'm afraid. I think part of the problem is that you spend too much time in the damn office."

Mac held up a hand to stop the lecture. "I am there as much as I'm needed."

"That's bull and you know it. It wasn't long ago you were picking on Jason for all of the time he spent in the office, and you're no better. Take some time off, Mac. The company won't fall apart without you."

"I can't right now; you're heading out of town."

William waved him off. "Please, I'm not talking about taking a monthlong vacation or anything…yet. But how about trying to leave by six? While the sun is still out."

"And do what?" Mac asked, confounded by the thought. Did he have to do all the thinking for his children?

William caught a glimpse of Gina as she climbed from the convertible, a smile of pure satisfaction on her face. "Look after Gina while your mother and I are out of town. This isn't going to be an easy visit for her, and as much as she says she's going to be fine, I'll feel better knowing that she's not alone."

Mac looked at his father as if he'd grown an extra head. *Look after Gina?* Was his father out of his mind? Did he see what Gina looked like? The last time he'd seen her, she'd been a kid; the woman walking around the garage right now was a living, breathing fantasy. Her long, curly hair and big, expressive eyes were slowly killing him. In the short span of time they'd been together today, he'd done his best not to look at her because when he did, he wanted to do more than just look.

His father was probably thinking it wasn't a big deal because Gina was like family, but for crying out loud, Mac was only human. Any man who had breath in his body would find it hard to look at Gina Micelli in a sisterly way. "She doesn't need a babysitter, Dad," he said a little too sharply.

"No," William said softly. "But I'm sure she could use a friend."

Mac eyed his father suspiciously. "You know, I'm not gullible like Lucas and Jason. If you think you're going to play matchmaker with me and Gina, you're seriously mistaken. It's not going to happen." He was shocked by his father's sudden outburst of laughter. "What? What's so funny?" he demanded.

"Oh, Mac, I'll admit I had a hand in getting your brothers married off, but this is different."

"Why?"

William reached out and put a strong hand on his son's shoulder. "As much as I want all of my boys happily married, you're just not right for Gina. Besides, do you really think now is the right time to be playing matchmaker for her, when her father is gravely ill?" He shook his head and tsked at Mac.

That only irritated Mac more. "Okay, I understand the timing is wrong, but are you telling me you wouldn't try to fix us up if she were here for any other reason?"

"It's a moot point," William began diplomatically.

"The hell it is!" Mac snapped and then noticed that Gina was watching them. He pulled his father farther away from the garage. "Let's be hypothetical then, okay? If Gina were here for a social visit, can you honestly tell me you wouldn't be doing everything in your power to get us together?"

"Yes," William said simply, enjoying this little turn of events. When Mac continued to glare, he decided to elaborate. "It was different for your brothers; Lucas was already attracted to Emma. I just gave them a nudge. And Jason and Maggie? Well, your brother needed to see that he wasn't as irresistible as he seemed to think. He needed a challenge like Maggie."

"And what? I don't need a nudge or a challenge?"

William laughed. "Oh, I'm sure you do, but I wouldn't do that to Gina."

There were a million thoughts racing through Mac's head at that moment, and yet he could barely make his voice function. "Care to explain that?" he growled.

With a dramatic sigh, William led Mac away from the garage and toward his car. "Your brothers were ready to settle down. They may not have realized it at first, but it was true. You? You're not ready for it and Gina needs someone who'll want to be there for her and take care of her—someone with staying power. That's not you." It pained him to say the words, but he was merely planting a seed.

"What do you mean I don't have staying power? When have I ever walked away from anything?"

"Mac, you are my son and I love you, but it's not that you walk away from anything; it's that you don't get attached to anything."

"That's not true." Mac's tone was deadly calm.

"When was the last time you were in a long-term relationship?" William asked.

He wanted to answer; the answer should have been on the tip of his tongue, and yet for the life of him, Mac couldn't remember the last time he'd had more than a couple of dates with the same woman. "How can I have a long-term relationship when I'm so involved with work?" Mac thought he was being clever by throwing the ball back in his father's court.

He was seriously mistaken.

"That just proves my earlier point!" William exclaimed with a smile. "Effective immediately, I'm putting you on a leave of absence."

"*WHAT?*" How the hell had he gotten to this point?

"You work too hard, you have no personal life, and you're too proud to admit that you need a break. There's nothing wrong with needing some time off, Son. We all do. Look at me; I'm taking your mother on this cruise because we needed some time away. I hate that the timing is what it is; I hate to leave Gina here to take care of things with Arthur, but we'll only be gone for ten days."

"Dad, I don't need a leave of absence, especially while you're away. I'll be needed at the office while you're gone."

"Nonsense. Jason is there, and we have a very capable team of executives that can handle things if you take some time off."

"I don't *want* any time off!" Dammit, why didn't his father ever listen? "I promise to cut back a little, but there's no need to do anything drastic."

William watched as Mac's features ran from panic to anger to uncertainty. Just for fun, he took a long pause to make his son sweat it out a little bit more. Finally, he spoke. "Okay, we'll put off the leave of absence for now, but if I don't see some changes in you and your work habits, I will enforce it. Am I making myself clear?" he asked in a tone he'd used on his sons since they were little, and it gave him great joy to see that it still had the desired effect.

"Yes, sir," Mac answered begrudgingly.

"Good. Now it's getting late. I want to walk Gina back to the guesthouse and make sure she's settled. Make sure you stop by and see her tomorrow night after she gets home from the hospital and see that she's okay."

Mac nodded, hating how he felt like he was ten years old and getting his punishment handed down to him. On the upside, at least by doing this he could get his father off his back. The last thing he needed was forced time off. Work was very fulfilling for him, and the thought of being cut off from it was not the least bit appealing.

For now he'd humor his father and make himself leave the office before dark. He'd check in on Gina—briefly—and make sure she was all right.

And maybe, just maybe, he'd be able to forget she was a beautiful woman who he was apparently all wrong for.

Chapter 3

THE LARGE HOSPITAL LOOMED IN FRONT OF GINA, AND although the doors kept opening and closing, she couldn't seem to make herself walk through them. She didn't think she'd be this freaked out at the thought of seeing her father, but for some reason the thought of her robust father lying in a hospital bed frightened her. They may not have had the best relationship, but he was always larger than life to her, and she was afraid to see him in this weakened state.

Standing on the sidewalk, Gina watched as people came and went: visitors, staff, and patients getting to go home. She smiled as a young couple came out with their new baby and wished she were there for a joyous event. She let out a sigh and decided that standing outside wasn't going to change what was going on inside.

"This is just a visit," she said quietly, taking one slow step at a time. "It happens to be in a hospital but other than that, I'm just spending the day with my dad." She repeated those words in her head all the way up to the fifth floor and down the hall to Arthur's room. The hesitation was there, and Gina didn't realize how long she'd been standing frozen to the spot until a nurse came up beside her.

"You must be Gina," the woman said, and Gina looked at her in confusion. "Your father has been talking about you all morning. He made sure he was looking his best for your arrival."

She tried to smile, she truly did, but Gina knew it didn't quite reach her eyes. "Is it okay to go in?" she finally asked. The nurse nodded and walked away. Gina longed to call her back, to talk to her, to do anything humanly possible to prolong having to go in and face the unknown.

Standing up straight and plastering what she hoped was a genuine smile on her face, she walked through the door to her father's private room and said a silent prayer that she was going to be all right.

—⁓—

She wasn't all right.

Hours later, back at the Montgomerys' guesthouse, Gina collapsed on the sofa and cried. The first glimpse of her father had nearly brought her to her knees. He looked pale and fragile, and her tower of strength was suddenly desperately in need of someone to lean on. It had been a swift role reversal and while she was there, Gina had done everything she could think of to make him comfortable. They'd shared lunch and talked nonstop for almost six hours. Arthur had been exhausted by the time she'd left and Gina hated to admit she'd felt the same way.

When her body began to ache from the sobs that seemed to come from a place inside her she hadn't known existed, Gina knew she had to stop. Yes, seeing her father and knowing his condition was much worse than he'd let on had come as a complete shock, but she had to be strong. She needed to be able to function and focus on the positive so he wouldn't know how devastated she truly was.

She stood up and walked to the kitchen in search of

something to eat. Monica had been considerate enough to have it stocked with homemade meals for her to heat up as needed, but nothing was appealing at the moment. Suddenly Gina wanted to break free of her normal, healthy, boring habits and indulge in a junk-food binge. Cheeseburgers, French fries, soda…her stomach growled loudly in agreement.

Grabbing a bottle of water, she moved on to the bathroom and washed her face to try and recover from her crying jag. She was tense and on edge and needed something to do. It was an unseasonably warm night, and without letting herself doubt her decision, Gina walked down the short hallway to the bedroom and grabbed her swimsuit.

She'd go for a swim to burn off the energy and then maybe she'd decide what to eat. Changing into the blue bikini that she had never been brave enough to wear back home, she admired her reflection.

Her mother had always said that she was too curvy to wear a bikini "decently, " so Gina had stuck to wearing modest one-piece bathing suits to avoid arguments. Why she had brought the bikini with her she wasn't sure, but right now it made her feel good. A quick rummage through her things had her pulling out a teal-blue sarong that she wrapped around herself before heading out the door.

—✍—

It was six o'clock in the evening and Mac was feeling ridiculous. He'd left the office thirty minutes ago and was making good on his promise to his father by checking up on Gina. As a peace offering, he had stopped and picked up a pizza for them to share for dinner. It smelled delicious and as much as he wanted nothing more than to go home, Mac figured there was no harm in sharing a quick meal.

"Just a pizza," he said as he grabbed the box and climbed from his car. "Just a pizza and some beer. Just a friendly meal between friends, and then I'm out of here." He walked through the gate leading to the back part of the property where the pool and guesthouse were. At this point, he felt some of the tension leaving his body. The weather was being particularly cooperative, so he placed the pizza on one of the tables by the pool, figuring it might be nice to eat outside. "Just pizza and some beer and…a bikini."

A bikini?

Mac almost swallowed his tongue. There, walking out of the French doors of the guesthouse was Gina— wrapped up in scraps of blue Lycra and green silk.

He should have taken the leave of absence.

Gina didn't notice Mac at first, and for that he was glad. He took his time looking his fill. She was curvy in all the right places, and between the long, curly hair and the jewel colors she was wearing, she was bewitching. He could picture her with gold bangles on her wrists and maybe one of those barely there gold chains around her waist…and found himself breaking out in a cold sweat. He was just about to clear his throat to alert her to his presence when she looked up.

"Mac? What are you doing here?"

"I come bearing gifts," he said lightly, hoping she didn't notice that he was standing in a puddle of his own drool. "I hope you haven't eaten."

Gina looked beyond Mac to the pizza box on the table

and nearly screeched with delight. "You are a lifesaver! I was just wishing for some junk food and here you are with pizza. It's perfect!"

"You were wishing for junk food?"

"Your mother stocked the kitchen for me with all kinds of wonderful home-cooked meals and stuff to make salads but right now, after the day I had, all I want is comfort food." She walked over to the table and opened the box as she sat down. "Oh, pepperoni is my favorite! Thank you, Mac; this was very thoughtful of you."

Had he known he was going to have to sit and eat with a half-naked Gina, he would have gone straight home. As it was, he was thinking he should run while he could and take a cold shower. He eyed the pool and considered his options.

"Aren't you going to join me?" she asked, grabbing a slice from the box and not waiting for him before taking a bite. She moaned in pure ecstasy. "Now *that* is what I'm talking about."

He was in hell. There was no other way to describe it. He was tired, hungry, and now he was horny too.

Perfect.

Not having any other choice, Mac pulled out the chair opposite Gina's and sat down. She handed him a slice of pizza and a beer, and Mac took a long swallow before he could make himself speak. "So how did it go with your dad today?"

Gina finished chewing and then sighed. "He's worse than I expected."

"Did you talk to the doctors?"

She shook her head. "Today was just about spending time together." She stopped and considered her next words. "I guess I wasn't sure what I anticipated, but once I walked in and saw him, I knew he was worse than he had let on."

Mac didn't know what to say, so he simply nodded and waited for her to go on.

"I had said I didn't want to know; I didn't want to focus on his prognosis, but I realize now that's just being in a state of denial. There's nothing I can do for him except be here, and that's hard to deal with because I feel so helpless." Her breath caught on the last word and more tears sprang to her eyes. She had thought she'd gotten them all out earlier but apparently she was wrong.

Without conscious thought, Mac reached across the table and placed his hand on top of Gina's. She looked up at him at the contact, and he felt like he'd been struck by lightning, so powerful was the connection. "I wish there was something I could say that would make you feel better," he began, carefully removing his hand from hers. "I've never been in your position but I imagine if it were my father, I'd feel the same way. Talking to his doctors might not change the outcome, but you might find some comfort in knowing exactly what he's going to need."

—⁓—

What Mac was saying made sense and Gina was grateful for both his words and the distraction. Right now she didn't want to think about her father's illness because it was still too raw and devastating. Sitting and sharing this simple meal with Mackenzie Montgomery was exactly what she needed.

A thought entered her mind and she wasn't sure if

she was being clever or stupid. Gina knew she was going to be in North Carolina for at least a couple of weeks and it would be nice to have a distraction when things with her father threatened to overwhelm her. Why couldn't Mac be that distraction? Granted, they hadn't gotten off on the best footing last night, but judging by the way he had looked at her when she'd come out in her bikini, and the way he had just looked when he held her hand, he wasn't completely unaffected by her.

She smiled to herself. It wasn't as if she thought Mac was going to fall in love with her, and if she were completely honest with herself, the timing was just plain wrong. But for once, Gina wanted to be reckless. Her mother controlled every aspect of her life, and right now Gina wanted to experience having the control. Convincing iron-willed Mac to have a short fling might not be easy, but Gina had no doubt in her mind that it was exactly what she wanted.

Reclining in her chair, she finished her second slice of pizza in silence and then looked over and smiled at Mac. "This was way better than my plan."

"What was your plan?"

"I was going to swim a bunch of laps until I was exhausted and then sort of close my eyes and reach into the refrigerator and eat whatever I grabbed." They both laughed. "So I thank you for saving me from myself." She smiled at him and was relieved to see that he had relaxed. "Of course, now I just feel ridiculous sitting here in a bathing suit with a pool five feet away and not swimming."

She didn't miss the fact that his gaze skimmed over her bikini-clad body. Gina stood and stretched. "I'm certainly too full to swim but I don't think a relaxing soak in the hot tub would be a bad idea." The words were said lightly and she turned and looked at Mac. "Care to join me?"

———

In that moment, Mac realized that he must have been a horrible person in a previous life to be tempted like this. Gina was staring at him expectantly and he knew he'd have to come up with a viable excuse. "I'm not particularly dressed for the hot tub," he said and then wanted to smack himself in the head. What the hell was that? *Lame*, he cursed himself. *Very, very lame*.

Gina chuckled and shook her head. "Correct me if I'm wrong, but this is your parents' house; you grew up here. I'm sure you keep some extra clothes here."

"Well sure, but—"

"Go get changed. It's still early and it's a beautiful night. We can sit and relax, and you can tell me what you've been up to for the last ten years or so." Without waiting for an answer, she picked up the pizza box and headed toward the guesthouse. "I'll meet you back here in ten minutes," she said over her shoulder as she kept walking.

Mac watched her go. He couldn't take his eyes off her; the sway of her hips was mesmerizing. The smart thing to do was run; get in his car and go home. He was an intelligent man and knew that staying and climbing into the Jacuzzi with Gina was going to test his endurance in ways that he really had no interest in testing.

Like a convicted man walking to his own execution, Mac turned and headed toward the main house in search of a pair of swimming trunks.

It was going to be a long night.

———

Gina hid in the shadows until she saw Mac exiting his parents' house. Then, as if she didn't have a care in the world, she walked over to the Jacuzzi. Daintily, she stepped up the stone stairs leading to the heated tub and dropped her sarong to the ground. Next, she gathered up her long hair and clipped it in a way that left random tendrils framing her face but kept the bulk of it off her shoulders and out of the water.

She sensed more than heard Mac's approach, and she gave him a beaming smile. "Perfect timing," she said.

He made a noncommittal sound, tossed a towel down, and climbed into the tub. The water did feel good, but his damn eyes hurt from forcing them away from the sight of Gina sans sarong. Mac had just gotten comfortable when he saw Gina carefully stepping in to join him. He was about to close his eyes when he heard her soft cry and then felt her fall directly into his lap.

Instinctively, his arms went around her and Gina's hands were on his shoulders, her breasts pressed against his chest—her mouth mere inches from his. Mac's tongue felt like it was the size of his fist but he forced himself to speak. "Are you okay?" he asked, his voice low and gravelly.

Gina blushed. "I'm not normally such a klutz. I took that first step in and just lost my footing. Sorry." She made no attempt to move; she couldn't. The feel of Mac's arms around her was even better than she had ever imagined. The hardness pressing against her thigh told her he was enjoying it too. She was hoping he'd pull her closer.

Mac gently moved Gina off of his lap.

Sigh.

"So," she began as she shifted away from him slightly, "tell me what you've been up to."

"For the last ten years?" he joked. "That could take a while."

Gina relaxed down in the jetted water and sighed. "Believe me, this feels so good," she purred, "that won't be a problem."

Mac almost groaned out loud at the sight. Instead, he cleared his throat and told her about finishing college and his early days working with his father. Gina's eyes were closed, and Mac took the opportunity just to look at her. Was she doing this to him on purpose? Was she trying to tease him? Her breasts were barely covered by the bubbling water, and with her head thrown back to lean against the side of the tub, the sight of her slender throat had him itching to lean forward and lick the droplets of water glistening there. He felt himself fighting the urge when Gina spoke.

"It must be nice working with family," she said softly, almost sleepily, and Mac could envision her using that voice on him in bed.

"There are good days and bad," he admitted, trying to take his focus off her half-naked form sitting so close beside him. "After Lucas's career ended, he was bitter, and there were times it was difficult to have him around. But once he and Emma got together, he was a completely different man."

Gina smiled. "I can't wait to see him and to meet Emma and Lily. I hope once they're all settled in at home, I can go over and visit."

Mac shrugged; he was sure that once his parents got home from their trip, they'd take Gina with them to see his brother and his family.

"I see Jason from time to time when he's in Cali. There's never a lot of time to talk, but it's always nice to see a face from home. I hear his wife is a sweetheart. I hope to meet her too."

"Believe me, I'm sure there will be a family gathering or two before you leave."

"I hope you realize how lucky you are," she said, opening her eyes and turning to face Mac.

"For what?" he asked, thoroughly confused.

"You have a wonderful family; you have no idea what it's like to have no one to support you."

"Your father supports you, Gina. He's always been very proud of you."

She sat up a little straighter, her tone a little sharper than she intended. "I never doubted that my father was proud of me. By support I meant siblings who were there when you needed them. I'm an only child, and during my parents' whole divorce debacle, I had no one to commiserate with, no one to share my fears with. I was terrified to move across the country, and my mother was so busy hating my father that I was alone a lot."

Mac wasn't sure if he was supposed to say anything or not but decided to keep quiet, because clearly Gina needed to get some things off her chest.

"You have wonderful parents and brothers you're close to. And now," she added with a halfhearted laugh, "you have two sisters and a niece! I mean, I really hope you appreciate them, Mac, because I can tell you, it is no fun being alone."

Reaching out, Mac placed a calming hand on her shoulder. "I do appreciate them; maybe not all the time, but I know I'm lucky. I'm sorry your folks made things so hard for you. Honestly, I don't know what I'd do without my brothers, even though there have been times I wanted to strangle them."

"At least there was someone there to strangle," she mumbled.

"I'm sorry you were alone, Gina, but know that while you're here, you're not."

"Thank you," she said softly. Gina was about to say more but felt maybe what she really needed was to get some sleep. Her emotions were all over the place and being this close to Mac had her on sensory overload. She didn't want to argue with him, and he certainly didn't seem too interested in making a move on her, so she decided to cut her losses for now and call it a night.

"This was wonderful," she said as she stood, water cascading down her body. She smiled as she noticed Mac's jaw drop. "But I am exhausted and I think I'm going to head in, put on my jammies, and watch a movie." Turning, she leaned down and gently kissed Mac on the cheek. He closed his eyes and she lingered for just an extra moment before standing and climbing out. "I really appreciate the pizza and the company, Mac. I'm sure I'll see you again soon."

He could only stay seated and watch her glistening body as she walked slowly back toward the French doors she'd come through earlier. There was a towel draped on a chair next to the doorway and she wrapped it around her hips as she walked through the arch. Turning one last time, she waved to Mac and then closed the doors.

His head dropped back against the stones and he let out a low growl, counting backward from one hundred.

And it still wasn't enough to wipe the image of Gina Micelli's curvy, wet body from his mind.

Chapter 4

GINA ARRIVED AT THE HOSPITAL THE NEXT AFTERNOON after two, as the nurses had instructed. Her father was asleep when she walked into his room, so she made herself comfortable, content to just look at him for a while.

"When you were a little girl," he said sleepily, "I used to sit and watch you sleep too. It's nice to see that we've come full circle."

"How are you feeling?"

"Like I've been poked and prodded by too many people," he said lightly, his voice gaining a little strength. "They're going to be doing that sort of thing more and more often so I guess I better get used to it."

"Is it really necessary?" she asked quietly.

"If you mean is it going to help me get better, then no," he said seriously. "It's more for the doctors to track the cancer and make sure that it's not getting any worse or spreading."

Gina nodded and willed herself to not cry. "I hate that they are making you more uncomfortable when they need to be doing everything they can to help you."

He smiled sadly. "In their world, they are helping me. By making sure I'm not getting worse, they are helping me."

"It still doesn't seem right."

"Let's talk about something more fun than my illness. Tell me what you did last night after you left

STAY WITH ME 51

here. Anything exciting? Have you looked up any of your old friends?"

Gina smiled. "Mac came by and we shared a pizza by the pool." She stopped and blushed. "I think his folks asked him to look in on me."

Arthur chuckled. "I wouldn't doubt it. I'm glad they didn't cancel their trip on my account. I know you didn't want to stay at my place because you've never been there, but if you change your mind, just say the word."

"I appreciate that, Dad, but the Montgomerys' guest-house is just fine."

He nodded in understanding. "Actually, I have a favor to ask."

"Anything," she said, leaning forward and taking his hand. "What can I do?"

"Well, there are just some things from home I'd like: a couple different pairs of pajamas, some of my books…I've got a list made. Would you mind stopping by there and bringing them with you when you come back tomorrow?" He looked both hopeful and wary at the same time.

"Of course I don't mind," Gina said sincerely. "Is there anything else you need? I don't mind going shopping if you're missing something."

"That won't be necessary," he said, leaning over to his bedside table and opening the drawer. He pulled out a yellow legal pad, ripped off the top page, and handed it to his daughter. "I put directions to the house on there too, even though I am sure you have a navigation system in whatever car you're driving."

Gina told him about William lending her his beloved convertible and they laughed. "I know Monica gave him hell for buying that car," Arthur said. "He felt so proud of himself for buying such a hip car, but he really did look a little ridiculous."

"Well, his loss is my gain while I'm here," Gina said with a sassy smile. "My car back home will never be the same to me."

"So get rid of it," he suggested. "Go out and get yourself whatever car you want!"

She waved him off. "Please, you know that Mom is a safety fanatic. If I came home with a sports car, she'd have a coronary."

"Gina," he said solemnly, "isn't it time you stopped letting your mother dictate your life to you? You are an intelligent, grown woman. You are entitled to have happiness in your life and if that damn car makes you happy, then you should have one."

Reaching out, she patted her father's other hand. "It's just a car, Dad. It's not a big deal."

Arthur grabbed her hand and looked straight into her eyes.

"You are a good daughter, Gina; no parent could ask for a better child. But it is time for you to start living your own life. I sat back and held my tongue for far too long, and while I thought I was doing the right thing and making your life easier, it seems like all I did was allow your mother to take away your right to think for yourself." Gina started to interrupt him but he held up a hand to stop her. "I blame myself for not fighting more for you, Gina, and I regret my cowardice more than anything. All I ever wanted in this world was for you to be happy."

"I am happy, Dad," she began.

"Are you? Because I'll tell you what I see when I look at you: I see a beautiful, intelligent woman who is unsure of herself. You look to others for approval rather than taking action and doing what feels right for you. I know you hate your job; hell, I know you hate being an accountant! Your mother pushed you to do that too, but you don't have to stay with it. You can be anything you want, Gina!" His eyes were pleading with her for understanding. "What is it that you want to be? Honestly."

A wave of panic rose in her. No one had ever asked her that before, and the thought of saying it out loud to anyone terrified her.

"Tell me, sweetheart. What would make you happy?" Tears flooded Arthur's eyes.

"I…" she began hesitantly. "I want to paint."

Arthur smiled, his face immediately looking younger. "You were always a talented artist, Gina. Why don't you paint?"

"I don't have the time," she said sadly. "My job is pretty demanding, and when I'm not working I have other commitments. There just aren't enough hours in the day."

He reached out for Gina's hand again and she grabbed on to him and held on tight. "Promise me something."

"Anything."

"Promise me that while you're here, you'll paint."

She smiled at him with such love that her heart actually hurt. "I'm here to spend time with you, Dad, not paint."

"There is nothing that would help me feel better than knowing you were doing something that gave you joy. Besides, there is only so much we can sit here and talk about. As much as I want to spend every moment I can with you, there are going to be times when I'm just not up for company, so I want you to use that time doing what makes you happy. Promise?"

"I promise."

———⁓———

Four hours later, Gina left the hospital. Her father had eaten an early, light dinner and she had placed a gentle kiss on his forehead as he dozed off. With paper in hand, she made the drive to his home to gather the items he had requested.

It felt weird to know she was driving to the house that belonged to her father and yet it was a place she had never seen. Once she had moved to California, Arthur had always come to visit her; her mother had never allowed her to come back to North Carolina. Gina had always hated that; there had been friends she would have liked to have seen and visited with over the years, but she had been forced to do it simply by phone or email. Arthur had sold their family home once his wife and daughter left, and Gina had no idea what kind of place he had moved to.

The house surprised Gina. It was a large Tudor set back on several acres of property. There were huge trees lining the long driveway, and it was immaculately landscaped. She parked and climbed out of the car. Her immediate impression was that this was a home that would be perfect for a family.

She used the keypad to enter the house and stepped into an enormous foyer. Immediately she kicked off her shoes, not wanting to mark up the beautiful hardwood floors. For the next several minutes she toured the main floor in wonder. Windows all along the back of the house looked out over a custom deck, a large expanse of green grass, and then ultimately a lake. The kitchen was modern with all top-of-the-line appliances.

Her father's room was right off of the family room. She took out the piece of paper he had given her and found most of the items on the list with relative ease. His room was filled with dark furniture, very masculine, but it really seemed to suit him. There were pictures of her scattered around the room from various stages of her life and it saddened her that this was how their relationship was: mostly a collection of photographs.

The last of the items he had said she'd find up on the second floor. Gina wondered why her father would choose such a large home when it was just him. Clearly he had to have a cleaning staff come in to maintain it all; it seemed a waste to have all of this room and no one to share it with.

At the foot of the stairs she stopped to compose herself; looking around, Gina knew she would have loved living in this house. Even now she knew she could easily pack up from the Montgomerys' guest home and stay here, but it didn't seem right. It was too late. All too soon, this home would not belong to her father. He would be gone, and it would be too hard to make any memories here without remembering all that she had lost.

Taking a fortifying breath, she headed up the curved staircase. There was a sitting area at the top of the stairs, and as she walked down the hallway, she counted five bedrooms. He'd told her there was a box in the bedroom at the end of the hall that had some things he wanted her to have. Gina had been curious what he could possibly have for her but had no idea what it could be.

Opening the door to the bedroom, she gasped. A look around the room had her placing a hand over her rapidly beating heart. It was the room of her dreams; it was the room that her father had set up for her but she had never been allowed to use. She cautiously stepped farther inside as tears rolled down her face.

Arthur couldn't fall asleep after Gina left. There were so many things he wanted to say to her, so much he wanted to apologize for and make up to her. Unfortunately, time was not on his side. He turned his head and caught a glimpse of something shiny. Gina had forgotten her cell phone. Reaching over, he picked it up and smiled. She may try to come off as conservative, but her bejeweled phone case showed a different side and it made him smile. There was hope for his daughter yet.

Without thinking, he reached for his own phone and dialed a familiar number. "Hey, it's Arthur," he said cheerily. "I need a favor…"

There were times when you had to do things you didn't want to do and you did them with a smile; then there were times you could bitch and grumble and be miserable. This was somewhere in between, Mac decided.

When Arthur had called to tell him that Gina had left her phone at the hospital and asked if Mac could bring it to her at his house, there was no way he could say no. With everything the man was going through, how could

Mac possibly complain about doing this small favor? So he'd left the office, driven the short distance to the hospital, and sat and visited with the man who'd always been like a beloved uncle to him.

Now Mac sat in his car in the driveway of Arthur's home and contemplated his options. He could easily put the phone in Gina's car and let her think it had slipped out of her purse, or he could knock on the door and have to see her face to face.

The images from the previous evening had kept him awake well into the night. Gina in a bikini, Gina laughing, Gina in the hot tub and in his lap… Just thinking about it even now was enough to make him hard. With a growl of frustration, Mac knew what he wanted to do, but he also knew what he needed to do.

"Dammit," he grumbled as he rose from the car and slammed the door. "If I make it through this, I should be given an award for restraint." He knocked on the front door but no one answered. He tested the knob and found it unlocked, so he let himself in. "Gina?" he called out. Silence. Calling her name several more times without getting a response, Mac felt a small wave of panic rising in him. Where was she? Why wasn't she answering? Had something happened to her?

He quickly walked through the entire lower level and then took the stairs two at a time, calling her name. "Gina!" At the top of the stairs he stopped and listened and finally heard a sound. He walked toward the end of the hall and stopped in the doorway. There, in the corner of the room and on the floor, sat Gina. Tears were streaming down her face and he rushed to her side. "Are you hurt?" he asked frantically, scanning her for any signs of injury.

Her sad green eyes met his. "He remembered everything," she said softly. "Every hobby I ever had, every interest I ever mentioned, he had in this room just waiting for me to come home." This brought on another wave of tears and Mac sat down beside her and pulled her into his arms. Gina burrowed into him and clung to him as if her life depended on it.

Mac searched his brain for what he could possibly say when Gina was so clearly distraught. So rather than talking about her father, he took another approach. "Tell me about your hobbies," he said softly.

Gina raised her head and looked at him as if she'd just realized he was truly there. "What are you doing here?" She started to wipe away her tears but Mac carefully pulled her hands away and did the job for her.

"You left your phone at the hospital," he said, mesmerized by the deep green of her eyes that were slowly starting to become addictive to him. "Your father called and asked me to bring it to you because he was concerned about you being alone without a way to call for help if you needed to."

"I didn't even realize."

Mac couldn't help staring at her while she was talking. If he leaned just a little closer, he could easily kiss her. He cleared his throat. "Did you have a lot of hobbies growing up?" he asked, breaking the spell.

Gina looked away and nodded. "I was always trying something new; most of the things I did made my mother crazy. She wanted a little porcelain doll for a daughter, someone to dress up in frilly dresses, who always looked neat and pristine. Instead she got me." She gave a small laugh. "She wanted me to play the piano and I took up guitar. I was really into painting, and so she wanted me to paint formal portraits and landscapes, and instead I was doing all kinds of abstract stuff. She wanted my hair straight and sleek, and it's a mess of curls." She stopped after that last comment and shrugged. "That wasn't about hobbies, but the sentiment is the same. I was never the daughter she wanted."

"Then she's a fool," Mac said firmly. "There is nothing wrong with you, Gina. Nothing." He placed a finger under her chin and forced her to look at him. "Those were her issues, not yours. Don't ever be sorry for being who you are."

"You sound just like my father."

"I'll take that as a compliment because he's a very smart man."

Gina smiled, removing herself from his loose embrace and standing. "He gave me a list of things that he wanted me to bring to him from the house. At the end of it was a box of stuff he said he wanted me to have. I came up here and it wasn't simply a box; it was a room." She walked around, clearly still in awe.

"He set up this room for *me*," she said as she continued to walk and touch. "There are paint supplies in the closet to use with this easel set up by the window. He must have bought every size of canvas available so I'd have a selection. There's a guitar over there." She nodded her head toward the far corner of the room. "I went through a cowboy phase and there, on top of that wardrobe, is a selection of cowboy hats." Gina pulled one down, put it on, and posed for Mac, then giggled. "It was silly and just a phase, but he remembered." She placed the hat on the bed.

"I took a photography class during my sophomore year of high school, right before we moved; there are three different cameras on this shelf. He remembered authors I loved and kept up with their titles. There's even a collection of teen movies from the eighties because he remembered how much I enjoyed them. They're all on DVD and Blu-ray, so he's been doing this recently." She looked around the room as tears welled up again. "All those years I wasn't allowed to come home and he was doing all of this for me. I was such a brat and thought that he didn't care, and yet he did all of this."

"You weren't being a brat, Gina. You were a child who was put in the middle of a really sucky situation. How could you know that he was doing all of this for you? Why didn't he just bring these things to you or send them to you as gifts?"

"My mother would have had a fit."

Mac stood and began to pace. He remembered Gina's mother; she wasn't the warm and fuzzy type. Arthur would always play games with Mac and his brothers, but Barbara Micelli looked at them like they were nuisances; she didn't want to interact with them and she certainly never did more than tolerate their presence for very short amounts of time. "Then shame on her," he said roughly. "You were a child and you were entitled to do things that you enjoyed doing. That's not a crime. What she did to you? Now that was a crime."

"She was angry and hurt—"

"And it had nothing to do with you!" he interrupted. "If she wanted to be angry with your father for whatever she deemed his faults to be, that's one thing, but to take

it out on you is irresponsible." He almost kicked himself when he saw Gina wince. She was upset enough
and didn't need him yelling at her for things that were
beyond her control.

He took a deep, steadying breath before speaking
again. "So, what are you going to do with this stuff? We
can move some of it over to the guesthouse if you'd like."

She looked at him in surprise. "Seriously? You'd
help me do that?"

"Of course," he said simply. "I think we can bring
the easel and the paints and maybe just a couple of the
canvases to start. Then we can take the guitar and the
cameras…" He looked around the room. "It looks like
that's a fairly new laptop over there, and he's probably
loaded it with photo-editing software so we can set up a
workspace for you. There's plenty of room."

"You don't think your parents will mind?"

Mac laughed. "Are you kidding me? They would
be thrilled to know you are using the space and doing
something you enjoy. Plus, you know your father would
love knowing you're using his gifts."

Apparently unable to speak, she simply nodded
and began to collect some art supplies. Together they
worked in silence to get the things that she wanted down
the stairs and into their cars. Thirty minutes later, it was
dark out and they were ready to go.

"Have you eaten dinner?" he asked as they stood in
the driveway.

She looked at her watch. "Goodness, no. I didn't even
realize how late it was! I'm so sorry! You must have
missed dinner too!"

"Not a problem. We did pizza last night so why

don't I grab us some burgers and meet you back at the guesthouse?"

"Are you sure? I feel bad about stealing two of your evenings. I'm sure you have better things to do than babysit me."

With another woman, Mac might have thought that she was fishing for compliments, but he knew Gina was genuinely concerned about being a burden. He could smack both of her parents for making her feel that way. "You aren't stealing my evenings. If anything, you're saving me from myself."

"What exactly does that mean?"

He smiled and walked over to his car. "We'll discuss it over dinner." Opening the door, he climbed in and turned the key. He lowered the window as he was about to pull away. "I'll meet you there in about thirty minutes. Don't move anything without me."

And then he was gone.

When Gina arrived back at the guesthouse, she did not unload the car. Much. She carried one box with her as she went inside and then screamed at her own reflection. No wonder the man didn't kiss her; she looked like some sort of deranged lunatic with raccoon eyes! "What man in his right mind would want to kiss that?" she said with disgust. She washed her face and brushed her teeth and grabbed a clip for her hair. Knowing that her chances with Mac were growing dimmer by the second, Gina decided maybe luck just wasn't on her side and this was never meant to be. She was used to disappointments; this would just be one more to add to the list.

She walked into the bedroom to change into a pair of yoga pants and an oversized T-shirt. Her feet were bare and the only makeup she put on was a little bit of lip gloss. The night was a total loss, so she might as well be comfortable.

Before long, she heard a knock on the French doors and yelled for Mac to come in. Her first thought had been to set everything up for them to eat outside as they had the previous evening, but that seemed like too much effort. She was physically and emotionally wrung out for the second night in a row. Simplicity was better.

"I hope you don't mind eating in here," she said as she set up paper plates and napkins on a coffee table in the small living room area. Then, reaching into the small box she had carried in, she fished around until she found what she was looking for and popped a disc in the DVD player.

Mac watched the opening credits of *The Breakfast Club* for a moment in silence. "Are you all right?" he finally asked as he placed their bag of food down on the table. "I mean, I know I kind of invited myself over but if you'd rather be alone, I can take my share of the food and go." His tone indicated he was simply offering her an out if she truly didn't want him there.

"What? No. Why would you even think that?"

Mac reached for the remote and shut off the television. "We don't need to have the TV on while we eat, for starters. I don't know about you, but I kind of enjoy talking with you. You asked me a question before we left your father's place and I thought we were going to talk about it when I got here."

Gina's shoulders relaxed from their stiff and defensive position. "I enjoy talking with you too. I just feel bad about monopolizing your time."

"Ah," he said with a chuckle as he began to dole out their food. "I believe that was where we left off."

They sat on the floor and feasted on cheeseburgers and fries and milk shakes. Gina was in junk food heaven! If they kept up this pace, she'd gain ten pounds before going back home. She wasn't going to focus on that tonight, however. Tonight was about relaxing with a friend—a friend she wanted to be much more with, but clearly that wasn't on the agenda.

"So how am I saving you from yourself?" she asked before indulging in her chocolate milk shake.

Mac shared how his father was concerned about his work habits, and how his brothers had all been like him at one point and now had wives to go home to. "I used to pick on Jason for being such a workaholic, but my dad swears that I put him to shame with my hours."

Gina nodded in understanding. "I work a lot too. Do you like what you do?"

Now Mac nodded. "I love what I do and working with my father and brothers really isn't a hardship. I love being able to put my ideas out there, knowing that if they're good, I'll get honest feedback, and if they're bad, no one is going to hold back."

"That must be wonderful. I hate my job. It's boring and not particularly challenging."

"So why don't you quit?"

Gina shrugged. "I don't know what else I'd do."

"Anything you want, I'd imagine. You're an

intelligent woman; I'm sure you'd be an asset no matter where you went."

She beamed under his kind words and she could only hope that he truly meant them. "So what do you do in your spare time?"

Mac laughed. "That's the problem. I don't seem to have any. I work all the time. That's why my father has been after me. He wants me to find a hobby or something to do that isn't work related, or he's going to make me take a leave of absence."

Gina almost choked on her fries. "He can't make you do that, can he?"

"He's the boss; he can do whatever he wants."

"So I'm saving you by…?"

"Making sure that I have something to do and leaving the office while the sun is still out." He took a bite of his burger. "It's not as painful as I thought it would be."

"I'm sure your father's heart is in the right place and that you'll find something to do that relaxes you and brings you joy." Gina looked around the room. "My father asked me to paint while I'm here. I'm trying to figure out where the best place would be to set up."

They finished their meal and began bringing the supplies in from the cars. Mac did all of the carrying while Gina told him where to set everything up. The guitar went into the bedroom along with the cowboy hats. The cameras and laptop went on the coffee table, and Mac set up her easel and paints next to a large window that overlooked his mother's garden. The room was large enough for all of the supplies without overwhelming the space, and once everything was inside and set up, they stood back and admired their handiwork.

"Thank you, Mac," she said with a smile. "I couldn't have done this without you." Gina stood on tiptoe to kiss him on the cheek at the same time Mac turned his head to look at her. Their lips met and held for just a second before his arm snaked around her and pulled her flush against him.

———∼∼∼———

His lips sipped from hers gently at first, as if testing her response, until her arms came up and wrapped around his neck with a soft whimper. Next thing Mac knew, he was devouring her. His tongue licked at her bottom lip as she opened for him. It was all heat and passion and wildness; their tongues were tentative at first, but then they settled in as if they'd kissed a thousand times before. Mac pulled his mouth from hers and kissed her cheek, her jaw, and then her throat. Gina threw her head back, and Mac reached up and pulled the clip from her hair, letting those luxurious curls flow over his hands. The feel of the silky tresses was as erotic as he'd imagined.

She whispered his name and raked her fingers through his hair to hold him to her. "Mac, please," she said and did her best to get even closer to him. She felt the evidence of his arousal, but just as she was mentally congratulating herself on finally getting the man to notice her, he released her and turned away.

It took a moment for Gina to catch her breath. She reached out and touched Mac's shoulder but he flinched and took a step farther away from her. "Mac?"

When he finally turned, his expression was one of cool indifference. "I'm sorry. That shouldn't have happened."

She hated that phrase. Why did men feel the need to use that as their go-to line? "Really? Why not?"

Mac kept his face neutral; if Gina had any idea how much he had wanted that to happen and more, she'd be shocked. "You're a family friend and you're here to visit your ailing father. The last thing you need is someone mauling you when you were simply offering a small kiss of gratitude. I'm sorry. It won't happen again." There. He'd said it. Mac was known for his iron-clad control, so he had no doubt that he could pull this off.

"What if I want it to happen again?" she asked defiantly. "What if I want that to happen…and more?"

"It's not going to happen, Gina. It can't."

"So you've said," she snapped. "I'm a grown woman, Mackenzie. And for the record, you weren't mauling me. I don't need you getting all righteous and whatnot. I knew what I was doing and I know what I want. I don't see why, if we're both attracted to one another, we can't explore that while I'm here."

He raked a hand through his hair. This was not going the way he had planned. She was supposed to be grateful to him for showing some self-control—they would agree that it was a mistake and he'd be on his way. Why was she tempting him with things he couldn't have?

"Gina, you can't stand there and tell me that you honestly think it's okay for us to have a short-term affair while you're in town. That's crazy."

"Why?" she demanded. "Why is it crazy? Do you have long-lasting relationships with all of the women you date?" His lack of response said it all. "That's what I thought. So tell me why this would be so different?"

She was going to keep poking at him until he gave her a response, so he gave her one that was certain to stop her in her tracks. "Because you're Arthur's daughter!"

he yelled. "Your father is like an uncle to me. We grew up together, and I am not so self-centered that I would sleep with you while you're in town because your father is dying! I'm not that much of a bastard, no matter what people may think!"

Gina could only stare at him for a long time, and when she finally spoke, it was with a level of calmness that she really didn't feel. "Okay. I didn't realize that you felt that way, and I'm sorry if I've put you in an awkward position. It won't happen again." She looked around the room again. "If you don't mind, I think I'll watch that movie now, and I'd like to check out some of the photography software. Thank you again, for helping me get all of my things over here."

He was being dismissed, and as much as he wanted to tell her that it was all a lie and that he wanted her, he knew that she needed more. Hell, everyone knew that she needed and deserved someone better than him. His father had been right when he'd said that Mac didn't have staying power.

It just had never bothered him until now.

Chapter 5

FOUR DAYS LATER, GINA WAS STANDING AT HER EASEL painting. She had gone through half of the canvases they had brought over as she tried to find her muse. She considered what she'd done so far: there was a landscape of Monica's garden, a still life with the requisite bowl of fruit, and numerous random abstracts. And then there was what she was working on now, a semi-abstract portrait of a man with an intense gaze and short hair who looked ready to jump right off the canvas at her.

Mac.

She painted him as she saw him most in her mind, looking like he wanted to devour her.

They hadn't seen or spoken to each other since he'd left that night, and Gina found that she missed him. Not just his physical, sexy presence, but their conversations. Now, when she wasn't at the hospital with her father, she was familiarizing herself with her passions. Music was playing in the background and she swayed in time with it as she painted. She was wearing one of her cowboy hats, a pair of shorts, and a tank top. She had actually gone to the craft store and bought herself a smock to protect her clothing. It was now covered in paint, so Gina considered that money well spent.

With a final stroke of her brush, she added a touch of red behind the painted man's head and smiled at the finished product. It was good. It was more than good.

It was possibly one of the best pieces she'd ever done. Stepping back, she studied it and then headed to the kitchen to pour herself a glass of wine. The sun was setting, and Gina decided that after a quick shower, she'd heat herself up some dinner and maybe go soak in the hot tub to ease her sore muscles. Standing up for so long while painting was hell on her body.

She showered and threw on a pair of panties and a ribbed tank; the hot shower had eased some of her tension, so she might not need the hot tub. She was heating up her dinner when her phone rang. She looked at the screen and groaned. Her mother was calling.

"Gina, sweetheart," her mother began, "aren't you done in North Carolina yet? You really should be back home. I'm sure your bosses are not happy with you being away for so long."

She sighed. "They are fine with me being away, Mom. I told them, just like I told you, that I'd be gone a couple of weeks. I've only been gone one."

"Don't argue with me, Gina. Your job is important. Surely by now you've had a chance to visit with your father. What more can you possibly do?"

Reaching for her wineglass, she took a long drink and then refilled it before answering. "I'm here to spend time with him. He's dying. Can't you even be gracious enough to understand that we'd want to spend time together?"

"Please, you are always so dramatic. Lord knows where you get that from," her mother said bitterly. "It would have been nice if he'd spent time with you *before* he found out he was dying."

Gina wanted to reach through the phone and slap her

mother. "How dare you!" she snapped. "How could he spend time with me when you did everything you possibly could to keep that from happening?"

"Is that what he told you? Because he's lying. Your father is a liar, Gina!"

"No, that's not what he told me; that's what I know. I wasn't a child when we moved away, Mom. I was a teenager, old enough to know what was going on. I know you did everything you could to make him pay for not being who you wanted him to be. You used me to get even with him. Well, you can't do that anymore. I'm here in North Carolina, and I don't know when I'll be home."

Her mother sputtered. "You can't do that! Think about your job, your commitments—"

"Right now the only commitment I have is to spend time with Dad, and if you don't like that, then it's too bad. It's not your decision to make."

"Gina, be reasonable! After all these years and all I've sacrificed for you—"

"Sacrificed? Are you kidding me? I was the one who had to sacrifice! I had to leave my father and my friends and my school and everything I loved to move to the other side of the country! You started up a whole new life and didn't care about how you ruined mine!" Gina had no idea what had spurred this act of bravery on her part, but it certainly felt good.

"And this is why I didn't want you spending time with your father; he's poisoned you against me! You never spoke like this before…you are being highly disrespectful and I demand an apology."

Gina laughed. It wasn't a cheery laugh, but one

filled with disbelief. "You can demand all you want but you are not going to get your way. I'm here and I'm not sure when I'll be home." Before her mother could interrupt, she added, "And as for my job, I'll deal with that as well. I'm a grown woman, and it's time you remembered that."

They were silent for long moments. Finally, Barbara cleared her throat. "Well, I guess that sums it all up, doesn't it? If that's what you feel you have to do, then fine; stay in North Carolina for however long you like. Just don't expect to lean on me when you come home and have no job. As you pointed out, you're a grown woman; I won't be supporting you."

Gina rolled her eyes and took another long drink of wine. "I don't believe I ever asked you to, but thanks for the reminder." She pulled her now-cooled dinner from the microwave and looked at it with disgust. "Look, let's just take some time to calm down. I'll call you next week, okay?"

For a minute, Gina didn't think her mother was even going to respond. Finally she said, "That's fine. We'll talk then." Gina wished her mother a good night and hung up. Carefully, she placed her phone down on the cool granite countertop and then walked to the center of the room and screamed. She screamed until she couldn't breathe and then she took a deep breath and screamed again. Luckily no one lived close by or they'd probably be calling the police, but right now that was the least of her problems.

She dropped to her knees and did her best to catch her breath. Why? Why did her mother have to make everything so complicated and why did Gina allow it for so long? It had felt so good to get those things off of her chest tonight, but now she worried about how long she would be punished for it. For too many years, Gina had sat back and let her mother make all of her decisions because it was easier than arguing with her, but now that she'd had a little taste of freedom, she knew that there was no way she could return to that way of living.

Rising to her feet, Gina went back to the kitchen and bypassed her dinner, instead pouring herself another glass of wine. With a grimace, she noticed that the bottle was empty.

The wine was making her more than a little tipsy, and she couldn't help but sway as she made her way to the stereo to turn the music back on. "Ooo…classic rock," she said with a giggle and began to sing along to Elton John's "Crocodile Rock." "Hear that, Mom?" she called out into the room. "I've got the music on way too loud and it's that rock 'n' roll you hate." That made her break out into a fit of giggles. Then, in another act of rebellion, she turned on the TV, hit the play button on the DVD player, and smiled at the beginning of *Say Anything*.

A look around the room a little too quickly made her dizzy. "I really should eat something," she mumbled, but her dinner was no longer what she wanted. She danced her way back into the kitchen, singing off-key. Rummaging through the cabinets, she found a pack of Oreos and grabbed a few, sighing at how good they tasted. "And I'm not eating a balanced diet either, how about that? I'm an adult, dammit! It's my life and from now on, I am going to do what I want. No one is going to tell me what to do, no one is going to bully me into being where I don't want to be, and if I want to have wine for dinner, then I damn well will!" She slammed the glass down on the counter and it shattered.

Gina cursed and made a feeble attempt to clean it up. The shards of glass cut her finger and she winced from the pain. Her finger was bleeding, so she carefully walked over to the sink to rinse it out and wrap it with a paper towel. She headed back to her bedroom in search of a Band-Aid. There was one small lamp lit, and she started to sway to the slow sounds of Rod Stewart. "Maybe I'll order a pizza," she said out loud, and looked around the room for her phone before remembering that it was back in the kitchen.

Turning too quickly, she banged her knee on the bedside table and cried out in pain.

And then she just began to cry.

If anyone had been there to ask, Gina knew she wouldn't have been able to put into words what the exact cause of her tears was. Maybe it was the pain from hurting her knee, maybe it was the fact that she was away from home and visiting her dying father, maybe it was because there wouldn't ever be enough time for them to make up for all the time they had lost. Or maybe, just maybe, it was because she knew deep down that she was never going to get her mother's approval no matter how hard she tried.

Gina collapsed onto the bed and curled up in the fetal position. She was a mess. None of this was fair. She had done everything she could to please her mother and yet nothing ever did. She had missed out on years with her father and now they weren't going to have even one more together. She didn't know who she was or where she belonged. Right now, Gina felt like a child who was completely alone in the world.

Turning her face in to the pillow, she cried harder.

—◇◇◇—

Mac slammed the car door and cursed. All he wanted was some peace and quiet, and to just have the final say in how he spent his time. Unfortunately, his father had called, found out that he was working late at the office, and reminded him of their deal.

Dammit.

When William had asked how Gina was doing, Mac told him that he hadn't seen her in days. Of course, he didn't elaborate on why he hadn't seen her, but his father had been incensed just the same. "Her father is dying and she has no one there to help her through this!" William had lectured. "I expected a little more from you, Mac. I thought I could trust you to make sure Gina was okay. Maybe your mother and I need to cut our trip short and come home."

Mac groaned. True, they were due back in three days, but he wouldn't be able to live with himself if he was the reason they had to come home. "That won't be necessary," he had assured his father. "I just thought that Gina might want a little time to herself. I didn't want her to feel like we were watching over her as if we were afraid she was going to steal the family silver or something."

They had argued a little more and in the end, Mac had promised his father that he'd leave the office immediately and go and check on her. So here he was, in his parents' driveway against his will, going to see a woman who he both dreaded seeing and yet couldn't wait to feast his eyes on.

The first thing he noticed as he approached the guest-house was that all of the lights were on and there was music playing. He knocked on the door and waited. And waited. And waited. Trying the doorknob, he found it to be unlocked and cursed. Didn't the woman ever lock a door? "Gina?" he called out with a sense of déjà vu. He stepped inside and took a look around the room. There was no sign of her.

Mac walked over to the paintings lined up against the wall and admired her work. He could clearly pick out his mother's garden and the view of the sunrise coming through the French doors. He smiled at her abstracts and then turned to the easel and stopped.

It was him.

Gina had painted him.

Why?

He stood there for countless minutes, staring at his own face, in awe of her talent. If this was what she could do after not picking up a paintbrush in years, how much better would she be if she were allowed to do this all the time? Mac pulled his gaze away from her paintings and scanned the room. The stereo was on and so was the TV. "*Say Anything*?" Mac murmured. "What the hell is that?" He turned off the television, DVD player, and stereo.

Upon further inspection of the room, he noticed that there was a plate of food on the kitchen counter with a stack of cookies next to it. He walked over and jumped as he heard glass crunching under his feet. He thought he saw blood on the broken glass and felt a wave of panic begin to wash over him.

"What the…?" he muttered and took a closer look

around the room. Something was wrong. "Gina?" he called out again, suddenly nervous. "This isn't funny, dammit."

He strode down the hall to the bedroom and stopped dead in his tracks. The lights were dim and there, sprawled on her belly across the bed, in a tiny pair of navy-blue panties and a tight, white tank top, lay Gina. Her hair was fanned out beside her, one leg was bent, and the overall view was spectacular.

"Gina? Are you okay? I'm sorry for walking out on you the other night; I was wrong. I can't fight this anymore," he said to her as he walked farther into the room. "I know I said that it couldn't happen again, but I'm just not strong enough to resist you, Gina." And the truth was that he had known it all along. Somehow, from the first moment he'd seen her in the airport, Mac had been drawn to her, and it was only fitting that he finally admit to it and enjoy it. Mac was standing next to the bed and heard Gina's shuddering sigh.

She was asleep.

Here he was thinking he was coming clean, and she didn't even know he was here. He brushed her hair back from her face and felt her forehead, and she stirred and sighed. Her face was wet with tears. He looked around at the tissues scattered on the bed and on the floor—some of them had blood on them. Stepping away from the bed, he walked back to the kitchen where he noticed the empty bottle of wine on the counter. What the hell had gone on here?

Gina's phone was on the counter, and he didn't think twice about picking it up and seeing if she had maybe gotten a call from the hospital about her father. He scrolled and saw that the only call she had received

today was from her mother. From everything Gina had
shared with him, he knew that it was completely plau-
sible that there had been some sort of argument that led
to her being upset.

He just couldn't imagine what could have possibly
been said to make Gina *this* upset. Placing the phone
back on the counter, Mac walked back to the bedroom
and looked at the woman who was slowly working her
way into his life, his mind, and his heart. It angered
him that anyone would upset her to this point, and he
couldn't remember the last time he had felt this protec-
tive about a woman.

Gently, he checked her over but other than a cut on
her finger, she seemed okay. Except for being out cold.
He moved her gently so that he could get the blankets
pulled up over her, then sighed and went about cleaning
up the place. By the time he had cleaned the mess in the
kitchen, it was nearing eleven. He suspected Gina was
going to be feeling like hell come morning. He could
only hope that she would simply sleep it off. He knew
he should leave.

Mac stood in the door of the bedroom and thought
about it. There was a large chaise lounge in the corner
of the room and Mac kicked off his shoes, removed his
tie, unbuttoned his shirt, and made himself comfortable.
Whatever it was that had happened, he didn't want Gina
to wake up alone—especially if she was sick.

With the lights off and only the glow of the moon
coming through the windows, Mac let himself relax. He
had known when he'd driven over earlier that he wasn't
going home tonight; he had just hoped that meant he
wasn't sleeping alone. Or sleeping at all, for that matter.

This was new territory for him, and as much as he wanted to obsess about it and come up with a plan for how it was all going to pan out, he realized he was far more exhausted than he had thought.

The woman was tiring as hell and all she'd done was pass out before he could get to her.

He could only imagine what she was going to be like once she was awake.

Chapter 6

WHOEVER WAS POUNDING ON THE DOOR WAS GOING TO get an earful. Gina slowly rolled onto her back and stretched, wondering who would be knocking on the door at…well, she wasn't ready to open her eyes to see exactly what time it was, but she was sure it was an ungodly hour.

Several things occurred to her at once: she didn't remember crawling under the blankets, the pounding wasn't someone at the door but going on in her head, and the room was spinning. "Crap," she mumbled and placed both of her hands on her head in hopes of making the spinning stop. "Crap, crap, crap…"

And that's when she heard the chuckle.

Glancing in between the fingers that were now shielding her eyes from the light, she saw Mac standing in the corner of the room. "What are you doing here?" she asked, her voice raw and scratchy.

Mac stretched and walked to the side of the bed. "I came to check on you last night and found you passed out cold. I cleaned up the broken glass and threw out the uneaten food, and figured there'd be a good chance of you not feeling so hot either overnight or this morning. I wanted to make sure that you were okay."

She should have been touched by his considerateness, but right now it just pissed her off. He was here to babysit her. Again. He hadn't come here because of the kiss the other night; he hadn't come because he was going crazy without her; he was here because he felt obligated to check on her. That thought made her frown, and frowning caused her head to throb even more. "Fabulous," she grumbled and kicked the blankets off, heedless of the fact that she was half-naked.

When she sat up too quickly, she groaned and then almost punched Mac when she heard him chuckle again. Without opening her eyes, she heard him leave the room and breathed a sigh of relief. Her throat was dry and her tongue felt like it was the size of her fist. Why did she even think drinking so much wine on an empty stomach was a good idea? That's what she got for being rebellious.

Gina did her best to pry her eyes open and there, standing before her in all of his bare-chested glory, stood Mac. He had a glass of water in one hand and held the other out toward her. She saw the ibuprofen tablets and greedily reached for them. He handed her the water and she drank the entire glass down as if she'd been walking in the desert for days. "Thank you."

Mac helped her to her feet and she stumbled into him. When her hand touched his chest, she stopped and leaned her head against him, waiting for the spinning to stop. Well, that and she really wanted to touch him. She must be a glutton for punishment. "Are you okay?" he whispered.

Rather than answer or even look at him, Gina forced herself to move. Doing her best to focus on taking one step at a time, she walked away from where she most wanted to be and headed toward the bathroom to try and put herself back together again. Mac didn't speak or follow, and she didn't look back at him. Gingerly closing the door behind her, Gina merely groaned at her appearance. Her hair was wild, her eyes were puffy, and basically the only thing she had to be grateful for was the fact that she had already washed her makeup off before her crying jag, because otherwise she was certain she'd look like a hungover drag queen.

It was no wonder Mac had no trouble staying away from her; every time he saw her it seemed like she was a wreck of some kind. Refusing to let her mind go there right now, she did her best to start to feel more human again. The cold water on her face had the desired effect of waking her up, and brushing her teeth made her able to swallow without grimacing. They were baby steps, but she'd take them. Her robe was back in the bedroom so she had no choice but to walk back out there in her underwear and hope that Mac had had the decency to leave.

He hadn't.

She found him placing a cup of tea on the night stand, waiting for her return. As she approached, she refused to make eye contact with him. When Gina sat back down on the bed, she noticed the plate of toast beside the tea. "Thank you," she said quietly and reached for the steaming mug first. The first sip was heavenly, and she twisted around so that she was reclining against the pillows that Mac had stacked for her.

Why did he have to be considerate on top of everything else? And why wouldn't he just leave? The last thing Gina wanted was an audience to her pathetic life. "As you can tell, I'm not going to be sick. I feel like hell but other than that, I'm fine. I'm sure you need to get to work, so please don't feel like you need to stay and babysit."

He walked around the side of the bed and sat down

beside her. He stretched out his feet and stacked his hands behind his head on the pillow, not looking at her either. "Want to talk about it?" he asked casually.

"About what?" Gina placed the mug down and reached for the toast.

"About whatever it was that had you so upset last night?"

She finished the half slice of toast before answering him. How could she possibly explain what she didn't understand herself? "How do you know I don't binge every night?" she snapped and when he looked at her with disbelief, she plunged ahead. "Don't worry, it wasn't about you."

He gave a mirthless laugh. "I didn't think that it was, but thanks for the ego boost." Mac turned his head toward her. "Seriously, what happened?"

Why wouldn't he just leave? Why did he have to now be lying beside her, his shirt unbuttoned and revealing a very well-muscled chest that she wanted to lay her head down on until her world was okay again? "My mother called. We argued. I drank more than I should on an empty stomach. End of story."

—◦◦◦—

Mac stared at her. She still wouldn't meet his eyes. There was more to it than that simple explanation. "Really?" he asked.

Gina finally looked at him, her face full of defiance. "Yes, really. Now you've done your good deed for the day and you can leave."

He tensed at her dismissal, and although he wanted to lash out, he knew that wasn't what Gina needed right now, and she was all that mattered. "I saw your paint-ings. You've been busy."

She paled. "So…what, you came over, let yourself in, and then snooped around?"

"The door was unlocked, the music was playing, there was a movie on the television, every light in the place was on, and the paintings are right out there in the middle of the room. That's hardly snooping."

"Don't you have someplace to be?" she moaned. "I mean really, aren't you a workaholic or something?"

"I'm taking the morning off."

She eyed him suspiciously. "Your father found out you were working late, and that's why you came over and why you can't go into work this morning. That's it, isn't it?"

He smiled sheepishly. "That's part of it, but that doesn't change the fact that I want to be here."

"Why?" she asked with a dramatic sigh. "Is it enter-taining for you to watch a train wreck?"

"You're not a train wreck, Gina; you're someone who is going through a tough time right now. We're friends, right? I just wanted to make sure that you're okay."

From the look on Gina's face, Mac was sure he'd said something wrong. Why didn't women come with a manual? He thought he was being a good guy, and it pissed her off. He thought he was being a good son by working hard, and it pissed his father off. Hell, it seemed like no matter what he did, someone was pissed off at him! He was just about to rant about it but noticed a single tear slowly making its way down Gina's cheek.

At thirty-five, Mac had thought he was immune to a woman's tears. At this stage in his life, he thought he was okay with being alone. Somehow, over the last week, his time with Gina had changed him. Back when they were growing up, he really hadn't paid much attention to her; she was the very young daughter of his father's friend. But now? Her parentage hadn't changed, but he couldn't seem to make himself *stop* paying attention to her.

Mac turned on his side and reached out to cup Gina's face so that she was forced to look at him. His dark gaze met hers and he wiped that single tear away with the pad of his thumb. "I hate to see you cry," he said, his voice a deep whisper. "I hate to think of anyone upsetting you, and more than anything, I hate to think that I can't make it better."

Gina was taken aback by his words. Never in her life had anyone wanted to defend her or even seemed to care about the things that had hurt her. She leaned her cheek into his large hand, closed her eyes, and sighed. It was a good feeling. The skin of his palm was rough—he had the hands of a man who wasn't afraid to do a hard day's work.

"If you really want me to leave, I'll go," he said softly, leaning toward her. "But I'd really like to stay."

She reached for him, and at first he just took her in his arms and held her. She nestled against that broad chest, closing her eyes and savoring his warmth and the scent of his skin. Maybe she even dozed for a while, so safe did she feel. When she opened her eyes, it was the most natural thing in the world to turn her face up to his. She knew he was about to kiss her, but that didn't stop her from holding her breath in anticipation. Mac's lips were soft and gentle on hers, taking the time to simply place tiny kisses on her lips, her jaw, and her cheek. He rested his cheek against hers and simply let the skin-on-skin sensation wash over him. His breath was hot on her ear as he said, "I never should have left the other night. I thought I was doing the right thing, but the truth is, I wanted to stay then, just like I want to stay now." He pulled back and waited until Gina opened her eyes. "Ask me to stay."

A shy smile crossed her lips and she blushed. "Stay with me."

━━━

No three words had ever had a more powerful effect.

What had been gentle before was now heated; what was sweet was now frantic. Mac rolled Gina under him and growled at the feel of her curvy body underneath his. Her scantily clad, curvy body. How had he managed to lie beside her when she wore little more than her underwear? How had he been able to sit and have casual conversation when there was more of her golden skin bared to him than was hidden?

As close as they were, he wanted to be closer. It was torture to take his mouth from hers, but he straddled her hips, sat up to take his shirt off, and then dove back over her. The feel of her breasts pressed against his chest was sexy as hell, and he was just settling back in with a kiss so hot that his skin felt scorched when he felt Gina push at his shoulders.

"Mac," she sighed, tearing her mouth from his. He pulled back and looked at her, his breathing ragged. Gina could see the heat and the uncertainty in his gaze, like he was afraid she was going to tell him to stop. Without breaking eye contact, Gina sat up and slowly crossed her arms in front of herself before lifting the tank top over her head. She didn't think Mac's gaze could get any darker, but the sight of her bared for him did just that.

She offered him another smile and reached out and raked her fingers through his hair. Leaning forward until her mouth was a breath away from his, she simply said, "Stay with me."

The feeling of Gina's breath on his chest and her head on his shoulder was something that Mac knew he could become addicted to. Hours had gone by, and in that time, he had explored every inch of her body. She was wrapped around him now, both of them near exhaustion, and yet as her hand gently explored his chest, Mac knew he was more than willing to go another round.

He pulled her closer and sighed with contentment as he placed a kiss on top of her head. "Why did you come here last night?" Gina asked quietly. "Was it only because your father asked you to?"

Mac chuckled lightly. "That was what I was telling myself, but the truth was I couldn't stay away. I didn't want to. Ever since I left here that night, I've been making myself crazy trying to stay away."

She pulled back and looked at him. "You didn't have to stay away, Mac. I told you that."

He trailed a finger down her cheek to her chin. "I didn't want to feel like I was taking advantage of you. You're dealing with so much now, and I didn't want you to feel like I was...I don't know...using that to my advantage."

Gina laughed. "But that's crazy! You weren't taking

advantage of me; I wanted you just as much as you wanted me." Her gaze darkened as a sexy smile played at her mouth. "I still want you." She bent down and kissed her way across his chest, enjoying his sharp intake of breath. "I've always wanted you." There were a million thoughts racing through Mac's head, many things he wanted to say, and yet the sight of her beautiful face simply staggered him. He hadn't realized he had said the words out loud until she reached up and caressed his face. "No one's ever told me that I'm beautiful."

"You are. When I saw you in the airport, I was mesmerized by you. I had no idea who you were, but I couldn't take my eyes off of you." He leaned down and placed a kiss on her forehead. "I still can't."

Gina began to shift underneath him to better align their bodies. "I don't want you to take your eyes, or anything else for that matter, off of me."

And then she kissed him.

Chapter 7

"ARE YOU SURE THEY AREN'T GOING TO MIND?" GINA asked, fidgeting with her skirt, her hair, her necklace… anything she could get her hands on. She and Mac were on the walk in front of the home of Mac's brother Lucas and his wife, Emma.

"The whole family is going to be here and you were invited. Of course they aren't going to mind."

"But it's a family thing, Mac."

Reaching for her hand, Mac gave it a gentle squeeze. "Gina, relax. You are like family to us. Lucas is excited to see you, and Emma can't wait to meet you. It's all okay."

Then the door opened, and there stood Lucas with a big grin on his face. He pulled Gina into his embrace, lifting her off her feet and spinning her around.

"It is so good to see you!" Lucas said. "I'm sorry for the circumstances that brought you here, but Emma and I are thrilled that you're here with all of us today."

He put her down and gave Mac a quick hug before ushering Gina inside to greet the rest of the family. Mac stood in the doorway, unsure of what he was supposed to do. It had been three days since he and Gina had first made love and no one knew about the change in their relationship. As far as everyone was concerned, he had just offered to drive her over for the family barbecue. He wasn't ashamed of their relationship, but he wasn't sure he was ready to let everyone know either. What he and Gina shared was private.

And incredible.

Just thinking about the last couple of nights was almost enough to make him blush. Gina was his every fantasy as well as being a kind and considerate friend. He loved talking with her and hearing about her day. She spent a great deal of time at the hospital and seemed to be reconnecting well with her father. She and Mac talked a lot about her relationship with her parents, and he found he never knew what to expect when he showed up at the guesthouse.

Music was always playing and her taste was quite eclectic; one time she'd be listening to seventies rock, the next night it was Motown. The Jackson Five were her personal favorite, but then he'd find her with head-banging metal on five minutes later. She wore cowboy hats and yet hated country music. He smiled at the image of her wearing nothing but a cowboy hat last night while they made love in the hot tub.

"Mac? Are you going to join us?" he heard Emma call from the next room. He loved his family and spending time with them, but right now he'd rather have Gina all to himself instead of sitting through an afternoon with everyone.

In the kitchen, Mac found his parents—his mother holding Lily—Jason and Maggie, and then he saw Lucas and Emma talking with Gina. Lucas had his arm around Gina and even though Mac knew it didn't mean anything, he still wanted to go and push his brother aside and be the one holding her. The thought of any man with his hands on Gina filled him with a rage he hadn't known he possessed.

"What are you scowling about? Surely you aren't

mad that your brother invited Gina over, are you?" Mac turned his head and saw his father standing beside him.

"What? No. What made you think that?"

"Well, the way you're looking at them, for starters."

"No, it's not that. I was distracted, that's all."

"If you tell me you're thinking about work, I'm not going to be happy. You know that, right?"

Mac nodded. "So how was your trip?"

"Nice change of subject," his father chuckled. "Listen, I was thinking, I hate for Gina to spend so much of her time at the hospital and then home alone. I know she's only here for a short time but I'm thinking of setting her up with—"

"I told you not to play matchmaker with us, Dad," Mac growled so that only his father could hear.

William looked at his son with indignation. "And I already told you that I wouldn't do that. No, I was thinking of asking Todd from Operations to take her out. He's a great guy and I trust him. Maybe I'll set them up with tickets to a show or something. You've spent some time with Gina; do you think she'd be open to something like that?"

Mac stared at his father with disbelief. Was he crazy? Setting Gina up with a total stranger? What was the matter with him? "Don't you think you're being a little presumptuous? I mean, wouldn't it make more sense for you to maybe get Emma or Maggie to go out with her for one of those girls' night things?"

William appeared to consider Mac's suggestion. "I suppose I could plant the idea with the girls and see what happens, but I think Gina would appreciate a night out with a nice guy. I think Arthur would approve."

Unable to speak freely in the middle of the kitchen, Mac pulled his father into the living room before responding. When they were alone, however, he let it all out. "Don't you think it's a little rude to be pimping Gina out? I mean, who put you in charge of her social life? If she wanted to go out on a date, she is more than capable of doing that on her own! She's had her mother making all of her decisions for her and her father sitting back letting it happen; she certainly doesn't need you joining in on it!" His tone was low but intense, and by the look on his father's face, Mac knew he sounded a bit unreasonable.

"First of all, I don't think I'm 'pimping Gina out.' Secondly, I was just trying to make sure she didn't spend all of her time sitting vigil by her father's bed. I know that her mother is a control freak; I don't think what I was considering is the same thing."

"Well, it is," Mac snapped. "Let Gina be the one to decide when and where and *who* she wants to go out with. She doesn't need any more people controlling her social life."

"I still think that Todd would be a good choice," William said.

"Todd is a kiss-ass and a complete tech-geek. Gina would have nothing in common with him."

"Opposites attract," William countered. "I'll talk to her about it but leave the decision completely up to her." And with that, he turned and strode away to rejoin his family, leaving Mac fuming.

When Mac joined them several minutes later, his anger had simmered down to a low boil. Everyone was laughing and smiling. Lucas was taking a platter piled with steaks out to the barbecue and Jason was following. Rather than get sucked into another awkward conversation with his father, who was now cooing at Lily, he decided to join his brothers out on the deck.

"Everything okay?" Lucas asked as he opened the massive grill and began placing the steaks on it. "You and Dad looked pretty intense in there."

Mac took the beer Jason was holding out to him. "Yeah, sure, everything's fine. He wants to set Gina up with Todd in Operations." Lucas and Jason exchanged looks and then smiled. "What? What was that about?" he asked, gesturing between the two of them.

"What's it to you if he sets Gina up with Todd? He seems to be a decent guy," Jason said.

Lucas nodded in agreement. "Plus, I'm sure it might be nice for her to go out a bit while she's here. It can't be easy being away from home and spending all of her time at the hospital, watching her father's health deteriorate."

Mac huffed impatiently. "She doesn't spend *all* of her time at the hospital," he told them. "She's painting and playing guitar and learning about photography!" He explained to his brothers about the room Arthur had set up for his daughter. "So you see, she's not sitting around bored; there's no reason for Dad to be setting her up on dates."

Jason took a long pull from his beer and then, with a straight face, turned to Mac. "You look real pretty when you pout like that. Anyone ever tell you that?" Lucas burst out laughing and Jason took a step back as Mac lunged for him. "What?" Jason said, leaping just out of Mac's grip. "It was a compliment!"

"Screw you," Mac muttered as he turned and pulled out a chair from the large redwood set on the deck.

"What is your problem?" Jason asked.

"Right now? You!"

Jason turned to Lucas and shrugged. Lucas lowered the flame on the grill, picked up his beer, and joined his brother at the table. "Clearly something is bugging you. Now, you can simply tell us what it is, or I can guarantee that we're going to spend the entire day ragging on you. It's your choice, bro."

Mac threw his head back and sighed. "Look, I've spent some time with Gina at Dad's insistence and I just know that having people setting her up or making decisions for her is a real sore point."

"So you're concerned about Gina," Jason said diplomatically, and Mac nodded.

"Or," Lucas said, dragging the word out, "are you concerned that Dad is playing matchmaker again and you don't approve of who he's setting her up with?"

Mac considered his answer. "Look, I'm not saying that Todd's not a nice guy; I'm sure he is. I'm just saying that it's not Dad's place to set Gina up. Hell, Gina doesn't *need* to be set up!"

"Because she has you," Jason said quickly.

"Exactly," Mac said without thinking and then cursed. His brothers high-fived each other before returning their expectant gazes toward him. "This is none of your business."

"Oh, really?" Lucas said with a smirk. "And why not?"

"Did I get involved when you were on-again and off-again with Emma?" he said before turning to his other brother. "Or how about with you and Maggie?"

"Well," Jason countered, "you did sort of badger me about my time at the office."

"That's different and you damn well know it! I didn't ask for any details of your relationships and I would appreciate it if you showed me the same respect." He leaned back in his chair and slouched a bit. Taking another long drink from the icy bottle of beer in his hand, Mac thought the discussion was over.

"Here's the thing," Lucas said, leaning forward with his elbows braced on the table, "Emma and Maggie weren't close family friends. If you are just having your usual three-date fling, that could make things awkward. I mean, she's staying at Mom and Dad's! What are you thinking?"

"Emma and Maggie were both employees of Montgomerys, or have you both forgotten that?" He felt vindicated when they had the grace to look a bit sheepish. "I know that Gina and her father have been part of our lives for what seems like forever but"—he paused—"I can't explain it. I saw her in the airport and before I even knew it was her, I was drawn to her."

"And you don't think this is Dad playing matchmaker with the two of you?" Jason asked.

Mac shrugged. "I doubt it. He told me from the get-go that he didn't think I was right for Gina because I don't have staying power. I mean, what the hell does he know?"

"He knows that he's been married to Mom for almost forty years," Lucas responded. "He's not blind, Mac; he knows that you don't date long term and that your position with the company is your whole life. Why? Are you pissed that he's *not* matching you up with anyone like he did with me and Jace?"

"Hell no! I don't want him interfering in my life. As it

is he's been on my case because I work too much. He's been threatening me with a forced leave of absence! I think if he's going to play matchmaker, he probably feels like he's got to get me out of the office first."

"Maybe," Jason said, unconvinced. "He's sneaky. I mean with Lucas and Emma, it was just a matter of giving them a little nudge, but with me and Maggie? I was blindsided."

"Well, he's not going to blindside me," Mac said confidently. "I watched the both of you fall and now I know what to look for. Dad's not going to snag me a wife; I'll find her myself without anyone's help, thank you very much."

His brothers laughed and although Mac joined them, he suddenly wondered if the joke was on him.

—∿∿—

Gina helped Maggie and Emma set the large dining room table and found that she felt really at ease with them, as if they could be good friends. She had told her father of her plans for the day and although she felt guilty for missing the time with him, he had encouraged her to go.

"So how is Arthur feeling?" Emma asked as they worked together folding napkins and putting out plates and silverware.

"He has good days and bad," Gina said, trying not to get choked up. "His doctors have all been wonderful and they seem pleased with how he's been responding to his treatments."

"Will he get to come home anytime soon?" Maggie asked.

Gina shook her head. "It's not likely. I talked to one of his doctors yesterday and he said that they may allow him to go home at the end with a trained, live-in staff, if that's what Dad wants, but I haven't discussed it with him yet. I'm trying very hard not to think about the end and just focus on the time we have together now." As much as she tried to stop them, the tears began to fall and she suddenly found herself embraced by the two women.

"I cannot even imagine what you must be feeling," Emma said quietly. "We shouldn't have brought it up. I didn't mean to upset you. I'm sorry." She squeezed Gina a little more.

"It's okay; it's sort of like the elephant in the room. I know I can't ignore what's happening and I have to learn to deal with talking about him without breaking down, especially to the people who are so close to him."

They released her, and Maggie reached for a napkin and handed it to Gina. It was at that moment that Mac walked in. "What the hell's going on here?" He immediately stepped to Gina's side. "Are you all right?" he asked gently.

"We were just talking about my dad and I got a little emotional."

He looked at both Maggie and Emma accusingly. "Maybe you can find something a little more cheery to talk about?" His tone was firm and both women looked a little bit shocked to hear it directed at them.

"We already apologized, Mac," Emma said defensively, crossing her arms over her chest. She was married to a stubborn Montgomery man and she knew how to stare one down when needed. It didn't take long for Mac to cave.

"Sorry, I just… Lucas said the steaks are about done," he said as he exited the room.

Maggie and Emma looked at each other knowingly, and then looked at Gina and saw her staring at Mac's retreating back. Maggie leaned toward Gina. "So, you and Mac, huh?"

Gina blushed. "What? No…no…um…yeah, no." The two women in front of her did not look convinced. "I mean, I used to have a massive crush on Mac when I was younger, but he never even noticed me."

"I'm pretty sure he's noticing you now," Maggie said, placing the last of the silverware on the table. "You don't need to hide it; I think you would be great for Mac. He never dates a woman more than a handful of times, but I think you could be the one to make him consider the long term."

"It's not like that," Gina said, her blush heating up even more.

"We're not trying to embarrass you," Emma said. "We've both been there. Those Montgomery boys are irresistible. And I agree with Maggie; I think you and Mac would be wonderful together."

Gina wanted to talk to them about it but suddenly the entire Montgomery clan was piling into the dining room. "We'll talk later," Maggie whispered as everyone worked together to get the food on the table and settled in to eat.

By the time everyone was seated and all the food had been served, Gina felt oddly overwhelmed. Meals with her family were always quiet and sedate; she couldn't remember the last time there had been laughter around the table. Lucas and Emma shared how they were adjusting to being new parents, William and Monica talked about their cruise, and then Maggie and Jason talked about their plan to start looking for a new home because they wanted to start a family.

It was all very uplifting, and everyone was so encouraging that Gina wanted to just flee. She knew she was very emotional these days and even when surrounded by happy stories, she felt the need to escape. After her reaction at the mention of her father earlier, everyone seemed to silently agree not to bring him up.

Conversation continued to flow around her, and she found herself simply smiling and nodding rather than actively participating. Finally, Monica attempted to draw her in. "So I saw you carrying in some canvases yesterday. Are you painting again?"

Gina nodded. "I am. I hadn't picked up a paintbrush in years, but when I went to get some things at my father's house, he had some there for me as a surprise. I hope you don't mind that I'm painting in the house?"

Monica waved her off. "Don't be silly, sweetheart; you can do whatever you want there. Who knows, maybe we'll even hang some of them in there? Those walls have always been a little too vacant for me."

"I didn't know you painted," Emma said with a big smile. "Would you consider doing something for the nursery? We have it ninety percent done but I'm afraid I procrastinated a little too much and didn't finish before Lily was born. She's sleeping in our room for now, but I would love to have something original in her room."

"I would be honored," Gina said shyly. "But maybe you should see some of my work before you get your hopes up. You may not like it."

"Of course she'll like it," Mac said, looking at his plate. "You're extremely talented."

His comment would have meant more to Gina if he had looked at her when he said it, or if he had said it with a little more gentleness. He was being brusque, and for the life of her, she couldn't understand his change in attitude from earlier today. She mumbled her thanks and looked back at Emma with a smile. "We can get together and talk about what you'd like."

"You used to like photography when you were younger too," William interjected. "Do you still enjoy it?"

"Ah, that's another hobby I'm rediscovering, thanks to my dad. It's all done on computers now, with photo-editing software. I'm trying to figure it out, but I'm not all that tech-savvy."

"Funny you should mention that," William said. "I know someone who could probably help you. He works for us; his name is Todd. If you want, I can give him your number and the two of you could get together and figure out some of that software."

"I really could use the help," Gina said, considering William's offer. "I just don't seem to have the knack for anything computer related."

"Then Todd is the man for you," William said with a big smile. "I think the two of you will really hit it off. I'll give him your number and have him call you. Is that all right with you?"

Gina nodded but felt a weird sense of disappointment. She was sleeping with Mac, but she knew it was tempo-rary. Although by temporary she thought it was implied that it would last as long as she was in North Carolina. Then she thought about Maggie's earlier comment about how Mac only dated women a handful of times. Was this how he was going to stop their relationship? By letting his father set her up with someone else so she wouldn't bother him anymore? If that was the case, then she'd let him know she was fine with it. "That would be wonderful, William. Tell Todd that I look forward to his call."

—∿∿—

Mac continued to stew. Gina *wanted* to go out with Todd? What in the world was going on? Had he said or done something wrong? He wanted to stand up and tell his father to back off and then tell Gina that she couldn't see anyone else.

But he didn't, of course.

First, he wasn't one to make a scene. And second, what he shared with Gina was private, just like he had told his brothers earlier. Clearly, however, they weren't on the same page, because she was willing to go out with another man and practically made the date right in front of him! Well, he'd just see about that. When they left later, they would discuss this in the car like rational adults. He'd just have to bide his time and get through the rest of this day without letting anyone know there was a beast raging within him.

When lunch was finished, everyone dispersed. The men went back out onto the deck and Gina found herself sitting in the den with Maggie, Emma, and Monica. Lily had long since gone down for a nap, and the four of them were happy to have the time to relax.

"Don't let William push you into going out with Todd," Monica began. "He played matchmaker with

Maggie and Jace after doing it with Lucas and Emma, and I'm afraid he's making it his life's ambition to fix people up."

"Matchmaking? Seriously?" Gina said with a laugh. "Why would he want to match me up with anyone?"

"Maybe to make Mac jealous?" Emma said mischievously.

"Make Mac jealous?" Monica repeated, confused. "Why would he…? Oh no." She looked at her two daughters-in-law. "You don't think that's what he's doing, do you?"

Both women nodded. "It makes perfect sense," Maggie began. "Mac's the last Montgomery standing and William clearly loves Gina like a daughter. It just makes sense."

Gina was beyond mortified. It was one thing to mention that she used to have a crush on Mac to Emma and Maggie, but to talk about it in front of his mother was another story altogether. "If it's all the same to you—" she began.

Monica interrupted. "Gina, I remember how you used to have a crush on Mac back when you were a young girl and I'm sure William does too. It's nothing to be embarrassed about. I'll talk to him when we get home later and make him back off. You have enough on your plate without my husband trying to marry you off."

Sagging with relief, Gina relaxed into the sofa cushion. "Thank you, Monica. I appreciate that."

"But should you ever want our interference, you just say the word and we'll gladly do our best to make that stubborn son of ours open his eyes." They all laughed and soon the talk was focused on babies and houses. Gina sat back and enjoyed it, and secretly hoped that those were topics she'd get to talk about someday.

Chapter 8

IT WAS AFTER DARK BY THE TIME EVERYONE WAS getting ready to leave. Gina was so thankful to have had a day just to relax. She hadn't realized how much she had needed it until now.

"It's crazy for Mac to drive you home when that's where we're going," William was saying as he came to stand beside her. "I told him that you'll ride with us."

"Oh," she said, looking over her shoulder to where Mac was standing a few feet behind her. He hadn't spoken more than a handful of words to her all afternoon, and her heart sank. He was clearly severing ties with her, and although their time together had been short, it still hurt. Turning back to William, she smiled. "Okay then. Ready when you are!"

Hugging Lucas and Emma, she thanked them for including her. "You'll come for lunch tomorrow, right?" Emma asked. "Maggie will be here, and it will be a lot less chaotic. We can discuss the painting for the nursery."

"That sounds wonderful. I'll have to leave by one thirty to get to the hospital, but I think it will be fine. Thank you again, for everything."

"It was our pleasure, Gina," Lucas said as he hugged her. "It was really good to see you and I'm sure we'll be seeing you again before you head back to California."

"I'm sure of it," she said. Jason and Maggie came and hugged her good-bye as well, and next thing she knew, she was being ushered out the door and into William's car.

Mac hadn't said good-bye.

The drive back to the Montgomerys' wasn't very long, and once back at the house, William and Monica invited her to have some coffee with them. Gina agreed, even though she wanted to be alone and think about where she had gone wrong and misread how things were with Mac.

They were seated at the large table in the kitchen when Gina realized how serious they both looked. "Is everything all right?" she asked.

William looked at his wife before facing Gina. "I was wondering if you've talked to Arthur's doctors in the last couple of days."

Gina shook her head. "Not at any great length. Honestly, I've just been trying to focus on spending time with him and making the most of the time we have together. His spirits have been up, and he's gained a little weight back. From the conversations that I have had with them, I've learned his scans are showing that nothing has spread."

William nodded. "That's all really great news, sweetheart, and I know that your father loves having you here." He paused and fidgeted slightly in his seat. "There are just some things that you are going to need to start thinking about, and maybe now isn't the time to be having this discussion, but I wanted to at least put it out there for you."

She reached across the table and placed her hand on top of his. "You've always been so kind and considerate. I know you are looking out for me and I do appreciate it. Dad has already told me you are the executor of his estate and I trust you." Taking a sip of her coffee, Gina took a moment to compose her thoughts.

"Dad and I have been apart for so long and honestly, I didn't know what to expect when I came back here. We're getting to know each other again and I spend most of the time trying to ignore the fact that he's in the hospital." She looked at the Montgomerys and smiled sadly. "I'd love to be able to take him out for the day just so that we can have that memory together." She shrugged. "But the doctors aren't fully on board with the idea."

"I can talk to them," William suggested.

"I would appreciate that."

"The thing is, Gina, there's the house, the business… your father wants—"

Gina cut him off. "I'd really rather not do this right now. I know we are eventually going to have to talk about it, but I'm not ready. I'm sorry. I hope you don't think that I'm being selfish or naive about the whole thing; I'm not. It's just that it's been such a wonderful day and it's been so long since I've been around such a joyful family. I'd like to have that memory."

William nodded. "Of course. I'm sorry. I didn't mean to spoil your day. I just figured we've been away, and you may have questions or concerns—"

"I'm good, really." She finished her coffee and gently pushed the cup aside and smiled at the two people she'd always wished for as parents. "You are so blessed to have such a wonderful family. I really enjoyed watching the way you all interact, and the love on your faces today as you held Lily was absolutely precious."

It was a nice segue to happier topics, and they talked

for a while about everything and nothing. It was one of the most relaxing parental conversations she'd ever had. A glance at the clock showed it was after ten. "It's been a long day, and if you don't mind, I'd like to try and get a head start on some ideas for Lily's nursery." She wished them both a good night and walked across the expanse of the yard to the guesthouse. All the lights were off, but she already knew this place like the back of her hand.

Gina opened the door, stepped inside, and nearly screamed as she was grabbed and backed up against the wall.

Mac.

His mouth was hot and urgent on hers. Gina dropped her purse to the floor so that she could wrap her arms around him. He lifted her off the ground and soon her legs were around him as well. Their tongues mated while Gina raked her fingers through his hair. It was madness, and all she could think of was how she never wanted it to end.

When Mac finally broke the kiss, he rested his forehead on hers, his breathing ragged. "You are not going out with Todd."

"What?" Gina asked, confused.

"You're mine, Gina," he said with a low growl as he licked and kissed his way down her slender throat. "Mine."

She smiled and arched her neck to aid in the path he was trailing. She had no idea where this relationship with Mac was going, but right now she didn't care. She needed him, she wanted him, and if the hardness she felt pressing into her was any indication, Mac wanted her too. Gina tugged on his hair, pulled his mouth back to hers, and kissed him as if her life depended on it. She came up for air. "What are you doing here?"

—∿∿—

He didn't answer right away. Instead, his hands were busy skimming her body and his mouth was doing wicked things to any exposed skin he could find. Gina purred with delight and sighed his name. Mac lifted his head and looked into her sexy, slumberous eyes. She packed a powerful punch and she didn't even know it. His expression was serious as he put her gently back on her feet. "I'm sorry for the way I behaved today. My family makes me a little crazy and I know I didn't act the way I should have. We never talked about…us and how we wanted to handle it. I wasn't ready to put it out there to everyone because…" Mac was always confident and self-assured in everything he did, but for some reason, this woman turned his carefully organized world upside down.

Gina reached up and cupped his face in her hands. "What we have is private," she said, and he nodded. "I get that. I honestly do. I don't expect you to announce to everyone that we've slept together, but I wouldn't have minded you speaking up when your father was trying to set me up with another man."

"It won't happen again," he said seriously. "I'm sorry if I hurt you."

With a shy smile, she pulled his head down to hers. "Thank you," she whispered.

"Can I stay?"

"Yes."

Scooping her up into his arms, he strode to the bedroom and took his time making things up to her.

Mac looked at the clock on the bedside table and saw that it was after three. Gina was sound asleep beside him with her back to him. Normally she fell asleep in his arms, but tonight she had rolled away. Maybe it wasn't intentional, but he had a feeling that it was. Had he come off as being too possessive? Was his apology not enough after the way he had treated her earlier at Lucas and Emma's? Hell if he knew.

What he did know was that he already missed the feel of her in his arms. While he knew that the cat was eventually going to come out of the bag, he didn't want it to be with him getting caught leaving the guesthouse when the sun came up. Hating what he had to do, he quietly rose from the bed and got dressed. Gina didn't stir and he was glad for that. If she so much as looked at him with her kiss-swollen lips and sleepy gaze, he'd be a goner.

What the hell was he going to do? He wanted Gina; heck, if he were honest, he would say that he needed her. Somehow he was missing something from his life, and it turned out that she was it. Mac hadn't considered himself lonely or incomplete, but these last two weeks with her told a different story.

Going to the office in the morning used to make Mac feel energized; now he found himself watching the clock and figuring out how and when he was going to see Gina again. Sleeping alone had never bothered him before, but now all he wanted was her close beside him.

He was a goner.

The biggest problem he had with the whole thing was

Gina herself. She had spent so much of her life not being able to be who she wanted to be; he didn't want to be an obstacle for her. She was just now starting to come into her own and if he made any demands on her or her time, she might never get to discover just who Gina Micelli really was. Did he truly want to be responsible for that?

"Mac?"

Her soft whisper brought him to her side. Leaning over, he kissed her softly on the cheek. "Go back to sleep, baby," he said quietly. "It's too early for you to be up."

"Why are you leaving?"

"I need to get to the office early and I have to go home and change. Plus, I didn't think you wanted my parents to see me leaving here in yesterday's clothes." The frown on her face told him that his explanation didn't thrill her. "Can I see you later?"

Gina nodded, then relaxed back into her pillow and rolled over. Mac kissed her on the top of her head before tiptoeing from the room.

She listened for the door to close and sighed. She wasn't sure how much longer she was willing to stay his dirty little secret.

"So there we were, in the middle of the mall parking lot, and my water breaks," Emma said with a laugh. "The look on Lucas's face was priceless. I don't think I'd ever seen him so panicked!"

"What did he do?" Gina asked, laughing along with her.

"First he dropped all our bags and tried to pick me

up! I yelled at him to put me down, that I could manage to walk the ten feet to the car, and then it took him three tries to pick up the bags. I think he was doing more Lamaze breathing than I was!"

"When we first saw him at the hospital, I thought they were going to have to shoot him with a tranquilizer dart," Maggie joked. "Jason wanted to slap him just to bring him back to reality."

"I'm telling you, you can take all of the birthing classes and read all of the books, but when you are actually going through it, all of that goes out the window."

"I can't wait," Maggie said with a smile. "We're trying and we're looking for a house. Having babies with Jace is everything I ever wanted."

"Is your place too small?" Gina asked.

Maggie shook her head. "Oh, good gracious, no. It's actually quite large, but it's just not…a home. We live in the townhouse that Jason was living in before we met, and it's beautiful but not very kid-friendly. We want a house with a yard, something that isn't so modern. We're on a golf course and there aren't a lot of families in the neighborhood. The more we talked about it, the more we realized we want to move and get settled before we have a baby."

"That makes sense." Gina changed the subject to Lily's nursery. "I did some sketches this morning I want you to look at. When you were showing me the nursery yesterday, I had an idea of what you were going for. If there's something that you like in the pile, great, and if not, we can figure something out."

Emma took the sketches from her and stared at them in awe. "You did all of this before you came here?"

"I was up early."

"You must have been to get all of this done." She handed them to Maggie, who marveled over them as well. "Gina, these are amazing! How is it that you're an accountant when you can draw like this?"

Gina shrugged. "My mother convinced me that art wasn't a bankable future, and if I wanted to have some financial security and meet a man who was stable and would take care of me, I needed to give up my art and go into business."

Both women looked at her as if she were crazy. "Let me tell you something," Emma said. "I went into business because I was afraid to be creative and do what I loved, which is baking. I'm glad I did, because otherwise I would never have met Lucas, but I enjoyed my job at Montgomerys. It doesn't seem as though you enjoy your job at all from what you've told us."

"I really don't, and I plan on resigning when I go back—if I go back." She put that last part out there to see what kind of reaction she got.

"Are you thinking of staying?" Emma asked excitedly. "Is it because of Mac? Are you two getting serious?"

Gina rolled her eyes. "This has nothing to do with Mac." That was only partially a lie. "I've never been happy in Cali. I never felt like I fit in. I have no idea what I'd do here, but I think if I gave myself the opportunity, I could really be happy."

"Well, you won't want to stay in the guesthouse forever, but I'm sure William and Monica would love it if you stayed. You could always move into your father's house," Maggie suggested.

Gina vehemently shook her head. "No, I couldn't.

I know he wants me to stay there, and it's a beautiful house, but it's not someplace I want to be. To me, it represents a lot of sadness. He created a life for me there, even though he knew I was never going to use it. And once he's gone, it will just be a place where he had to live alone." She looked up at both women and smiled sadly. "It's a truly lovely house, but I think it deserves a family with kids and a dog and to be filled with laughter. It's too big for one person. I don't know how he stood it for so long."

Not wanting to upset Gina further, Emma began to talk about which piece of art she wanted to use for the nursery. Gina was relieved by the change of subject, but at the same time, there was another subject that she needed advice on.

"I don't know what to do about Mac," she blurted out.

"Oh, thank God," Maggie sighed. "I was afraid you weren't ever going to talk about it!" All three women burst out laughing. "So you still have a thing for him?"

Gina nodded. "If anything, he's gotten better with age, and when I saw him at the airport? My heart actually stopped. He's just…" She couldn't find the words to accurately describe what she felt.

"He's a Montgomery," Emma supplied. "And Montgomery men have a way of grabbing your heart and not letting go."

"I thought it wouldn't be a big deal; you know, it was a childhood crush. But once I spent time with him, it grew into something more."

"You're in love with him," Maggie said simply. "We can completely understand because we both felt the same way. Still do."

"And I envy you both, but Mac… I don't think he wants a relationship. I know he wants me right now, but we have an expiration date. Once I go back to California, it's over."

"Are you sure?" Emma asked. "If he's anything like Lucas, it can be like pulling teeth to get him to talk about how he really feels."

"He came by last night upset about the whole Todd thing, and said straight up that he didn't like the idea of me dating somebody else. But at the same time, he didn't ask me for anything beyond right now. Does that make sense?"

Emma reached out and took Gina's hand. "They may be handsome and charming and sexy as hell, but they are also slow as molasses when it comes to making that big step toward commitment. Don't give up on him. He's not going to let you go back to California; I can guarantee it."

"I hope you're right. Because I already know that I'm losing my father; I don't think I could survive losing Mac at the same time too."

Unable to help herself, Emma went over and hugged her. "Give him time. I know he'll be worth the wait."

Later that night, Gina was busy experimenting in the kitchen. She had spent the afternoon with her father, but he was tired from a morning of getting poked and prodded by his medical team. William and Monica had invited her to join them for dinner, but she had declined and decided to go shopping and play around with some recipes. After her lunch with the girls, she had realized that her culinary skills were greatly lacking.

When Gina had graduated from college, she had dreamed of learning to cook and having a place of her own to decorate. Her mother had other plans for her and in the end, Gina had caved and moved back home, where there was a housekeeper who did all of the cooking and cleaning. She was almost giddy now at the prospect of picking out her own foods to create her own meals.

A small giggle escaped as she used the remote to put on some music—the Beatles this evening—and got to work organizing all she was going to need to make the soup, salad, quiche, and quick bread she had planned. The bread was a mix, and she had it put together and in the oven in no time. The quiche was a little more challenging, but she found that chopping and sautéing the vegetables was a lot of fun. It soon followed the bread into the oven.

After a quick pause to air drum to "Help," she went to work on the salad. She used her hip to shut the refrigerator door to let it chill and then started the soup. "Probably should have done this before the salad," she mumbled and then shrugged. Who cared? She wasn't on anyone's schedule but her own! The idea was empowering. She laughed and segued into a sing-along with John, Paul, George, and Ringo to "She Loves You."

—⁓—

That's when Mac came in. He stood in the doorway and smiled. Gina was dancing around the kitchen in total abandon, singing into a wooden spoon. He couldn't help but smile at the picture she made. The carefree woman before him was blossoming, and he knew it was because she was finally free to experience life on her own terms.

He was thrilled for her, a little less so for himself. The smile slowly faded to a frown. Deep down, Mac knew his greatest fault was that he was a bit of a control freak; he didn't go with the flow or do things on the spur of the moment. He was a meticulous planner; he made lists and crossed things off as he went along. Watching Gina dance and sing with abandon suddenly hit him like a punch in the gut.

His father was right; he wouldn't be good for her.

How soon before he was the one trying to get her to conform to his schedule and his rigid way of thinking? How soon before the music became too distracting for him or his schedule made him miss her excitement at preparing a meal for them? He wanted Gina with a fierceness he couldn't control and it scared him. She scared him. That was why when Gina left to go back to California, he would let her go. He had to. The only way for her to have the life she deserved was for him to step back and let her have it.

It just might kill him.

Just then she spun around and spotted him. She did a little jump of excitement and fairly skipped over to him, wrapping her arms around him and kissing him with all of the passion she put into everything she did. Mac welcomed it, savored it, because soon, all he would have was the memory of it.

Chapter 9

"SOME MIGHT CALL THIS A DATE," GINA TEASED A WEEK later as they stood outside Lucas and Emma's house. Mac looked down at her with an arched eyebrow. "It's true; when a man takes a woman out and they socialize with other couples, I've been told it can technically be called a date."

"Is that right?" he asked, smiling down at her.

She nodded. "It's not traditional, don't get me wrong, but I think this situation still applies."

"Traditional, huh? Anyone can do traditional. It takes a special knack to take someone to their brother's home for dinner."

"Careful…you may spoil me," she said with a big smile. Mac was glad he was finally able to arrange this. Between work and the fact that Arthur's health had been deteriorating this week for seemingly no reason, it had been difficult for them to spend any quality time together.

She had introduced him to the wonders of John Landis and the fabulous teen movies of the eighties. They had snuggled up together on the sofa for a movie marathon on more than one occasion while eating popcorn or pizza; he was really feeding into her junk-food craze. And while he watched everything from *Sixteen Candles* to *The Breakfast Club*, he couldn't quite get the appeal. What he did get, however, was how much those movies meant to Gina, and that for a couple of hours out of her day, she could relive a simpler, happier time in her life.

"Okay, I get the whole teenage angst thing and the shy, quiet girl getting the captain of the football team thing, but I don't get what the big deal is about this movie," Mac said the night before when Gina had finally made him watch *Say Anything*.

"It's a classic," she said simply.

"No, no, no…*Star Wars* is a classic; *The Dirty Dozen* is a classic. Anything with James Bond is a classic. But this? I just don't see it."

She rolled her eyes. "First of all, none of those movies you mentioned are romantic."

"There is always romance with 007," he countered.

"That's sex, not love, and yes, there is a difference!"

"Okay, okay, so tell me why you think this is a classic."

"It's about love conquering all. They fall in love against the odds and no one thinks that he's good enough for her, and yet in the end, he is exactly what she needs." She sighed. "Every woman wants that, and they all love this movie and think it's a classic. Everybody cries when John Cusack stands outside her window, holding up the boom box with Peter Gabriel singing 'In Your Eyes.' It's iconic. He's doing whatever he can think of to get her back, and he won't take no for an answer."

Mac still didn't agree, but it made her happy, so he was happy to sit and watch it with her.

Lucas opened the door and welcomed them in, and Gina kissed him on the cheek and went right to the kitchen with the tray of stuffed mushrooms she had made. After she had sashayed away, Lucas looked at his brother and grinned. "Man, do you have it bad."

Mac glared at him. "Don't start on me. It's been a hell of a week, and Gina needs a carefree night to relax and have fun. And so do I."

"Dad mentioned that Arthur's not doing well."

"He spoke to the doctors along with Gina this week. Although the cancer hasn't spread, Arthur's body is just shutting down. We all knew it was coming, but it's coming faster than anyone expected."

"I thought he was doing well, holding his own?"

Mac shrugged. "Those first two weeks that Gina was here he was doing great, but the body can only take so much and he wasn't in great health to begin with."

"How's she holding up?"

"She has good moments and bad. By the time I see her at night, she's had time to kick and scream and cry. She acts like she's handling it, but I can see it's getting to her."

"It would get to anyone. I hate that she's going through this alone."

Mac shoved Lucas hard. "What the hell does that mean? She's far from being alone!"

Jason heard the beginnings of the scuffle and walked over. "What's going on?"

"He's a jackass, that's what's going on," Mac said.

With a dramatic roll of his eyes, Lucas turned to Jason. "Mac was just telling me about Arthur and how Gina was doing, and all I said was I hate that she's dealing with this alone."

"And I reminded him that she's not alone," Mac countered.

Jason looked from one to the other and chose his words carefully. "Look, she's got all of us to lean on, and Mom and Dad have taken her in like surrogate parents, but at the end of the day, she's alone."

"No, she's not, dammit! I'm there!"

"Are you?" Jason asked, his tone serious.

"Why don't you just say what you have to say, Jace?" Mac growled.

"I don't have to ask if you're sleeping with her, because even though you don't talk about it and we haven't asked, we all kind of know. It's in the way the two of you look at each other and believe me, we're all fine with it. I get why you're keeping it a secret—you don't want Dad catching wind of it and putting on his matchmaking cap again. But the truth of the matter is, sneaking into her house after dark so that no one sees you and creeping out before the sun is up is *not* being there for her."

Mac wanted to argue, he wanted to tell his brothers they were wrong, but unfortunately, they were right. He was there for Gina physically, but was that really enough for her? Was he helping her or hurting her?

"Don't you think it would be better for her if you were there at the hospital with her? Maybe go with her to talk to the doctors? Dad says she still hesitates to ask them questions."

"And you think if I'm there with her she will? She doesn't want to hear what she already knows is going to happen. Would you find it easy to sit there and listen to some doctor tell you that Dad was going to die? That he only had a month or less to live?"

Both brothers shook their heads. "It's not a crime for

Gina not to want to sit with a team of medical professionals and their cool detachment, talking about her father like he's just a case to them," Mac went on. "He's her father; she loves him and she's dealing with a horrible situation the only way she knows how."

"We're not getting down on Gina," Lucas said. "All we're saying is that if you really care about her, then maybe you need to make her a little more of a priority."

"Oh, like the two of you did? Now you're experts?"

"When I walked away from Emma, I thought I was doing the right thing. If I had actually taken the time to talk to her, even though it was uncomfortable for me, it would have saved us both a lot of time and heartache."

Jason nodded. "I didn't make Maggie a priority, and I went and made decisions that directly affected her without talking to her about them. I almost lost her." He looked at Lucas and then back at Mac. "We don't claim to be experts; we're just guys who made the same stupid mistakes that we're watching you make, and we're trying to help."

"This is completely different, and if it's all the same to you, I'd like to drop the subject and just have a good time tonight without all of this hanging over our heads. Can we please do that?"

In silent agreement, the three of them headed toward the kitchen, where the sound of female laughter called out to them.

As the night went on, Mac realized he was enjoying himself more than he thought possible. Without the threat of his father's prying eyes, he was free to relax and enjoy his time with Gina. They held hands, they stood close, and he was able to put his arm around her and touch her as much as he pleased. He could tell that his brothers' wives approved, because whenever he caught their eyes, they smiled and nodded at him.

Emma stood when she heard Lily's soft cry over the baby monitor. Gina rose as well. "Would you mind if I went and got her?" she asked. "I know she doesn't know me, but if it's okay with you, I'd love to go and pick her up."

Emma sat back down and sighed. "That would be wonderful. I love this house, but by the end of the day, the thought of another trip up those stairs is just exhausting." Gina excused herself and walked up to the nursery. "You're a lucky man, Mackenzie," Emma said, reaching out for her husband's hand. "Gina's a wonderful girl."

"Who knows," Maggie interjected, "someday one of us could be running up a flight of stairs to pick up your crying baby." Everyone laughed, but Mac suddenly didn't feel so well. *Babies?* That would signify a future between him and Gina, and he was doing his best to come to grips with the fact that she'd be leaving him soon. Clearly no one else had gotten the memo.

"Not me, Maggie," he said as lightly as he could although his voice croaked. "No babies in my future."

"Oh come on, are you telling me that you're not thinking of you and Gina settling down and having a family?" Maggie asked, sounding stunned.

"Gina's going back to California; that's where her life is."

"Then what the hell are you doing with her?" Emma chimed in, full of indignation.

Well, shoot. He thought he had cleared the air by talking to his brothers earlier; he hadn't counted on their wives ganging up on him. "What's going on between me and Gina is just that, between me and Gina," he said a little too harshly.

"Mac," Lucas warned.

"Why is it anyone's damn business what is going on with me and Gina? We're doing fine and we both know where we stand. When things…get settled here, she's going back to California and to her life. End of story."

"You're not going to ask her to stay?" Maggie asked, her tone guarded.

"Why?" Mac asked, angry that they were still poking and prodding where they didn't belong. "Her job is back in California, her mother is there, her friends… There's nothing here tying her to North Carolina."

"You're here," Emma said softly.

Mac looked at her, his expression bleak. "Apparently I'm not." He stood and walked away from the table just as Gina was walking back into the dining room with Lily. One look at the woman—who was the topic of conversation and a constant presence in his mind—holding a baby was nearly his undoing. "Excuse me," he said gruffly and stalked out of the room.

—◆◆◆—

"Did I miss something?" Gina asked softly, handing Lily to Emma.

"Nothing important," Jason said as he stood and went after Mac. Lucas attempted to join him, but Jason waved him off.

Everyone began talking at once about Lily and dinner. It was the kind of conversation that Gina knew was intended to distract her. She wasn't an idiot by any stretch of the imagination, and she was light on her feet. She had heard the tail end of the conversation and knew that no matter how much she wished for it, and no matter how she and Mac clung to one another when they made love, it wasn't going to make a difference. He was going to let her go back to the West Coast without asking her to stay.

———ᴟᴟᴟ———

Jason closed the sliding glass door behind him and joined Mac on the deck. They stood in silence, staring out at a black, starless sky. He hoped Mac would say something, anything, but it soon became obvious that it was going to be up to him to get things moving.

"When we were kids, you used to love to climb trees. Do you remember that?" Mac turned his head and looked at him as if he were crazy but nodded before returning his gaze forward. "You taught me how to climb them and then I taught Lucas. Mom used to get so mad because whenever we got in trouble, we'd scatter and each climb up one of the big magnolia trees so she couldn't reach us." He chuckled at the memory.

"You taught me how to swim, how to play baseball and football... Hell, you were the one who coached me on how to ask out my first girlfriend, Katie Michaels. Remember her?"

"No," Mac said with a small shake of his head. "Is there a point to all of this?"

"Yeah," Jason said, turning to face his big brother. "Some of the most important and memorable things in my life, you taught me. Sure, Dad could have done all of that, but I looked up to you because you were my big brother and I thought that you were the coolest guy in the world. I watched you grow up and do amazing things with your life; you're a genius in the office and you're a whiz with numbers. And there are times, and I'll never admit this in front of anyone else so pay attention…there are times that I am just in freakin' awe of you. I think to myself, how can I ever compete or measure up to Mac?"

Mac looked at him, unsure of what to say. His jaw worked as if he was going to say something, but no words came out.

"When I planned out that expansion project? The one that Maggie came to work for me on? I was terrified, because all I could think about was how would I feel if I let you down?" Jason hung his head and shook it. "We may be equals around the office, but I know there is still so much I have to learn from you."

"Jace, that's not true," Mac finally said. "There isn't anything you can't do. You did an amazing job on the expansion, and you've kicked my ass on numerous projects. God, I don't want you to feel like it's a competition between us, because I sure don't."

"I know it's not a competition… I do. It's just that you gave me so much and I feel like I have nothing to give back." He paused and met his brother's gaze. "Except this. You're making a mistake. With Gina. I know why you think letting her go is the right thing to do; I honestly get it. But playing the martyr is only going to bring you so much satisfaction."

"She's spent her whole life…"

Jason held up a hand to stop him. "I know. She's got a mother who's a control freak and a father who wasn't strong enough to step in and stop it. That doesn't change the fact that she's crazy about you. After watching the two of you tonight, it's obvious how much you care about one another. Don't walk away and think that you're doing her a favor! All you're going to do is make the both of you miserable."

"Gina deserves a chance to make her own choices. If I ask her to stay," he said, stumbling over the words, "if I ask her to stay, then I might beg her to stay. And I know her well enough to know that if I did that, she'd stay. It wouldn't be her choice; she'd be doing it to make me happy. She needs to be happy, Jace. That's all I want."

Jace placed a hand on Mac's shoulder. "You make her happy."

"What if I don't? What if I'm…you know, me, and it doesn't work out?"

"Why would you even think that?"

"Please, I know my faults, Jace. I'm no saint. I'm mildly OCD. I like things orderly and done a certain way. She's just discovering herself." He laughed at all of the things Gina had been doing over the last couple of weeks. "When she's not at the hospital, she's either dancing or singing off-key, she's painting or taking pictures or cooking full-course meals at eleven o'clock at night! Things like that make her smile, make her forget she's here watching her father die. What happens when the dust settles, and I get annoyed with the distractions?"

"Do you love her?"

Mac couldn't answer. The thought terrified him.

"For once, I'd like you to learn something from me. I gave up; I watched Maggie walk away because I thought it was for the best and it damn near killed me. You deserve to be happy just as much as Gina does and together, you'll find a balance where you both work it out. It doesn't have to be all for her or all for you. It's not all black and white, man."

The sound of the door opening behind them had them both turning around. "Everything all right back here?" Lucas asked as he walked toward them. Jason looked at Mac, who nodded. "Well, it's no secret that you're upset, and I think Gina heard part of our conversation, so she's been a little quiet. Emma's putting coffee and dessert out now. Let's try and salvage the rest of the night." He faced Mac. "But know you're going to have to talk to her about this sooner or later."

Mac was afraid that there wasn't going to be an option for later.

———

It was nearly midnight when they pulled into the driveway of his parents' house. Mac turned the car off and sat in silence. Actually, the entire ride home had been in silence, but somehow now it seemed more profound.

"I'd ask you to come in, but I don't think it's a good idea," Gina finally said softly. She couldn't hide the sadness in her voice.

"I never meant to hurt you," he said, his tone equally soft.

"I know. I thought it wouldn't be a big deal to embark on something short term; it's my own fault that I let it become something more."

If she had kicked him in the chest, it wouldn't have hurt more. "It does mean something more, Gina; you mean more to me than anyone ever has. I just don't want to be another person taking charge of your life."

Sighing, she reached for the door handle. "I want you to know that I wouldn't trade these last weeks together for anything. I know that at first you resented having to spend time with me, but it meant the world to me to finally get to know you. Thank you for helping me through…well, everything." Gina turned and met his gaze. "I couldn't have come this far and handled all of this without you. You helped me to be strong, and I'll never forget you for that."

Mac hated the finality in her words, hated knowing that this was the way it had to be. Someday she'd be thanking him for stepping back and walking away. He just didn't know if he'd be able to bear hearing it then any more than he could bear hearing it now. "If you need anything, Gina—"

She cut him off. "Your parents are here for me. I think now that Dad's in the condition he's in, your father and I will be spending a lot of time together." Mac could tell she didn't want his pity. "I'm going to be fine." Unable to help herself, she leaned back into the car and placed a gentle kiss on his cheek. "Take care of yourself, Mackenzie."

And then she was gone. Mac couldn't watch her walk away; instead he kept his gaze on his white-knuckled grip on the steering wheel. It was for the best, he told himself. Maybe if he kept saying it over and over, one day he would be able to believe it.

Off in the distance, he saw a light go on in the guest-house. He longed to get out of the car, to chase after her and tell her that he was wrong; somehow he'd find a way for them to be together without ever interfering with her life. But he knew himself well enough to know it would be impossible. Hell, everyone knew that about him. Even his own father, who seemed hell-bent on playing Cupid to the masses, didn't have enough faith in him to want him with Gina. What did that tell him?

Unable to stand being so close to Gina any longer, Mac put the car in reverse and pulled away from the house. His chest hurt and his head ached. Driving into the night, he wondered if he'd ever have what his brothers had. Would he ever find a woman he could be himself with while letting her be who she needed to be? Lucas and Emma had found that balance, he reminded himself. They overcame the loss of Lucas's career and Emma starting a completely new one with her baking business. Jason and Maggie didn't have any major obstacles other than learning to trust in one another, and they were able to do it.

Why couldn't Mac? Where did his need to control everything come from?

And how could he let it go so that he could have a chance at finding happiness?

Chapter 10

FOR TWO WEEKS, MAC WENT THROUGH THE MOTIONS of working. He went in, did what had to be done, and left at a reasonable hour to keep his father off his back. It would have felt victorious if his father had been there to witness any of it. Arthur Micelli's health had taken a turn for the worse and William was spending the bulk of his time at the hospital. Mac wanted to call Gina or go and see her to make sure she was okay, but he knew that messing with her head was the last thing she needed.

"Mac? Do you have those numbers?" Jason asked, and by his tone Mac figured it wasn't the first time.

"Sorry, my mind wandered. What do you need?"

Jason and Lucas looked at one another with exasperation. "Look, all of this moping and staring off into space is getting old. If you're not going to work, then maybe take a little time off. No one would blame you. Just take a couple of days to get your head together," Lucas suggested.

"My head is fine," Mac snapped. "My mind wandered for a minute, so sue me." He reached into the file in front of him, pulled out the sales projections they were working on, and flung a copy at each of his brothers. "There. Satisfied?" Rather than argue with him, they all just went back to the meeting.

It was a little after three when Jason's phone rang. He looked at the caller ID and answered immediately. Mac wasn't paying much attention; there was a mountain of paperwork in front of him and he had to get through it just to keep himself sane. Soon Lucas stood and walked over to Jason, talking in hushed tones after Jason hung up the phone.

"Are the two of you done whispering like school-girls so we can get back to it? Dad needs this stuff by tomorrow, doesn't he?" Today was the one rare day that William wasn't at the hospital. He had driven to Raleigh to meet with a client, but had told each of them how important this particular project was and that he needed them to finish it.

Lucas stepped forward, his face somber. He looked at Jason, who nodded, before addressing Mac. "That was Dad on the phone. Arthur's doctors just called. They don't expect him to make it through the night. Dad's on his way back, but it will take him about three hours to get here and Gina's by herself…"

Mac didn't need to hear any more. He was on his feet and out the door.

――――※※――――

The fact that he wasn't pulled over for speeding was a miracle. Never in his life could Mac remember driving so fast to get to someone. If anything happened to Arthur before he got there, he would never forgive himself. The elevator seemed to take forever to get to the fifth floor, but once the doors opened, he flew toward the end of the hall to where he knew Gina was sitting, awaiting the worst news a child could get.

He stood in the doorway and just watched. Arthur was speaking softly; thank God he had made it here in time! Should he go in or wait outside? He decided to give them a few more minutes alone before announcing his presence.

—⁓⁓—

"I'm so sorry, Gina," Arthur said. His voice was weak. "I really thought we'd have more time."

Tears flowed openly in honor of her father for the first time since her arrival. There was no way to hold them back now. "I did too," she said, her voice trembling. "I wanted us to have a day outside together, even if it was just to sit in the park."

Arthur smiled. "That would have been nice. I remember when you were a little girl, we would go to the park and I would push you on the swings, and you would just giggle with excitement. You said you thought you were flying."

"To me, I was. I always loved those times together, just the two of us."

"I should have fought harder for you," he said. "I never should have let you go to California. I knew you didn't want to go, knew you wouldn't be happy. In the end I caved because I didn't want to fight anymore. I thought I was doing you a favor."

"I could have fought more too," she said quietly.

With a shaking hand, Arthur reached out and took Gina's hand in his. "Be happy, sweetheart. Just…be happy." His eyes closed, and Gina knew he was gone.

Mac stepped into the room and was immediately at her side, placing a strong hand on her shoulder. Gina didn't turn to face him, but reached up and put her trembling hand on his. "It's not fair," she sobbed. "He wasn't supposed to leave me yet."

"He didn't want to leave you," Mac said softly.

One hand held her father's while the other held Mac's—the two men she loved most in this world, and she couldn't have either of them. "I kept thinking that if I didn't sit with the doctors, if I didn't hear what they had to say, that he wouldn't go. Oh, Mac, I'm not ready for him to go!"

Mac knelt down beside her and gathered her in his arms while she cried. His heart broke for the way hers was breaking; he felt every shudder of her body as she cried for all she had lost. He lost track of time and was losing feeling in his knees from the position, but he'd stay like this forever if it brought her comfort.

Doctors and nurses surrounded the bed and Mac quietly asked them if they could please give her a little more time in the room with her father. No one argued. The door closed silently behind them and still he held on to her.

"There were so many things I wanted to say to him; I kept putting them off because I thought there'd be more time. Now he's gone and he'll never know how I felt!"

Mac pulled back and tucked a finger under her chin, forcing her to look at him. "He knew how you felt, Gina. All he wanted was the opportunity to spend time with you, to maybe make up for lost time. Arthur knew that you loved him."

"But I never had the chance—"

"Tell him now," Mac said and Gina looked at him like he was crazy. "Gina, you'll never have peace if you don't say what you wanted to. He's right there and you know it's just his body, but his soul is in a better place. He'll hear you."

—◦◦◦—

She didn't know if she fully believed him, but Gina
knew deep down in her heart that there was so much she
had to say and this would be her last chance. Standing,
she looked down at her father's face, finally at peace. A
quick glance over her shoulder at Mac had him nodding
his approval.

Gina cleared her throat and wiped tears from her face.
"Daddy," she began, "I miss you already. I'm so sorry
for all of the years together that we missed. I'm sorry
for being angry with you for so long for leaving me and
making me go to California. I know now that it wasn't
an easy decision for you and that you did what you
thought was best. My life wasn't as bad as I probably
make it out to be, but the truth is that I missed you. I
missed our time together, and I thought that maybe you
had forgotten about me."

She began to cry in earnest again and Mac handed
her some tissues. Gina composed herself and continued.
"I'm sorry for all the times I refused your calls or made
you feel like you weren't important to me; I was acting
out of anger and disappointment. Basically I was being
a brat. I'm sorry for not coming home sooner. I should
have been here with you long before you were forced to
come to the hospital. I hate to think that you didn't ever
get to go home again. I know you were disappointed that
I didn't want to stay at the house; it's a beautiful house
and I hope that a family will someday live there and fill
the rooms with laughter—the kind of laughter we should
have had there." Her knees threatened to give out, so
great was her grief.

Mac came up behind her and wrapped his arms around her for support. With a gentle kiss on her temple he whispered, "Keep going."

"I want to thank you for not giving up on me, for encouraging me to reconnect with the things I was once passionate about. If it wasn't for you, I would have gone on living in the dark and never remembered the light. You gave it back to me, and I only wish that you could see all that I've been creating because of you. I've made a beautiful picture for Lily's room." She let out a small laugh. "I wish you could see her, Daddy; she's such a sweet baby and Lucas is a wonderful father. William is just a gushing grandfather and I wish we had the opportunity to experience that for ourselves together. My babies will never know their grandfather…"

She turned into Mac's embrace, and he carefully pulled her close to him as he sat down in the chair she had vacated and cradled her in his arms. "He'll never see any of it," she cried. "He'll never see me get married or have children! Oh God, Mac, how am I going to get through this? I want him back! I want more time!"

He wished he had the answers. He wanted to take all of her pain away but knew that he was helpless. All Mac could do was be there for her now in her darkest hour and help her remember all her father had taught her.

They sat in that chair while Gina cried. The next time the doctor came in with the orderlies, Mac let them do what needed to be done. Together they stood, walked over to the window, and watched the sun setting so they didn't have to watch Arthur's body being wheeled from the room. Mac knew they were breaking some sort of protocol by still being in the room, but he was thankful for the graciousness of the staff.

He continued to hold her in his arms as she finally started to come to grips with what was going on. Every now and again, he would feel her shudder; the tears were coming less and less, but he knew it would be a long time before Gina would begin to feel anything other than grief.

The door opened again behind them, and Mac saw his father walk in, a look of utter devastation on his face. He came up to them and Gina went from Mac's embrace straight to William's and began to cry anew. Mac had never seen his father cry, and it was humbling to watch him do so now. He was whispering words of comfort to Gina, and Mac began to feel like an intruder.

"Come on, sweetheart," William said. "It's time to go. There are some arrangements that have to be made."

"Dad," Mac said cautiously, "right now? Can't they wait?"

William shook his head. "I'll take care of it and then I'll take you home," he said to Gina.

Before she could answer, Mac came forward. "I'll take her home. I don't want her to be alone."

"She won't be," William said with a sad smile. "Your mother and I are going to be there with her."

"It's okay, William," Gina whispered. "You go and be with Monica. I know that you're feeling this as much as I am. I just want to go home and crawl into bed. We'll talk in the morning, okay?" They hugged one more time, and walked out of the room arm in arm while Mac followed close behind.

Nurses and doctors who had been caring for Arthur

stopped to offer their condolences. William said good night to Gina and Mac before following one of the nurses. Arthur had taken care of the technicalities once he learned his prognosis. William had a copy of everything, and it was just a matter of signing some papers.

The elevator ride was made in silence, and Mac was proud of Gina for keeping her composure as so many people had stopped to talk with them. He led her out to his car and helped her in. The woman who had danced around to Rod Stewart and the Jackson Five now sat listlessly in her seat. He secured her seat belt as if she were a child. Gina kept her head bowed and Mac let her have that time to herself.

It wasn't until they pulled up in front of Mac's house that she spoke. "Why are we here?"

They had typically spent their time together at the guesthouse; he'd only brought Gina to his home once. "I thought you might appreciate a change of scenery tonight." He climbed from the car and went around to help her out. He pulled Gina close to his side and they made their way into the house. "Are you hungry? I can make us something to eat if you'd like."

Gina shook her head. "I don't think I could eat anything right now."

"You need your strength, Gina," he said as he gently caressed her cheek. "I know you don't want to eat but I'm sure you haven't taken the time for it today."

"I didn't want to leave his side," she said sadly. "I didn't want to take a chance..."

"Sshh..." he whispered as he pulled her close again. "It's okay. Come sit down and I'll make us some omelets. Just eat what you can, okay?"

She nodded and let Mac lead her to a stool at his breakfast bar. In their time together, Mac had never cooked for her; she wasn't even aware that he knew how. Watching him now was a good distraction. The entire time he chopped vegetables and scrambled eggs and placed bread in the toaster, he made small talk with her about random current events, and she was thankful to let her mind wander to things that didn't really even matter.

Before she knew it, a plate of food was in front of her and her stomach growled loudly. "I guess I was hungrier than I thought," she said shyly. Mac sat beside her and together they ate in silence. Gina managed to eat half of hers before pushing the plate away. "Thank you, Mac. That was delicious."

His own meal finished, he gathered their plates and quickly cleaned up before helping Gina up from the stool. Turning off the lights as they walked along, he led her to the master bedroom. Gently, he sat her down on the bed and then pulled one of his shirts from a drawer and handed it to her. "The bathroom is through there"—he pointed—"and if you need anything, just call me."

"Where are you sleeping?"

"I'm probably going to watch a little TV, so I'll either fall asleep on the couch or I'll go up to one of the spare bedrooms."

"I can take the spare room, Mac. It's okay." Gina stood but Mac's hands on her shoulders had her sitting back down quickly.

"I want you to stay in here tonight. I'd feel better knowing that you were in here." Gina stared at him as he leaned forward and kissed her forehead. "Get some sleep." Mac turned to walk away, but Gina's hand grabbing his stopped him.

"I don't want to be alone, Mac."

"Gina," he began hesitantly.

She shook her head. "I've been alone for so long, and right now I really want to be here with you." A single tear streaked down her cheek. "It's okay if you don't love me or if you don't want me anymore, but please don't make me be alone tonight." Her big green eyes stared up at him, and in that moment he would have given her everything that he had and more. "Stay with me. Please."

Mac pulled his hand from hers and walked away. He heard Gina gasp, but he simply closed the door and walked back to her side. Without a word, he stripped down to his briefs and then pulled her to her feet. Gina kicked off her shoes, and Mac helped her take off her skirt and blouse. When she stood before him in nothing but white lace, he kept his eyes on hers as he reached behind her for the shirt. Gina took it from his hands and dropped it on the floor.

Along with her bra.

"Just for tonight," she whispered. "I need you to love me just for tonight." Mac whispered her name, but she put her finger over his lips. "Please don't say anything. I don't expect you to make promises to me. I just need you." She reached up and wrapped one hand around his neck and pulled him toward her. The kiss was tentative at first, but once she brought her nearly naked body flush against him, Mac was lost.

He lay them down on the bed and sighed with the pleasure of feeling Gina's body against his again. He'd missed this, needed this. The kiss became greedy, but he couldn't be sure who was taking and who was giving, all he knew was that this wasn't one-sided. She may have been the one to ask him to stay, but he most certainly was the one who didn't want to leave.

———

Morning came far too soon. Mac hadn't let Gina leave his arms all night long. Several times she had disentangled herself from him but he managed to coax her back. He knew she was trying to distance herself from him, but Mac wouldn't allow it. They had made love numerous times before, but something about the way they connected last night went beyond anything Mac had ever experienced before.

They never said a word, and yet they had held each other's gazes the entire time. Mac didn't need Gina to tell him that she loved him; it was there in her eyes. He could only hope she read the same in his, because he knew that he was in love with Gina Micelli. Only now was not the time to throw that emotional curveball at her.

Today she was going to have enough to deal with; funeral arrangements had to be made, and he was sure there were legal matters dealing with Arthur's estate to be gone over. The last thing she needed was him confessing that he was in love with her. The timing was off; she'd probably think he was saying it out of pity, to make her feel better. No, he had to wait until she got through the funeral and all that went with it before they could sit down and talk about their future.

He would stay by her side, be whatever it was she needed him to be, everything he should have been from the moment he first laid eyes on her. With a sigh, Mac pulled Gina close and kissed her forehead. He whispered her name in an attempt to wake her up. Gina's eyes opened slowly, and when she looked up and saw him, she smiled warmly. Then the events of the day before came washing over her and Mac had to watch as that serene smile turned to sadness.

"You're not alone," he said to her. "The whole family is here to help you through this."

Confusion marked her face as her brows furrowed. "They're here now?"

Mac chuckled. "I didn't mean literally. Whenever you're ready, we'll go back to my parents' place and see what needs to be done. You don't have to rush. Dad knows that we'll be there at some point this morning."

—⁓—

Gina pushed the hair from her eyes and looked around the room as she held the sheet tightly to her chest. For a brief moment, she had forgotten all that had happened the previous day; waking up in Mac's arms was more than she'd ever thought she would experience again. Now all that was left was grief and remorse. She never should have asked him to stay with her last night, and she certainly shouldn't have made love with him.

Rising from the bed, Mac dressed quickly before turning to face Gina again. "I'm going to go and make us some coffee and call my parents. You can use the shower if you'd like. If you aren't ready to get dressed yet, there's a robe hanging on the bathroom door." He stepped up beside her and kissed her on the cheek. "Take your time."

Once she was alone, Gina didn't know where to begin. Everything was out of sorts; she wanted to burrow back under the blankets and just forget everything. She was so grateful to the Montgomerys, and she knew that William and Monica were going to do everything possible to help her through all of the planning and legalities she was sure to be faced with.

That just left Mac. When he had shown up at the hospital at the exact moment she needed him, she thought she had been dreaming. The way he had held her, calmed her, and taken care of her was in direct conflict to the way they had ended things. For someone who talked about their relationship being temporary, he was certainly doing everything that implied permanence.

Gina closed her eyes and remembered the intensity with which he had made love to her. The way he had looked at her, held her gaze as he loved her, told her that he felt more deeply for her than he was letting on. Unfortunately, unless he was able to open up to her and ask her to stay, Gina knew she would eventually have to leave.

By the time she met up with him in the kitchen, she had showered and dressed. Mac handed her a mug of steaming coffee while he spoke on the phone. Within minutes, he had hung up and sat beside her at the breakfast bar where they had eaten the previous evening. "Are you hungry? I think I can whip up some pancakes."

As tempting as it sounded, Gina had no appetite. She shook her head. "I'm not hungry." Mac nodded and they sat in companionable silence, sipping coffee.

"I spoke to my father and he said that whenever you're ready, we can go over and discuss all the arrangements."

It was Gina's turn to nod and then she rose. "Do you want to head over now?"

"I think I do," she said quietly. She gathered her few belongings, and when they were getting ready to head out the door, she stopped and placed a hand on Mac's arm. "In case I forget to say it later, I want to thank you for everything you're doing."

Mac smiled down at her. "You don't have to thank me, Gina." He trailed his fingers along the side of her face, relishing the softness of her skin. "Whatever you need, I'm here for you."

If only he knew that she needed him by her side forever.

For the next four days, Gina felt like she was caught in a whirlwind. Her father had planned everything for his own funeral, and Gina had been relieved not to have to even think about those decisions. As expected, there was a ton of paperwork to go over due to the size of her father's estate and, as promised, William Montgomery was by her side, holding her hand as he walked her through it.

The entire Montgomery family had been wonderful. While William helped her with the legal and financial decisions, Monica had been like a mother to her when her emotions began to overwhelm her. Emma had brought over every kind of baked treat from her bakery that she knew Gina loved, and Maggie had sat beside her and listened to stories of her childhood. Lucas and Jason had been overly attentive, and she found that she drew strength just from having them all around.

And then there was Mac.

He was never out of her sight. Mac had helped his father explain some of the countless legal documents. During the wake and funeral and reception afterward, he had been right by her side. She never had to lift a finger for anything because he seemed to know what she needed and when.

At night, when the lights were out and her memories threatened to overwhelm her, Mac was there to hold her close. They hadn't made love since the night at his home, but the time they spent clinging to each other was just as intimate to Gina. He comforted her when she needed it, and she found that it was getting easier to make it through each day with Mac beside her.

They were eating dinner with his family a few nights later when Jason mentioned that he was preparing to go to San Francisco for business. "It's beautiful there," Gina commented. "I always love going to Fisherman's Wharf. The food there is amazing."

"I've never been there," Maggie said, "and I'm hoping that we'll find time to do some sightseeing."

"I could recommend some great restaurants if you'd like," Gina said casually, and that's when it hit Mac. The funeral had merely been a distraction from real life. Now that Arthur was laid to rest and his estate was well on its way to being settled, Gina was going to head back to the West Coast. He could ask her to stay; they could talk about it tonight after they went back to the guest-house, but the thought of asking her to leave behind the life she knew was daunting.

Conversation continued to flow, but Mac chose not

to be a part of it. Everyone was so focused on keeping Gina's spirits up that no one seemed to notice his silence. When the meal was done and everyone was saying their good nights, William came to stand beside his eldest son. "Kind of quiet tonight," he said conversationally. They were standing alone in the family room while everyone else was heading for the door.

"Wasn't a whole lot to say."

"You've been to California a bunch of times. I'm sure you could have added a tip or two for your brother and Maggie."

Mac shrugged. "Gina's the native; she knows far more than I do."

"She's not a native; she was born and raised here in North Carolina. This is where she belongs; this is where her father wanted her to be."

Mac was desperate for a change of subject. "How are you doing with all of this, Dad? We've all been so focused on helping Gina, I feel we've sort of overlooked the fact that you lost your best friend."

His father's gaze softened. "I'm not going to lie to you, Son; it's pretty damn devastating. I can't remember a time in my life when I wasn't friends with Arthur. Knowing that I'm not ever going to see him again is more painful than I ever thought possible."

"I'm so sorry," Mac said gruffly. "I can't even imagine that."

"Pray that you never do, Mac. I'm trying to do everything I can for Gina, everything that Arthur would want me to do, but I'm battling my own grief at the same time, and I don't know what else I'm supposed to do."

"Just love her, Dad. She's lost her father, and now you're the closest thing that she has to one."

"It's a big responsibility, Mac. It's easy to love your own kids; as a parent you can't help it. Gina has always been special to me. She's the daughter your mother and I never had. It's easy to keep thinking of her that way and love her." Mac smiled and nodded. "You're in love with her too. Aren't you?"

Mac's eyes shot to his father's. "I don't know what you're talking about."

William reached out and placed a reassuring hand on his son's shoulder. "Someday you won't be so afraid of it."

"Of what?"

"Letting go of the control. You were always one to want to control everything and everybody, and loving someone means that you're not always in control. But you know what? It's worth it, Mac. Don't fight it so damn hard."

"I'm not like Lucas and Jason, Dad," Mac said adamantly. "You're not going to play that game with me. It won't work."

"There's no game here," William assured him. "I could tell how you felt about Gina every time I saw the two of you together. It's obvious that you're crazy about each other."

"Oh, you'd love that, wouldn't you? Then you could tell everyone how you played matchmaker to all three of your sons who were too stupid to realize how you were setting them up." With every word, Mac was getting more and more agitated, all his pent-up frustration pouring out. "I don't like being played, Dad; you know that. Is that why you left it up to me to check in on Gina? Pick her up from the airport?"

Now it was William's turn to be angry. "In case you've forgotten, that poor girl came here to watch her father die. How dare you make this about you or me or something as trivial as me putting a damn feather in my cap? I told you from the get-go that you weren't right for Gina. I told you that I wouldn't do that to her, and judging by the way you're behaving right now, I'm glad I didn't." He stepped away from his son. "Grow up, Mac. None of this was about you." William strode from the room and Mac was left standing alone and wondering what the hell had just happened.

It took a few minutes for him to settle down and go in search of whoever was left in the house. His father was nowhere to be seen, but he found his mother and Gina sitting at the kitchen table, talking quietly to one another. "Oh, Mac," his mother said, smiling with surprise. "I thought you must have snuck out with the crowd. We didn't realize you were still here." She gestured to the chair beside her. "Gina and I were just talking about which of her paintings I want to hang in the guesthouse."

The smile that crept across his face couldn't be helped. He was proud of her. Plain and simple, he was proud of how Gina had transformed herself since she had arrived. If only he could be certain that she wouldn't regress back to her former timid self once she was back in California and under her mother's influence. "They're all amazing," he said as he sat down. "I'm sure that no matter which ones you choose, you'll be pleased."

Gina beamed under his praise. "Thank you." They

talked about her artwork for a little longer before Monica looked at the time. "As much as I enjoy sitting and talking with you both, I'm afraid it's getting a bit late for me. William's already gone up."

Mac wanted to point out that his father hadn't gone up to bed because he was tired as much as he was pissed off, but he decided to keep that bit of information to himself. Rising to his feet, he leaned over and kissed his mother good night. Gina did the same. "Thank you for everything, Monica. Dinner was delicious."

They made their way across the yard in silence, and Mac knew that the woman walking beside him was stronger today than she had ever been. When they got to the front door of the guesthouse, he paused. "You seemed to enjoy yourself tonight."

"I did. But then again I always have a good time with your family; they're easy to get along with."

"I was thinking that I should probably go back to my place tonight," he said finally, hating the words even as he said them.

"Oh…okay."

"I haven't been to the office in almost a week, and I'm sure you have things to do as well."

"Yeah, sure." She didn't. Unfortunately, all she had left to do was decide whether or not she was going to relocate here to North Carolina or go home to California and back to her old life. It was on the tip of her tongue to share that with Mac, to ask him to help her decide, but he was already pulling away from her again. Physically and emotionally.

Gina couldn't do it anymore.

"I was hoping we would have time to talk," she

blurted out. "I mean, I can see that you're anxious to leave and all, but I have to know something before you go."

"Anything," he said cautiously.

"Do you want me to go back to California?" Her eyes were wide and her back was stiff as she asked it. No matter what his answer was, Gina would never have peace if she didn't take the risk and find out.

Mac weighed his words carefully. "I think you need to do what you want to do. I mean, if you think you'll be happy back there and in your old job, then you should do it. Of course you could go back there and start fresh, get a new job, move out of your mother's house, and experience life being independent."

Gina stared at him. Just stared. "I'm not asking you for the Miss America, politically correct answer, dammit! I want to know what you, Mackenzie Montgomery, want me to do!"

"I want you to do what makes you happy, Gina," he said stiffly. "I think you need to experience all of the things you've denied yourself. You deserve that."

Well, she had her answer. She didn't like it, but at least she had her answer. With a regal nod of her head, she turned and opened the front door. "Thank you for seeing me home. I'm sorry if I kept you from your job. I know how important it is to you."

His patience snapped. "Dammit, Gina, what is it you want from me?" Mac reached out and grabbed her upper arm, spinning her around to look at him.

She pulled out of his grasp. "I want honesty. I want to know how you feel. But all you can do is hand me this line of bull. Well, congratulations, you're like

Switzerland. You managed to be so neutral that you can't actually form a personal opinion."

"You have no idea, do you?" he said roughly. "I've sat here on multiple occasions listening to you go on and on about how tired you were of people making decisions for you. You yelled, you screamed, and you cried about it. Now, when I'm standing here, giving you the opportunity to make your own decision, I end up being the bad guy! I can't win!"

"Don't you dare put this on me!" she yelled. "This isn't about me making my own decisions. This is about you using that as your excuse not to have to change your way of life. Perfect Mackenzie who likes everything neat, tidy, and orderly. By letting someone else in, you'd have to give up some of your precious control, and that just isn't something you're willing to do—not for me and not for anyone. Well, you know what? That's fine. Because I deserve someone who doesn't see having me in their life as a sacrifice, but as a blessing."

"Gina—"

"Don't," she spat at him. "Just…don't. I can't make you love me. I can't make you change, and you know what? I never wanted you to. I love you because of who you are. You look at me and you see all of the ways that I'll inconvenience you. I'm tired of people treating me like that. I am a good person, dammit. And if you can't see that, if you can't appreciate that, then you don't deserve me."

She stepped inside and slammed the door, and in that moment, Mac realized just how much he had lost.

Chapter 11

ALL OF HER ART SUPPLIES WERE PACKED UP. THE PLAN was to have UPS come and pick them up and ship them to her mother's house. Temporarily. In the week since she'd last seen Mac, Gina had done some serious soul-searching and started forging the path of her new life.

Gone was her life as an accountant. That was the first and easiest decision she had to make. As much as she'd hated doing it by phone, she had called her boss and tendered her resignation. Surprisingly, the sky did not fall and the Earth kept spinning. After she hung up, Gina had felt as though a giant weight had been lifted off her.

The next thing she had done was call her mother. Another thing she had contemplated doing in person, but decided that the only way she could return to California was if the air was cleared between the two of them first. Of course her mother had ranted on and on about what a mistake Gina was making in leaving her job and how irresponsible it was of her, but when she realized that her daughter wasn't going to be swayed from her decision, her attitude changed.

"I didn't think I raised you to be so defiant, Gina."

"No, you didn't. You raised me to simply fall in line with whatever it was that *you* wanted. That's why your marriage failed; Dad wouldn't fall in line and become the man you thought he should be. You cannot control people like that. I am my own person and for the first time in my life, I am discovering who I am. You can support me in that or you can ignore me; the choice is yours. Either way, I'm going to do things the way that I see fit from this point on."

"It's just so drastic…I don't understand why you can't just come home and we can talk about this!"

"Because we don't talk; you talk. So the ball is in your court, Mom. You can have a relationship with me or not." Gina had learned to be bold, to say exactly what was on her mind. She spoke calmly. "I would have thought you, more than anyone, would have learned that when you push people too far, they eventually walk away. You pushed Dad until he was willing to let us leave. He didn't want to fight with you anymore. Did that make you any happier than you were when you were with him?"

Barbara was silent for a long moment. "No," she said quietly. "You may not believe me, Gina, but I missed your father every day."

Tears began to run down Gina's face. "So because you wanted to punish him for not letting you tell him how to live his life, you destroyed our family. Are you really surprised that I don't want to follow that same path?"

"I never thought he'd let us go. On some level, I thought that he'd either stop me before we could leave or that he'd come to his senses and come for us in California. And if I'm being totally honest, I truly believed right up until the end," she said with a sob, "that maybe he'd even just sell the company and move across the country to be with us." She was crying so hard she couldn't speak but Gina waited her out, needing to finally hear the reasons why her mother acted the way she had. "Oh, Gina,

I made a mess of our lives! I never stopped loving your father and when he didn't come for me or fight for me, I became angry and bitter. I wanted to punish him. I didn't realize how much I was hurting you. I'm so sorry!"

She knew it wasn't going to be easy, but from this point on, the two of them were going to have to work at building a new relationship. And while Gina was certain her mother would insist the way to do that was to spend a lot of time together, Gina had other ideas.

By the time the conversation ended, she felt as if she were floating on air, so light was she after removing what she considered dead weight. A look around the guesthouse had Gina feeling nostalgic. The Montgomery home had always been a haven to her as a child, and it was even more so now. Leaving here was going to be harder than she ever could have imagined. She looked at the two pieces of art that Monica had chosen for the walls: the landscape of the garden and a sunset over the lake at her father's house. Both made Gina smile and she was honored that Monica had wanted them hung on the walls here.

Wrapped by the front door was the painting she had done for Emma for Lily's nursery. She was planning on taking it over to her this afternoon, and now that she was finished with the majority of her packing, she would shower and take the drive over.

As she got ready, Gina realized how happy she was for Lucas. They had been friends since they were kids, and it was so wonderful that he had married someone like Emma, who seemed to truly understand him and was so obviously in love with him. Plus, she was thankful Emma was someone she'd easily bonded with and now considered a friend. It may have been ten years since she'd last seen Lucas, but now that she was older, Gina knew she wouldn't let that much time pass ever again.

It was a beautiful, crisp fall day, perfect for late October. The leaves on the trees were so vibrant that Gina's hands fairly twitched with the need to paint. Inspiration struck, and instead of loading the painting into the car, she grabbed her camera and a sweater and walked outside. There was a light breeze swirling the mutlicolored leaves around her, and Gina lifted the camera and just started shooting.

The Montgomerys' property was several acres large and with no direction or plan in mind, Gina let the leaves and the wind guide her. The golds and the reds flew by, and she almost couldn't keep up with everything she wanted to capture. She cursed as her long hair kept blowing in her eyes, wishing she had thought to bring a clip with her. A small leaf landed on the zoom lens of her camera, and without even missing a beat, she continued to shoot through her partially obscured view and captured a magnificent sunset.

Sunset?

"Shoot," she murmured and looked at her watch. Unable to believe her eyes, the watch told her that she'd been walking the property for almost three hours. "Too late to head over to Emma's now, dang it." Feeling invigorated from the fresh air and excited to get back to her computer to see what she'd captured, Gina headed back to the guesthouse. The thought of disappointing Emma made her frown, but William and Monica were throwing her a going-away barbecue on Sunday. She'd call Emma and let her know she'd give her the painting then.

Unable to contain her joy, Gina booted up the computer and kicked off her shoes as she clicked on some Motown to listen to while she created what she was sure would be a masterpiece.

———ᴧᴧᴧ———

Sunday was bittersweet. Gina appreciated that William and Monica wanted to throw her a farewell dinner, but the thought of leaving the people she considered family was harder than she'd ever imagined it would be.

"I can't believe you opted for a barbecue," Maggie said, handing Gina a glass of iced tea.

Gina shrugged. "To you a barbecue is no big deal, but for me? This is a treat. We never barbecue back home; my mother thinks it's uncivilized to eat with your hands." She burst out laughing and Maggie joined her.

"It's amazing that you are as normal as you are. Every time you tell me another tale from your life in California, I cringe."

"You get used to it." Looking up, she saw Emma walking toward her with Lily in her arms. Without hesitation, she scooped the infant up and cuddled her close. "I think I'm going to miss you most of all," she whispered to Lily and placed a kiss on her tiny head. She missed the look exchanged between the two Montgomery women.

"I know I said it earlier but Lucas and I are just thrilled with the painting you did for Lily. It's just… spectacular. I can't even believe that I know someone this talented!"

Gina had done a whimsical painting with teddy bears and butterflies. It wasn't that she was being original; she was following the small theme she noticed that Emma had started in the nursery. "I'm so glad you like it; if you want me to change anything or if you'd rather have something else, please tell me. I won't be offended."

Emma rolled her eyes. "Please. It's perfect, absolutely perfect. I know exactly where I want it hung and I've already told Lucas he's taking care of that as soon as we get home tonight." She reached out and gently stroked her daughter's head. "Promise me you're going to come back and visit. I want you to see where your masterpiece is hanging."

There was a moment of hesitation on Gina's part. She had barely come to grips with leaving. Would she ever be able to come back? Rather than commit to it outright, she did her best to sound encouraging yet vague. "I would love that."

"So you're all packed?" Emma asked, and Gina nodded. "Is there anything you need help with? A ride to the airport?"

"William and Monica are driving me there and I'll be flying out with Jason and Maggie on the company plane."

"Well, that's new information," Emma said with delight. "When did this happen?"

"Maggie called me yesterday; she knew I was procrastinating on booking my flight home, and with her and Jason flying out to California anyway, it just made sense." She smiled at her friends. "It will be nice to travel with some familiar faces."

"I'm sure." Emma looked at Maggie, her grin wide. "That was a great idea."

"Well," Maggie began, "it was a little selfish on my part. I'm hoping we'll have the chance to visit with each other a little more and that Gina can show us around while we're there. Jason will be in meetings a lot of the time, and now I'll have someone to sightsee with!"

Gina didn't want to admit that it was a little selfish on her part as well. With the distraction of Jason and Maggie, she wouldn't be spending so much time at home being spoon-fed a guilt trip at the hands of her mother.

"It's just hamburgers and hot dogs for crying out loud!" they heard Lucas yell from behind them. "It doesn't take three men to man a grill!" The women laughed and watched as Lucas did his best to shoo his father and Jason aside. "Amazingly enough, you don't seem too anxious to help when I'm grilling steaks."

"There's an art to this," Jason argued. "That's all I'm saying." The women turned back around and decided to let the men argue among themselves. No one mentioned the fact that there was one Montgomery man missing. Gina wasn't sure what Mac's absence signified, but she wasn't going to let herself go there. Today she was going to focus on the friends who were here around her and enjoy the day.

"So what are your plans for when you get home?" Emma asked. "Other than sightseeing with Maggie?"

They all laughed again and Gina knew she was going to miss this; it had been a long time since she'd had girlfriends to hang out and have fun with. "I think I'm going to travel a little bit. There are some places I've always wanted to go and now, thanks to my father and his generosity, I'll be able to take the time off and not have to worry." She smiled sadly at all she was gaining and at what cost. "I think I want to go someplace warm and tropical first."

"Ooh, maybe a cruise?" Maggie suggested.

"No, cruises don't do it for me. I want to be on the beach and sleep with the sound of the waves crashing on the shore." She sighed. "I'm thinking Hawaii or Fiji."

"You can't go wrong with either of those places." Emma sighed. "I'll have to live vicariously through you because I think it's going to be a long time before Lucas and I can go on a vacation alone together."

"Yes, but you have this beautiful baby girl to make up for it. I'd trade that for a vacation any day of the week," Gina replied. "Plus you never know; you're blessed with wonderful in-laws who, I am sure, would love an opportunity to babysit for you if you and Lucas wanted a little time away."

"Not to mention a brother and sister-in-law who would gladly help out too," Maggie added.

"See?" Gina said with a nod. "Blessed."

"Don't I know it," Emma said and stepped forward as Lily started to fuss. "I think she's hungry." She headed back toward the house, and Maggie and Gina followed. They all settled in the family room and Monica soon joined them.

"I cannot believe they are still out there fighting about how to grill a hot dog; this isn't brain surgery," Monica said, laying her head back on the sofa. "My children are grown men who still act like children." There was a comfortable silence as Emma settled in to nurse Lily. "So Gina, are you all packed and ready to go home?"

"I'm packed, not sure I'm ready," she admitted. "Actually, I have to meet with the realtor for Dad's house later this afternoon, but that's the last bit of business I have to deal with in person. After that, it's all stuff I can do over the phone or by mail."

"What time do you have to meet her?" Emma asked. "Do we need to rush the men along?"

"No, I'm not meeting Robin until around five." She looked over at Maggie. "I was hoping you'd take the ride with me. I'd rather not do this alone; I'm afraid I'll get overwhelmed. I need someone with me to keep me on task."

"I am just the girl to do it!" Maggie assured her as she reached out and squeezed Gina's hand. "We'll eat, help clean up, and then head over to the house, and by the time we get back, it will be time for dessert." She turned to Emma. "Please tell me you brought something with chocolate with you?"

"Don't I always?"

—–ⱳⱳ—–

The drive over to Arthur's house was filled with conversation, and Gina was happy for the distraction. Once they pulled into the driveway and she saw the "For Sale" sign, a wave of sadness washed over her.

"Oh my gosh!" Maggie said in awe. "This is your father's house?"

Gina nodded. "That's why we're here, remember?"

They climbed out of the car and Maggie stood, mouth gaping, looking at the modern Tudor-style home. She walked back and forth, examining the front of the house while Gina greeted her realtor, Robin. Gina called out to Maggie. "We're heading inside; are you coming?" Maggie nodded anxiously and followed them through the front door.

"As you know," Robin began, "we'll be going through and taking pictures of the entire house and property to put up on the website. I know you worked hard to clear out all of your father's personal belongings and anything that you didn't want, and I cannot thank you enough for being so efficient."

"There was no point in putting it off," Gina said, trying her best to remember that this was a good thing she was doing.

"We'll take probably about two dozen photos of the outside and focus on the architecture: steeply pitched gables, large stone chimney; tall, narrow windows arranged in pairs; decorative half-timbering against stucco surface…then we'll go into great detail on the property itself. It really is spectacular with the acreage and the pond in the back."

Maggie cleared her throat. "Um…what, what is the acreage?"

"You're looking at about seven acres total. The view out the back is just breathtaking, and you can see it all through the massive windows and glass doors that Arthur had custom made for the entire rear of the house. And what makes it even more appealing is that there are no homes behind you on the other side of the pond. That's a wildlife preserve, and it will never be built on. Whoever buys this property is going to love the privacy."

Robin turned her attention back to Gina, but noticed that Maggie was lingering at the foot of the stairs. "You can go up," she suggested. "There are five bedrooms upstairs but the master is down here on the first floor."

Before Gina could stop her, Maggie excused herself and ran up the stairs. She smiled and looked at Robin.

"I knew she'd love this place; that's why I brought her along. If you play your cards right, this could be the easiest commission you've ever made."

An hour later, they were climbing back into the car. "You didn't need me here with you at all," Maggie said suspiciously. "You wanted me to see that house."

Gina couldn't deny it. "Well, I knew what you were looking for, and I think it would be perfect for you and Jason! I'm right, aren't I?"

"Of course you're right. Jason's been here before, and he's always loved the house. He's probably on the phone with Robin now, getting everything together to make an offer."

"Whatever you offer, I'll accept," Gina said.

"One dollar!" Maggie teased.

Gina laughed. "And I'd take it."

Maggie smacked her on the arm. "Don't be ridiculous. This house is your future; you want to travel and be independent. This house is going to make that possible."

"And I think that my father would be very pleased to know that the house is staying in the family." True, Arthur Micelli had probably hoped his daughter would live in the house he had purchased in hopes of her coming back to live with him, but Gina didn't want a house that was marred by such sad memories. She knew that Jason and Maggie would make the house their own and fill it with love and children and laughter.

And that made Gina happy. Which is what Arthur had wanted all along.

Chapter 12

MAC WAS MISERABLE. IT WAS A SUNDAY, AND HE WAS at the office when he should have been with his family saying good-bye to Gina. What did it say about him that he blatantly blew her off in favor of work after all they had shared? Hell, take the physical part of their relationship out of the equation, and she was still a dear friend of the family.

He despised himself right now.

There didn't need to be anyone there to tell him he was a coward because he already knew it. Gina had been right when she had told him off. *Perfect Mackenzie who likes everything neat, tidy, and orderly.* Great; look where that had gotten him. Sure, everything around him certainly was neat and tidy; hell, he was even wearing dress slacks and a button-down shirt when it was a Sunday and no one was in the office! For years, all of this had made him happy. At least he thought he had been happy.

But he wasn't happy.

Not one damn bit.

Leaning back in his chair with his hands folded behind his head, Mac thought about the things that did make him happy.

A gypsy with wide, expressive green eyes.

A petite and curvy woman who danced to the Jackson Five and sang into wooden spoons.

An artist who painted with abandon while wearing cowboy hats.

A woman who loved him, who he didn't deserve.

Running a weary hand over his face, he reached for his phone. It was almost nine o'clock on Sunday night, and he was sure everyone would have left his parents' house by now. His first thought was to call Lucas, but with a baby in the house, Mac was afraid he'd wake her up. He pressed Jason's name on his phone and waited.

"You missed one hell of a barbecue," Jason said by way of greeting. "Don't ever let Lucas offer to grill hamburgers and hot dogs; apparently there is a right way and a wrong way to grill them, and he got it all wrong."

"Sorry I missed it," Mac said even though he wasn't. "Do you have time to talk?"

"Yeah, sure," Jason said and then whispered something to Maggie. "What's up?"

"I messed up."

"No kidding."

"What am I supposed to do? Gina's ticked off at me; she probably wouldn't answer the phone if I called her. I blew off the barbecue, so you know Mom and Dad are going to get on me for that one on top of everything else."

"I bought a house today," Jason said, interrupting Mac's rant.

"Excuse me?"

"A house. Today. Maggie and I bought a house today."

Mac pinched the bridge of his nose and counted to ten. "What exactly does this have to do with anything I was saying?"

"I'm not sure. I'm just stoked about the whole thing

and thought you might need a distraction from all of the ranting and kicking yourself."

"I'm not kicking myself," Mac grumbled. "Much."

Jason laughed. "Bro, you are totally kicking yourself right now and you totally should. You messed up in a big way and then, after you did all that, you heaped more on top of it. I'm telling you, it was epic."

Now Mac was getting angry. "You know, I called you because I thought you could help me, but if all you're going to do is be a jackass…"

"No, no, no…that title, big brother, belongs solely to you."

"Never freaking mind," Mac snapped and was about to hang up when he heard Jason yell out.

"Okay, you want me to help you? Then you have to listen. Get out of your own damn head for a little while and maybe you can learn something from me. Okay?"

Mac inhaled sharply. "Okay."

"Good. So Maggie and I bought this house—"

"Are we back to that again?"

"Aren't you supposed to be listening?"

"Fine, but this better have a point."

"It does," Jason assured him. "So we bought this house today. She actually toured it and called me, and the next thing I know I'm on the phone with the realtor talking offers and contracts. Now, why would I agree to buy a house when I wasn't even there with her?"

"Because you're stupid?"

"Ha, funny. Good to see there is still a little sense of humor left in you. But no. I bought the house because I trust Maggie. She toured it, she talked to the realtor, and it was exactly what we both wanted. We have been looking at houses for months, and before that we talked about what we wanted in a house for months. When she saw this place, she knew it was the one."

"Okay, so now you have a house. I'm still not seeing how this relates to me."

Jason sighed. "Sometimes you are so thickheaded it's painful, you know that, right? Anyway, there are several ways that this applies to you. First off, there's trust. Maggie and I trust one another. Some guys would have been pretty ticked off if their wives went off and made an offer on a house without discussing it with them first. I mean, I have to live in the house too, and although she didn't do it completely without me and I had the final say, I knew that in her mind it was a done deal."

"Trust," Mac repeated. "No, that's not an issue. I trust Gina."

"Do you? Because it seems to me like you don't."

"How could you even say that?"

"You don't trust her to fit into your world. In your mind she's going to change and morph into some kind of woman who all of a sudden will realize that you're a completely annoying control freak and decide to leave. Well, news flash, brother; she's known you most of her life and knows that you're a control freak and she still loves you! And in all of the time the two of you were together, did she once ask you to change?"

"Well, no but—"

"Of course she didn't," Jason barreled on. "Okay, so trust is number one. Next is communication. Maggie and I had talked about what we wanted in a house and where we wanted to live, and sometimes we agreed and sometimes we didn't but the bottom line is, we talked."

"Gina and I talked all the damn time!" Mac snapped. "God, I love talking to her; we would sit and talk for hours."

"Yeah, yeah, you talk, but do you actually listen? Do you talk about real things or just generalizations? From what you've told me—and that's not much—it seems to me like you decided from the get-go that this was a short-term relationship, and then somewhere along the way, that changed. Did you talk to her about it?"

"Well, no, but she didn't talk to me about it either!"

"Man, are you stupid," Jason said with disgust. "Do you even hear yourself? So because she didn't say anything, you couldn't say anything? You know what that leaves? A whole lot of silence."

"Fine, I should have told Gina how I felt. The last time we were together I tried talking to her, but she wouldn't listen!"

"Mac, you are my brother and I love you. You are a gifted businessman and you know how to talk to clients and put their minds at ease, but on a personal level, you are a mess."

Mac had to wonder why he had thought talking to his brother would make him feel better.

"I'm serious. I have watched you negotiate with clients and calm even the most skittish of them. But in all of the times I observed you with Gina? Hell, I'll even go so far as to say all of the times I've seen you with women, you aren't comfortable in your own skin. What are you afraid of?"

"I'm not afraid of anything; you just don't know what you're talking about."

"Okay, fine. I'm the dumbass here, but let me remind

you of this: I'm the dumbass who managed to find myself the woman of my dreams."

"You mean Dad found you the woman of your dreams," Mac reminded.

"He simply nudged. I almost let her walk away, but I listened to some advice and learned from my mistakes. Now I'm married, buying a house, and planning a family." He paused and chose his next words carefully. "Aren't you tired of being alone?"

Mac was, but the thought of admitting that out loud was too much for him. "I get what you're saying, Jace. I really do. I just don't know what to do right now to win her back."

"Do you seriously want Gina back?"

"More than anything," he said desperately.

Jason smiled. "Well then, this is your lucky day, Mackenzie, because I happen to have the perfect plan for you."

Gina took one last look around the guesthouse and sighed. Her boxes were all labeled and Monica had promised to have them shipped out the following day. Her life had changed in this house, and as much as Gina felt she had grown, she had also suffered such great loss.

Her father.

And Mac.

She looked down at the large item wrapped in simple brown paper that she was leaving behind. Mac's portrait. All of her other paintings were coming with her, but this one she just couldn't bear to keep. Instead, she had wrapped it up and had simply written his name on the paper, knowing that Monica would get it to him. Gina really couldn't imagine him hanging it in his house, but she still wanted him to have it and hoped he would remember their time together.

Picking up her large, clunky purse that held her phone, her laptop, her e-reader, and miscellaneous odds and ends for the trip, Gina placed one of her favorite cowboy hats on her head and walked out the door. Pulling it closed, she kept her eyes forward, refusing to look back. That was her new motto: no looking back.

Big, dark sunglasses shaded her eyes, and she had dressed much like she had upon her arrival. It was all about comfort, and the long, black gauzy skirt, though impractical for early November in North Carolina, was perfect for her arrival back in California.

William had loaded her luggage in the car earlier, and both he and Monica were standing by the SUV waiting for her. William had his back to her while he argued heatedly with someone on the phone. Gina couldn't hear the words, but his body language spoke volumes.

"Everything okay?" she asked Monica as she put her bag on the backseat.

"Just a small issue at the office; nothing he can't handle. Don't worry; he'll be off in a minute and we'll be on our way."

"I appreciate the both of you driving me. I'm sure I could have just driven with Jason and Maggie and saved you the trip."

"Nonsense, we wanted to do this, and besides, Jason is a nightmare to travel with. Ask Maggie. You'll see for yourself on the plane, but I can guarantee you they'll be

late, so don't panic if it's close to your departure time
and they're not there yet."

"Well, that's good to know, because I think I would
have had a slight panic attack if the plane started to leave
without them." As much as Gina was going for the carefree approach to life, some habits died hard—such as
being a stickler about time. No matter what, she was
always prompt. That was something she had never worried about with Mac; they were in sync on that subject.

Disappointment speared through her at the thought of
him. Somewhere in the back of her mind, she had truly
believed he was going to come for her and ask her to
stay. Apparently that was something she shared with her
mother: loving a man who wasn't willing to fight for her.

Or just didn't love her enough.

Gina knew she'd survive; she'd survived when her
father had let them leave when she was a teenager, she'd
survived losing him to cancer, and she would survive
Mackenzie Montgomery not loving her enough to want
her in his life for more than a handful of weeks.

She silently prayed that it wouldn't cause her to live
the rest of her life being angry and bitter like her mother.

Maggie texted to say that they were finally on their
way, and as Gina and the Montgomerys made their way
to the airport, all she could think about was how much
she didn't want to leave. North Carolina had always been
home for her; even after all of the years she'd lived on
the West Coast, she had never felt like it was her home.

"I'll make sure all your boxes get shipped out to you
tomorrow," Monica said. "They said they'd arrive some
time after two, but I'll text you after they leave, so you
know they're on their way."

"I'm not really in a rush for any of it. It's mostly painting supplies and personal items from my father's house. I think for the next week or so I'm going to be too busy working out some logistics with my mom to have any time to paint."

"So you're really moving out?" William asked.

Gina nodded. "I should have done it a long time ago. I have a friend who is a realtor, and I'm going to give her a call when I get home and set up a time to go look at places. I want to travel some and I'm not sure if I want a house or a condo, but I'm sure when I find the right place, I'll know."

"Well, you've always got a place to stay here," Monica added. "The guesthouse hardly gets used; it was nice to see someone staying in it."

"Have you considered moving back here?" William asked, looking at Gina through the rearview mirror.

"I did, but I'm not sure it's the right thing to do. There's nothing really tying me to any one place, so my options are endless. Perhaps I'll just rent something in San Francisco for a while, so I don't have to worry much while I travel."

"What are your travel plans? Have you finalized anything yet?" Monica asked, turning in her seat to face Gina.

"I haven't booked anything as of yet, but I'm planning on starting someplace tropical and then perhaps heading to Europe. I think I'd like to spend about a month away. You know, playing tourist and contemplating life. I'll paint and take pictures and make it a real bohemian sort of trip."

Monica sighed and smiled. "That sounds absolutely heavenly."

Just then Gina's phone beeped, and she looked down at the incoming text and laughed. "False alarm. Jason forgot his tablet. Heading back to the house. See you soon!" Gina looked up and saw both William and Monica laughing.

"I told you he's a handful to travel with. Maggie is so organized, and he just can't seem to get himself together."

"She doesn't seem to mind. And now that I know they're running behind, I can relax when I get on the plane. I've got my iPod, a new book to read…I'm ready for any kind of delay."

They parked in the short-term parking lot. William led them through to a part of the airport where corporate and private planes were kept and assisted Gina with the check-in process. She looked out onto the tarmac and saw several cars near the planes. "People can drive right up to their planes?" she asked, looking over at William.

He nodded. "Some do. I still prefer to come in through the airport. Then I have the option if I want to wait in the lounge until the jet is ready or head out and wait on board."

Gina had never flown on anything other than a commercial airplane, and the sight of the tiny planes compared to the major airlines' massive planes was a bit daunting. "You're not nervous about flying are you?" Monica asked.

"They just look so small in comparison," she replied nervously.

"Don't think of it like that. You'll be amazed by how roomy they are inside, and the seats are wide and comfortable. I think you'll be pleasantly surprised."

Gina wasn't totally convinced.

Soon she found herself hugging the Montgomerys

good-bye and had to force herself not to cry. "This isn't good-bye," Monica said, holding on to Gina tightly. "We're going to stay in touch and you'll come and visit, and who knows? Maybe William and I will make it out to California soon."

"I would love that." She looked at William and her heart lurched. Here was her father's best friend, a man who had done everything possible to make sure she was well taken care of. "I can't even begin to thank you…"

William held up a hand to stop her. "You don't have to thank me; you're family and I always take care of my family. Your father meant the world to me and I'm always going to miss him. His friendship was a gift, and I know that he would want me to make sure you are well taken care of." He pulled her into his embrace and held her tight. "Be happy," he whispered and Gina almost burst into tears. Those had been her father's last words to her.

She pulled back, smiling sadly at him, and could only nod. With a final wave, she let a uniformed attendant lead her out onto the tarmac and over to the Montgomery jet. It was bigger than some of the private planes out there, but nowhere near the size of the commercial jets. Taking a deep breath, she climbed the stairs and marveled at the sight before her. There was seating for at least two dozen people with a full galley and an entertainment center. It was far more luxurious than she could ever have imagined.

Gina settled into a soft leather seat that was more comfortable than most of her furniture at home, and sighed with pleasure. They hadn't even taken off yet and she swore she'd never be able to fly commercial ever again.

A flight attendant approached with the mimosa she had offered Gina upon her arrival at the door. Yes, she could definitely get used to this. Taking a sip, she laid her head back and smiled. The need for a little bit of music came over her, and she placed her glass down on the table beside her and reached into her bag for her iPod. Within minutes, she had her shoes off and had clicked to a favorite playlist. Her phone beeped and she smiled, knowing that it would be Maggie with an update.

"Almost there!" the text read. Gina replied with a smiley face and put the phone down next to her champagne glass. The first earbud was just about in place when she heard music. Looking down, she saw that she hadn't pushed Play yet and was curious as to where it was coming from. She stood and walked over to a speaker mounted on the wall and listened. Nope, no music coming from there.

"Is everything all right?" the flight attendant asked.

"I'm sorry," Gina said, shaking her head and chuckling softly. "I swore that I heard music but didn't know where it was coming from."

The flight attendant smiled. "I think it's coming from outside," she said as she motioned toward the door and stepped aside.

Were Jason and Maggie pulling directly up to the plane with the radio blasting? That seemed a little out of character for them. Walking to the door, she peered out and froze. There, at the base of the stairs stood Mac, his iPod playing "Ain't Too Proud to Beg" with tiny speakers held up above his head.

"You once told me that this was a classic," Mac called out over the music. "I may have embellished a bit but I thought this was a little more appropriate."

Gina put a hand to her chest to try and quiet her rapidly beating heart. "You're crazy," she said as her smile reached from ear to ear. "What are you doing here?"

Mac turned down the volume, climbed up the first two steps toward her, and stopped. "If you have to ask, then maybe I'm not doing this right." His hair was a little askew, and he was wearing jeans, sneakers, a T-shirt, and a raincoat, looking better than anything had in a long time to Gina. He took in her perusal of his attire and grinned. "It wasn't easy finding a raincoat like this."

She broke out in a fit of giggles. "I wouldn't imagine so. I can't believe you found one!"

"It turns out that Maggie and Emma are huge fans of that movie too, and so they helped hunt one down for me."

Gina looked around the tarmac. "They know you're here?" she asked with confusion. "Are Maggie and Jason with you?"

Mac climbed up a few more steps until he was eye level with her. "No, they're not with me and they're not coming." Now she was thoroughly confused. Her brows furrowed, and Mac reached out and smoothed her forehead with his fingers. "They're leaving next week for California, and I told them to let us know when they arrive and we'll meet up with them."

Her head tilted as she considered him. "We?"

"Yeah, we," he said and put the iPod in his pocket and cupped her face in both hands. Unwilling to wait any longer, he brought her face close to his. "You and me," he whispered before kissing her with all of the pent-up passion of the last several weeks.

Gina meant to put up more of a fight; she really did.

But the feel of his lips on hers and his hands on her face, and she was lost. He was everything that she had ever wanted, and he was here. He had fought for her, and he wasn't going to let her leave.

When they finally broke apart, Gina took him by the hand and led him onto the plane. He was handed a mimosa and then the flight attendant stepped out of sight again. She sat down in her seat and Mac was right beside her. Gina took the glass from his hands and then turned to face him. "I don't understand what's going on," she said, drinking in the sight of him.

"I finally came to my senses, that's what's going on." He looked down to where their fingers were locked together and squeezed. "I thought I was doing what was right for you; I thought that by letting you go, you would have the chance to live the life you deserved. But then I realized I was no better than your parents; I took away your options." His expression was solemn as he looked up at her. "I think that deep down, I was afraid if I let you decide, you'd choose to leave me. So I took the coward's way out and walked away first. I'm so sorry, Gina."

"You don't have to be sorry. I've been such a mess, going on and on and on about how I never get to make any decisions about my own life, that you had every right to think the way you did." She lifted his hand to her lips and kissed it. "I'm just glad that you came to your senses and stopped me from leaving." She leaned in and rested her forehead against his and felt all of the tension leave her body.

Then she sprang upright. "Oh my goodness, I'll have to call your mother and tell her not to ship out my stuff."

"Already done."

She shot him a sideways glance. "Awfully confident in yourself, aren't you?"

He shrugged. "Let's just say that I was hopeful." Gina began to gather her belongings. "What are you doing?"

"Well, since you're here, I thought we were going home for now." *Home.* She liked the way that sounded when it applied to the two of them.

"Oh, no," he said, tugging her down onto his lap. "We have this flight booked and we're leaving for now."

"But we're coming back, right?" she asked, anxious to be back where she most wanted to be.

"Eventually," he said and drew her back in for another long kiss. He pulled back a minute later. "You should know this means that you're stuck with me. Forever."

"I want to be stuck with you," she whispered and cuddled in as close to him as she could get, hating that they weren't alone. Her hands moved all over him, unable to help herself. It seemed like a dream that he was here with her, that they were on a plane and actually talking about forever.

The pilot's voice came through the speakers, alerting them that they were ready to depart, and Gina settled herself back in her own seat and then looked over at Mac. "This is really happening," she said in wonder. "We're really doing this. You're coming to California with me."

Mac gave her a big smile and raised his glass. "We are really doing this." He clinked his glass to hers. "To our future."

"To our future," she agreed. Having Mac here with her finally allowed Gina to relax in a way she hadn't in weeks. They talked through the takeoff and for the first hour of the flight, but when she rested her head on his shoulder, all she wanted to do was nap.

"Sleep for a little while, sweetheart," he whispered as he shifted to make sure she was comfortable. Then he spent the next several hours enjoying the feel of her beside him and watching her sleep.

When Gina finally woke, she sat up and stretched and then looked at her watch. "Oh my gosh!" she cried. "Why are we still in the air? We were due to land in San Francisco more than three hours ago! What's going on?"

"We aren't going to San Francisco," he said simply.

Gina looked at him quizzically. "What do you mean we're not going to San Francisco? That was what we booked the flight for. Where are we going?"

"We booked the flight for wherever we wanted to go. Jason and Maggie just told you it was San Francisco. And while yes, we could have done that, I thought it might be better if we took a trip to Hawaii for a week before going to California."

"Hawaii? Are you serious? How did you know I wanted to go there?"

"I have my sources," he teased. "Are you disappointed that we're not stopping at your house first?"

"I'm not, but I should call my mother. She was supposed to pick me up at the airport. She must be frantic by now!"

Mac waved her off and laughed. "She knows exactly where you are. My father called her before he took you to the airport."

"Oh no. How did that go? Was she the person he was arguing with?"

Mac laughed again. "You know it. Dad told her I had

this planned, and she demanded that I bring you home first, but he really stood his ground and told her it was time she let you live your own life."

"I'm going to pay for that, you know."

Mac leaned forward and kissed her. "No, you won't. In the end he calmed her down, and she and my mother talked after we took off and everything is fine. She's disappointed that she won't be seeing you for another week because she does miss you, but she's fine."

"How did you find all of this out?"

"You're a heavy sleeper, Gina," he said and ran a finger down her cheek. "I talked to my parents and my brothers, and everyone is thrilled to be rid of me for a couple of weeks."

"Their loss is my gain," she said with a smile and leaned her head on his shoulder once again. "I am just so happy you came back for me."

Mac tipped her face up to his. "I couldn't let you leave, Gina. You're my heart and I love you. I'll always love you."

It was the first time he had said the words out loud. They wrapped their way around Gina, and she couldn't contain the smile that just seemed to widen. "I don't think I'll ever tire of you saying that."

"You might want to tell me that you love me too," he prompted.

"I thought you already knew that." She kissed him deeply and savored the feel of his lips on hers. "I love you, Mackenzie Montgomery. I always have and I always will."

Epilogue

A LIGHT SNOW WAS BEGINNING TO FALL, AND WILLIAM Montgomery stood and stared out as the snow began to blanket the field of green. "Well, Arthur, I think I would have made you proud," he said out loud, although he knew he wouldn't get a response. "Don't get me wrong, I'm a real pro at this matchmaking thing, but Gina and Mac were a little more challenging than I had expected."

The cemetery was quiet on this Friday morning, and William was thankful that he could stand at his friend's plot and talk to him privately. "I wish you could see them. They're so happy and I know they have a good life ahead of them. Gina is painting and taking pictures while they travel, and she's got some serious talent. And Mac? Well, he's finally learning to relax a little and enjoy life. Gina's good for him. They've been traveling quite a bit and Monica and I look forward to the postcards they send and hearing about all of the places they've seen."

The cool air burned a little as he inhaled deeply, but it was a welcome distraction. "She misses you, you know. Barb, I mean. We've spent some time talking with her, and she talks about how much she wishes she hadn't been so stubborn. It's too late, I know, but I thought you should know. Monica and I will look out for her, so you don't have to worry." William retrieved a handkerchief from his pocket and wiped at his eyes.

"Jason and Maggie are settled in the house now," he

said. "They kept some of the furniture but they had a lot of their own stuff that they wanted to keep too. Maggie is just over the moon at the thought of raising a family there, and if my calculations are correct, they'll be bringing their first child home in about seven months." William smiled with pride. "You always wanted to hear laughter in that house, and you should know that now there finally is.

"Lucas and Emma are doing well. Emma's had to hire more help at the bakery, and she has a manager in place so she doesn't have to work so much now that they have Lily. I'll tell you what, that child has me wrapped around her little finger and she's barely three months old! I think I've gotten the hang of this grandfather thing, and I can only hope there will be plenty more coming my way."

His voice clogged with emotion as he went on. "We would have made awesome grandfathers together, Art. When Gina and Mac have children, well…it's going to be hard not having you there to share it with me. How many years did we talk about growing old and having our kids get married and enjoying our grandchildren together?" He wiped at his eyes again. "I miss you. Sometimes I pick up the phone to call you, and I'm just devastated when I remember that you're not there to answer anymore.

"I want to thank you for the lifetime of friendship you blessed me with. I don't know how I could have gotten through some things I did without you by my side. I don't know how I'll get through some of the things that lie ahead of me without you either. I know that I have Monica and the boys, but there's nothing like a best friend."

With one final sweep of his eyes, William put the handkerchief away. "I'll never forget you, Art. And you can be sure that I'll be sharing stories of the many good times we had together with our kids and our grandkids for years to come. Thank you for being the best friend a guy could ever ask for." He laid a hand on the cold marble headstone and gave it a pat. "You were the best."

William walked back to the car and let it warm up a bit before pulling away. Mac and Gina were due back from London today, and he was picking them up at the airport. He looked forward to hearing about their trip and their plans for the future now that they were planning their wedding. Mac had proposed in front of Abbey Road Studio in honor of Gina's love of the Beatles.

His son had come a long way from the reserved businessman he was several months ago. If anyone would have told him that Mac would spontaneously propose in such a fashion, William would have laughed them off. But now he knew it wasn't impossible. Gina had been a wonderful influence on him, and he was for her too.

There were many more couples out there, nieces and nephews who could probably benefit from his gift of matchmaking, but William felt as though his work was done. He had accomplished what he set out to do; his sons had each found wonderful women and they were starting their own families. He could only hope that he had served as a good example to his sons of the kind of fathers they should be.

Life was good for William Montgomery, and he was more than happy to hang up his matchmaking cap.

For now.